Thirty(ology)

Thirty(ology)

Kathryn Graves

imPRESS
Greenville

Copyright © 2023 by Kathryn Graves
Developmental edits + proofread: imPRESS Millennial
Cover Design: Krys Marino
Author Headshot: Stef Claire Photography

Second paperback edition July 2024

Printed in Canada

ISBN 978-1-0689494-0-1 (Paperback)

For Charlie. I started writing this book when you were barely even a thought. It grew, as you grew in my belly, and I will forever cherish the quiet moments of just you, me, and my laptop, making this thing happen.

For Vera. I wouldn't have been able to write *this* book without you. You made me a mom and gave me the perspective and courage needed to write this story. You've toughened me up and softened me up all at once. I hope this makes you proud.

For Ryan. Thank you for getting excited when I get scared. Thank you for making me laugh. Thank you for building this life with me. And don't worry, none of the husbands in this book are you.

For all the women in my life. Whether you're approaching it, in the thick of it, or looking back on it, I hope whatever combination of mess and monotony your thirties throws at you, you come out on the other end a little lighter, a little more self-assured, and most of all, you experience it with your favorite people.

Thirty(ology)

Part One
Highlight Reel

Summer 2016

One

ELYSE

YOU ARE CORDIALLY INVITED TO ELYSE & MARKUS'
HOUSEWARMING PARTY
SATURDAY, APRIL 23RD, 2016 AT 7:30 P.M.
261 NORTH TERRACE ST.
PROVIDENCE, RHODE ISLAND

WE'RE HOMEOWNERS!
COME HELP US CELEBRATE OUR DREAM HOME.
WE'LL HAVE A SIGNATURE COCKTAIL, A CHAMPAGNE
TOAST, AND A FEW FINGER FOODS, BUT OTHERWISE
B.Y.O.B (NO RED WINE PLEASE)
WE CAN'T WAIT TO HOST YOU!
(NO GIFTS PLEASE)

The amount of white was jarring.

Crisp, clean lines. Not a drop of color to be seen. Like there were no actual plans to live in it. It was beautiful, uninviting, and teetered between sleek and boring. Exactly what you'd expect from two investment bankers.

Elyse and Mark's townhouse was part of a new build development located on the edge of Fox Point, just a couple blocks away from the growing downtown core of Providence, Rhode Island, where they both worked in high rise offices. Close by there were plenty of hipster-chic boutiques, and it seemed like a new elevated casual restaurant opened every other week. While others might worry about keeping a house this white clean, Mark's family money would likely pay for a regular cleaner, so that was something Elyse wouldn't have to think about.

The house came promptly after their wedding. Building was a tedious process, but the honeymoon gave Elyse plenty of time to consult celebrity home styles and start a detailed Excel spreadsheet and multiple Pinterest boards. She had eighty different options for cabinet hardware, and she loved it. The vastness of options, the process of elimination, the level of control, and decisions to be made would overwhelm most, but Elyse leaned into it. She loved pouring herself into projects, especially the ones that resulted in a tangible product where all of her effort and attention to detail could be seen and praised.

"Elyse, this place is awesome!" Alex said, as she eyed the granite countertops of one of the largest kitchen islands she had ever seen.

Awesome, that's it? Awesome didn't do it justice. Elyse would've been more offended if she actually valued Alex's opinion about her interior design choices. She loved her friend dearly, but she didn't love her taste. Elyse was very much into quiet luxury, and whatever Alex's style was, it was loud.

Elyse had invited her best girlfriends over before the housewarming party officially started to get the detailed, sober house tour. Sure it was Mark's house, too, but the party belonged to Elyse. She was the one who agonized over the color scheme, or lack thereof, and made every little decision about every little thing, down to the toilet paper holders—slender, black matte, wall-mounted, $250-a-pop toilet paper holders. So yeah, this was her party.

The five of them met a decade ago in their first year at Providence College. More specifically, Elyse, Alex, Rachel, Leah, and Brie all met in the bathroom of their dorm. Alex was throwing up from taking too many shots, Rachel, then a stranger, was holding her hair back, while Brie was in the next stall trying to roll a joint. Elyse came in to check her makeup, and Leah just legitimately had to pee. In that bathroom, they drunkenly complimented each other and bonded over the fact that none of them particularly liked their roommates, and they all thought Jake the RA was super hot. Now ten years later, their lives are still just as intertwined as when they were freshman. They were each other's chosen family and biggest cheerleaders.

"Love your dress, Alex," Leah said, as she let herself in the front door, heading to the kitchen island where Elyse and Alex were sitting.

Alex looked down at her body-hugging magenta dress that emphasized her small yet perfectly perky breasts, which she often felt didn't need a bra. Some people, namely Elyse, would say it was more stripper-chic, and somewhat inappropriate for a housewarming party in one of the more affluent areas of the city. But this was one of those rare opinions that Elyse chose to keep to herself.

Alex looked down and touched the tiny lycra strap covering her shoulder. "Thanks! I kept the tags on and am going to return it tomorrow. I need so many dresses for all the events coming up this summer. Ya gotta be creative, ya know?"

Leah watched as Elyse's head tilted and a knowing smirk found her lips, which thankfully Alex didn't catch. It wasn't that Elyse was judgey—she just sometimes struggled to understand her friends' decisions. But it was probably for the best that Elyse's friends weren't more like her. There was really only room for one hypercritical, self-righteous friend in the group.

"Well, at least the bridesmaids' dresses I picked can totally be worn again," Leah said pridefully, as she hopped up on what she was sure was a wildly overpriced barstool.

Her wedding was just a month away, and even though they all had major events coming up this summer, Leah couldn't help but feel that her wedding was the pinnacle, as every bride should.

"Rachel just texted and said she and Brie are stuck in traffic but should be here in ten," Elyse said, as she poured the girls some champagne into her new crystal flutes.

Elyse prided herself on being the "first" in her group of friends. She was the first to land a real job, the first to get engaged promptly after landing said job, the first to get married, and now the first to own a home. Sure, Rachel's wedding was just a month after hers last summer, but it was more low-key—fitting for Rachel. Not the spectacle that Elyse poured every non-working (and some working) hours into planning.

Elyse's streak of firsts was coming to an end with Rachel being pregnant. This was one first that Elyse was perfectly fine to let someone else have. Of course, kids were part of the eventual plan, just not any time soon. Elyse wanted to enjoy the fruits of her labor and was fully focused on climbing the ladder at the hedge fund firm where she worked. Mark had made lots of little mentions about nurseries and backyard space for kids to run around multiple times throughout the house-building process. And Elyse did her best to ignore the subtle but immediate way she'd clench every muscle in her body each time he brought it up.

"Shit, we really need to start planning Rachel's baby shower. She's going to pop that kid out before we know it," Alex said, scrunching her brows together.

"Plus, she probably doesn't want to be too big at her shower, ya know, for the photos," Elyse added, tipping her glass. "Now that we're in the house, I'll have more time to focus on that."

"Are you sure you can handle that and plan my bachelorette party at the same time?" Alex asked, flipping her long dark hair over her nearly bare shoulder.

She and Leah were both getting married this summer, and even though Alex was opting out of a traditional wedding, she was very much looking forward to a traditional bachelorette party. Leah's bachelorette happened earlier in the spring to work around her sister's schedule, and they also did the typical bachelorette itinerary—spa, dinner, hotel drinks, followed by clubbing—but they kept it local to downtown Providence. Alex's bachelorette was planned for Vegas, and she figured an elaborate bachelorette party would, in some ways, make up for the lack of a big fancy wedding. Alex was much more a party girl than a wedding girl anyway.

Leah laughed behind the rim of her champagne flute. "I mean, you wouldn't want to get those party details mixed up. I'm not sure how Rachel would feel about a stripper at her baby shower."

Leah was objectively the smartest but also low-key the funniest of the group. Even after all these years, Leah's subtle, quick wit often caught the girls by surprise, and the air was always a little lighter when she was around.

A few minutes later, Rachel and Brie arrived. Brie haphazardly flung her worn Birkenstocks off at the front door. She had a pair for every occasion. Unlike the rest of her friends, Brie's closet consisted of a mix of '70's boho-inspired clothing and some practical granola-girl pieces, like her many Birkenstocks, Blundstones, and baggy corduroy pants in every shade of brown you can imagine.

Rachel was wearing her signature comfortable flats, a flowy empire waist top that downplayed her growing baby bump, and navy chinos that were leaning dangerously close to frumpy. But they were one of the last pairs of pants Rachel could still fit into, and she was too practical to buy a whole new wardrobe for such a temporary period of time. She was twenty weeks pregnant and figured she could rely on flowy dresses she already owned to get her through the summer, then leggings for the early fall, until the baby came. It always seemed like the rest of the girls had no issue throwing money at the latest trends for clothes, shoes, home décor, brunch, and ridiculous skincare products that Rachel didn't buy into at all.

"Brie, you live a few blocks away, how are you the last one here?" Alex asked.

"Long meeting with my thesis supervisor," Brie said, referring to her Ph.D. in Economics and Behavioral Studies program, which she was finishing up at Brown University. "I can't wait to get this Ph.D. over with. Speaking of which, I need a drink." Brie grabbed one of Mark's beers from the fridge just as Elyse was about to pour her champagne in one of her fancy new flutes.

There goes my perfect cheers boomerang shot for my Instagram.

The girls made their way to the living room with their drinks.

Elyse flung her arms wide, using her usual subtle yet patronizing tone. "So, what do you guys think? Crazy that we own a home. It's such a good feeling. I can't wait for you guys to experience it, too."

Luckily, the girls had become desensitized to Elyse's little comments that were mostly unintentional—so it didn't cause the tension that it sometimes had during their college years.

"Truly amazing, Elyse. You did an incredible job," Rachel said, knowing that Elyse was dying for the recognition of her hard work.

The house was beautiful and modern. It was somehow minimalistic yet overdesigned. It was basically the opposite of Rachel's house, which was perfectly fine and always tidy but lacked any cohesive style.

Between the glass décor, sharp edges, and aggressive amount of white, Rachel struggled to see herself bringing a baby here to visit and wondered if Elyse would even allow it.

"Cool painting." Brie pointed to a large canvas hanging over a white marble fireplace. It was a mostly white abstract piece with a few scribbled black lines that could have been painted by a toddler.

"I love it!" Alex said, although the minutiae of it all overwhelmed her. She took a large gulp of her champagne.

"It's beautiful, really. It's perfect," Leah said with a huge smile, partially because she was happy for her friend, and partially because she couldn't help but find it hilarious that Brie had found her way to the couch, her bare feet up on the glass coffee table, and no coaster under her condensation-covered beer can. Luckily, Elyse was too in awe of her own work to notice.

Leah knew Elyse the best, being her roommate in their sophomore and junior years. She knew that deep, deep, down, past all the pretentiousness and the obnoxiously perfect exterior, Elyse's thoughtfulness extended much further than the superficial stuff she obsessed over. She was fiercely loyal and always took care of her friends—if caretaking meant supplying them with fine wines, lending her expensive clothes, and being brutally honest.

"How are my favorite ladies?" Mark chimed in, as he entered the room.

He made his way over to Elyse and playfully grabbed her around the waist, which was remarkably still the same size it was a decade ago.

Mark and Elyse were a traditionally attractive couple. She has olive skin, greenish blue eyes, and ultra shiny blonde hair that she wore in a lob to match her corporate aesthetic, while he boasted broad shoulders, a dark complexion, dark eyes and hair. He was the type of guy you just knew would get better looking with age. It was unfair, really. You could tell that with every wrinkle that Elyse would desperately be trying to stave off, Mark would get more attractive, not less. Every gray hair that Elyse will end up diligently dyeing every six weeks from now until eternity, will make him more distinguished, not less. Even the inevitable softening of his currently hard stomach— the same softening that will drive Elyse to spend a small fortune on shapewear, will make him seem more endearing, and not as though he's let himself go. Mark, through no fault of his own, can just simply exist while Elyse will have to defy biology. It wasn't the amount of work that it took to be an "attractive," well-kempt woman that bothered Elyse. It was that all that work was supposed to seem so damn effortless.

Despite the uptight, suit-wearing finance guy persona, Mark couldn't be further from it. He just played that guy Monday to Friday, nine-to-six, and the occasional evening and weekend. Mark didn't take it too seriously, though. His job was a means to an end for him. A way to provide for a family and live comfortably—very comfortably by most people's standards—like his dad who had also been in finance, so his career choice just made sense. Not like Elyse, who genuinely loved her job. She loved the high stakes, how good she was at it, and how her competitive nature was rewarded, rather than frowned upon. She also loved that she was one of the youngest and one of very few women at her firm. Nothing made her feel more powerful than being around a table with a bunch of older men and knowing she was as good—or better at her job. So, it frustrated her beyond belief that her tenacity was often overlooked. She figured that it was just one of several problems being a young female in an old boys' club.

Mark had always been enamored with Elyse and knew that, among other things, her attention to detail and ability to organize would make her an amazing mother. He saw how she was the unlikely caretaker for her friends and was often the mastermind behind every get-together, dinner out, and vacation. While the previous men in her life either found Elyse to be too high-maintenance or couldn't handle her competitive nature, Mark found it both endearing and admirable. He was laid back enough for the both of them.

"Good," Rachel answered, as she gave Mark a hug. "Just admiring your wife's hard work."

He smiled as his eyes immediately went to Rachel's barely noticeable baby bump. "You're glowing! You and Sean must be so stoked. He's coming tonight, right?"

"Of course. He wouldn't miss it for the world, especially now that he has a permanent designated driver. Well, at least for a few more months," Rachel replied.

"And what about Andrew and Scott?" he asked, referring to Alex and Leah's respective fiancés.

"They're on their way," Alex answered for both her and Leah and smiled.

"Oh, and uh, Peter, what about Peter?" Mark asked, realizing that he had rudely forgotten about Brie's boyfriend who rarely came to any group activities.

"He's away at a conference right now," Brie replied, seemingly unbothered by her boyfriend's absence.

"Crazy that there'll be a bunch of babies and kids at these parties soon," Mark said excitedly, turning back toward Rachel's stomach.

"Elyse, I'm dying to see the walk-in closet," Leah said, sensing Elyse's discomfort at Mark bringing up kids.

Elyse lit up at the mention of her closet. It was a stark contrast to her facial expression when talking about babies.

"Of course! Just wanted to save the best for last. Right this way ladies!" Elyse said, as she motioned toward the glass and white wooden staircase that looked like it was suspended from thin air. It was over-the-top elegant, with some sharp edges, not unlike its owner.

———

Three hours later, the party was in full swing. Aside from their group of friends, Mark and Elyse invited several coworkers, Mark's sister and brother-in-law, a couple of his cousins who lived nearby, and a few of the women that went to the same spin class as Elyse. It was a mixed bag of people, but luckily, the signature cocktails that Elyse had promised were strong, making the mix of different groups of people easy.

While most of the guests were in the living room at this point, Elyse found herself back in the kitchen to grab a bottle of chardonnay. She liked to walk around with an open bottle of wine so she could top guests' glasses up as she mingled. It was one of her signature hostessing shticks.

Elyse looked around and saw her husband, four best friends and their significant others, all gathered around her custom-built kitchen island, which was covered in a mix of empty wine and beer bottles, and a half-eaten charcuterie board. All her favorite people, and things, in one scene. Alex looked like she was ready to hit the club with Andrew's hand resting low on her hip. Rachel, who looked like she was ready to hit the supermarket, sitting on a bar stool while Sean stood hunched over the granite countertops beside her. Leah, whose cheeks were the same hue as the bottle of rosé she'd already drained, stood, leaning into Scott who towered over her. And Brie who was sitting next to them, twirling her curly hair, looking more comfortable than she would've if Peter was there with her. The image warmed Elyse's unsentimental heart.

"Ohhh guys, let's do a toast!" Elyse clapped her hands together—a telltale sign she should probably be toasting with water.

Just as Elyse was about to raise her glass she had filled with wine, Leah cut in—a telltale sign Leah should also be toasting with water.

"Here's to your new home," Leah blurted, raising her glass.

"Here's to Elyse for making this house a home!" Mark quickly followed up.

Elyse raised her glass. "Here's to kicking off the first of so many celebrations with my girls this summer."

"Here's to summer of sixteen!" Brie said, as they all clinked glasses, watching tiny splashes of wine land on Elyse's white luxury barstools.

Two

LEAH

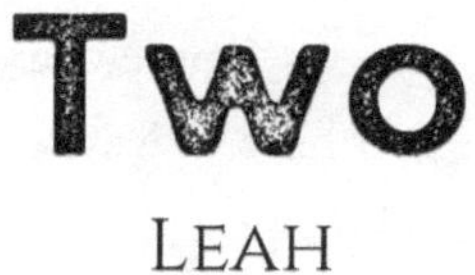

TOGETHER WITH THEIR PARENTS,
LEAH CAROL DAVIS & SCOTT JOSEPH EVANS
REQUEST YOUR PRESENCE AT THEIR WEDDING
SATURDAY, MAY 21ST, 2016 AT 4 P.M.
DINNER & DANCING TO FOLLOW

"Room service," Leah heard someone call from outside her door.

Rachel hurried to open the door, ensuring Leah didn't have to lift a finger. A concierge wheeled in a trolly of hot plates of bacon, eggs, and fresh fruit, enough coffee for a small conference, two carafes of orange juice, and five champagne flutes, as requested.

Alex began crafting mimosas, virgin for Rachel, while Brie started to pick at a plate of eggs.

"Leah, make sure you eat something!" Elyse said. "You don't want to faint walking down the aisle."

It was the morning of Leah's wedding, and she was a jittery mess, which surprised her. She and Scott had been together for eight years, the longest of all her friends' relationships. They already felt married in so many ways.

Leah wasn't usually overly stressed about the minute details of events, like Elyse was at her wedding, but she also wasn't as low-key as Rachel was at hers. She was somewhere right in the middle, which meant she needed to have at least one mimosa to calm her nerves. Purely for medicinal purposes.

"I think toast is the only food I can stomach right now," Leah said, holding up the now orange-colored glass. "Is it bad that I just want to fast forward through all the official stuff, like the ceremony and speeches, and just get to the fun part?"

"No, I think most wedding guests feel that way, to be honest," Brie quipped, grabbing a glass from Alex.

Leah smirked, appreciating her friend's accurate humor. "It's not that the official stuff isn't important. I just hate feeling like I'm under a microscope. And I know Scott does, too. Shit, is it too late to elope?" Leah asked, mostly joking.

Alex lifted her glass. "That's what mimosas are for. Drink up!"

Leah and Scott met in their first-year Intro to Engineering class at Providence College. Leah had always joked that she had a wide dating pool to choose from, being one of very few girls in the engineering department. They had every class together that first year, always sat next to each other in lectures, and shared study notes. They were so flirty that anyone who didn't know them and saw them together would just assume they were together.

They started officially dating in the summer going into their second year. After choosing different areas of specialization—industrial engineering for Leah and civil engineering for Scott—they realized they would only have a couple of classes together and would be seeing significantly less of each other, unless they made an intentional effort to do so. Leah had felt like she was dropping obvious hints to Scott the entire last month of classes that he just either wasn't picking up on, or he just wasn't as interested as she thought he was. Then, one night at one of the many end-of-the-semester parties, Scott finally made his move. He was walking Leah back to her dorm, and instead of asking her to come up to her room, or kissing his her at the door, he did something much more intimate; he held her hand.

They were both brilliant, laid back, go-with-the-flow type of people. Leah ended up going into industrial engineering and landed with a large management consulting company. She had been working her way up ever since, and Scott worked for the city as a civil engineer. It seemed like all their mental capacity was spent on being completely precise in their work, that outside of work, neither of them wanted to have to think, plan, calculate, or execute anything. But between Elyse, Leah's type A mother, and a full-service wedding planner, Leah pretty much just had to show up to her wedding, which suited her just fine.

Elyse accurately pointed out, "Don't be ridiculous, Leah! You and Scott have been together forever, and people are dying for you guys to finally be married. People have been waiting for this since you guys graduated. Plus, your parents have been planning this once they realized you were their only hope for a wedding."

Leah's older brother had eloped, which somehow meant that her sister-in-law would be fighting an uphill battle to get her parents' acceptance for the foreseeable future. And Leah's older sister, who was happily co-habitating with her long-time partner, Greg, and his two kids every other weekend, had sworn off marriage as an archaic institution not worthy of her time and money. Leah suspected it might have also had to do with Greg indicating he would never get married again.

"One ex-wife is enough," he would joke.

"Jesus, no pressure, huh, Elyse?" Brie said, as she leaned farther into the chair in the corner.

Elyse was inspecting her long satin bridesmaid's dress for wrinkles. "Oh, come on, Brie. You know I'm just being honest. You'll understand soon, anyway. You know you're next," Elyse replied, emphasizing the last part of her comment.

"Next for what?" Brie asked, knowing all too well what Elyse meant.

Elyse looked up from her dress and turned to Brie with wide eyes. "To get engaged!"

"Who says marriage is the end goal?" Brie quickly retorted, brows drawn together.

"What a fucked-up comment at a wedding," Alex observed from behind the safety of the room service cart.

"You guys haven't even moved in together yet. I mean, it's been a couple of years, right?" Leah asked, relieved to have some of the discussion not focused on her.

Brie shrugged. "We both like our own apartments."

Rachel shook her head and turned her attention back to the bride. "Leah, in all seriousness, we are so happy for you and Scott. He's one of the good ones."

"But I do feel bad that you'll have to birth his babies one day," Alex said, referring to Scott's large but proportionate head.

Scott is six-foot-two, a full foot taller than Leah, with a broad, naturally athletic frame. He was also one of those guys that actually looked better with a shaved head, which was fortunate since his dad started balding at twenty-five. Leah had long strawberry blonde hair, which she typically wore in a messy bun that always somehow looked put together.

She opted to switch it up and wear her hair down with soft curls for her wedding day. She wasn't one of those women that wanted to look like themselves on the most important day of her life. She wanted to go full princess mode and had selected a tulle ball gown and cathedral-length veil. Despite being only twenty-eight, it felt like she had been waiting forever to get married, or at least have the wedding. Like there was so much build-up to this day finally coming. She deserved that ball gown, dammit.

———

After a flurry of hair, makeup, taking the quintessential cute bridal party photos, and a couple more mimosas, Leah found herself linked arm-in-arm with her parents on either side, staring at Scott and no one else, as she walked down the aisle. She truly felt lucky she found Scott. She thankfully missed out on a lot of the relationship drama that comes with your twenties, because they'd been together, and things had just been so easy, so fun, and so natural for them. No breaks, or break-ups. No jealousy. No power struggles. Just two legitimate best friends and smooth relationship sailing.

Scott and Leah were the type of people that others always gravitated toward. They always made friends when they went on vacation and seemed like they were always getting invited to parties, weddings, and dinners. They both had that magnetic energy that people were just drawn to, and it drew them to each other.

Scott's a goofball, and Leah was laidback enough to tolerate it. He could also be romantic in his own way, which Leah appreciated. Not in the grand gesture way, but in a lots-of-little-gestures' way, like always grabbing her favorite candies when he got the groceries, always making sure her gas tank was full, waiting for her to watch the latest episode of whatever show they were watching at the time. All the little ways that say, "I'm thinking about you."

As her beautiful friend walked down the aisle, for just a quick second, Alex's eyes unintentionally went not to Leah, not to Scott, but to Leah's mother and father walking her down the aisle, looking the perfect mix of proud and happy for their daughter. In addition to having a seemingly perfect relationship, Leah also grew up with warm, loving parents. It was almost like maybe those things were related. Alex ignored the slight pang of jealousy she felt knowing her mother and stepfather wouldn't be walking her down the aisle, and even if they were, their expressions would probably read less proud and happy, and more inconvenienced and drunk.

She returned her attention to Leah as she met Scott at the altar and gave both of her parents hugs before taking Scott's hand.

The rest of the wedding went flawlessly. An elegant cocktail hour, a wonderful dinner, speeches that were the appropriate balance of sweet and funny, and most importantly, short. And it ended with practically every guest on the dance floor until the last song played.

Leah was filled with joy. She and Scott were finally married, and now they could just go on living their lives as they had been. They had already been together for so long, the wedding and the marriage certificate were just check boxes to legitimize their already solidified partnership— and have an epic party with their closest friends and families. They weren't looking for marriage to change anything—they were looking for it to keep things the same. The people who say marriage is hard probably just haven't found the right person, yet, Leah thought.

"That's my wife!" Scott yelled over the loud music as Leah danced in the middle of her group of friends.

Leah wasn't exactly shy, but she also hated to be the center of attention, unless she had a few drinks.

"Come on babe." Leah motioned for Scott to join her in the middle of the group once she realized she was literally in the center of attention.

Scott jumped in, pulling out all of his best dance moves. They were kind of goofy but so was Scott. It was one of the things Leah loved most about him. It was one of the things that *everyone* loved the most about Scott. He could make friends with anyone, and he could make any situation light and fun. Scott felt similarly about Leah. She was easygoing, fun, and ranked highest as one of the "cool" girlfriends/wives, according to all of Scott's friends. She wasn't one of those high-maintenance, naggy girls that he heard other guys complain about.

"Best night of my life!" Scott yelled near Leah's ear as they danced.

"I know, I don't want it to end!" Leah had yelled back.

After the final goodbyes, congratulations, and thank-you's were said, Leah and Scott piled into an Uber to take them to their hotel down the street.

"You know what's cooler than being married?" Scott asked, as he fumbled to fasten his seatbelt.

"What?" Leah lulled her head to the side to hear what drunken explanation Scott would give.

"That we've been together for so long. Like lots of people our age get married, but not a lot of them have been together for as long as we have," Scott said.

"Well, of all the stupid things I did in college, you were the best one," Leah said, shoving his shoulder playfully.

Scott leaned over, probably too far, from the light push Leah gave him. "I know this is corny, but I legitimately can't wait to grow old with you."

"Well, I'd hope so, since we just got married," Leah said, equally drunk.

"No, like I think we'd both be really great old people. Like we're really cut out for it," Scott said.

Leah laughed, because Scott was drunk but also because he was right. They were young and fun, and went through all the motions of being in their late twenties, but they both had old souls, too.

"Well, here's to getting old together," Leah said as she raised a champagne bottle.

Three

ALEX

ALEX'S LAST FLING BEFORE THE RING
WHEN: FRIDAY, JUNE 17TH – SUNDAY, JUNE 19TH, 2016
WHERE: VEGAS, BABY!!!
ALEX IS GETTING MARRIED!
LET'S CELEBRATE IN STYLE WITH A GIRLS' WEEKEND
GETAWAY.

FOR EASE OF COORDINATION, ELYSE MARSHALL WILL
DO GROUP BOOKINGS FOR FLIGHTS AND
ACCOMMODATIONS. PLEASE CONTACT ELYSE
DIRECTLY WITH ANY QUESTIONS.

Alex's eyes were wide as she took in the chic fireplace that was anchored by two modern white furry accent chairs and a slender glass side table with a fresh bouquet of white peonies. "This suite is amazing! Really, you guys went all out. You know I would've been just as happy with all of us crammed into a standard room, right?"

Brie followed suit. "You might've, but I wouldn't have been." She was notoriously particular about her sleep environment. It was the only fussy thing about her.

"Okay, Doctor Brie," Alex said jokingly.

"That's unofficial Doctor Brie to you! Still another month before it's legit," Brie said, referring to her long awaited Ph.D. defense.

Alex sunk into one of the white furry chairs, lowering her tone. "Well, I really appreciate you coming so close to your thesis defense. It means a lot. A weekend away with my favorite people is just what the doctor ordered, and by doctor, I mean me."

Leah sat across from Alex on the other white chair, amused as she pet the arm rest. "Like we were going to let you get married without a proper send-off?"

The girls were in Vegas for Alex's bachelorette party, and despite Alex opting out of a traditional wedding, her friends wanted to make sure she felt every bit as special as she deserved to feel. Plus, they knew Alex was the last person who would want to skip the quintessential debauchery that is a bachelorette party in Vegas. Elyse had taken the reins on planning the party, naturally. Alex compromised by letting Elyse do a formal invite for it, and Elyse compromised by including a penis border around the invitations, but she chose the most elegant penises she could find.

Alex was more than happy it was just her and her four best friends on this trip. There were other peripheral friends invited—a couple coworkers, a cousin, and a couple girls from her spin class—but an entire weekend away and the cost of flights and hotels was an easy out for them to decline the invite. It was actually amazing that Alex had as many female friends as she did. She was one of those women that other women saw and automatically hated and felt threatened by. The kind you hope isn't your husband's co-worker. The kind you don't want to stand next to in photos.

Alex was hot, and she knew it, which made her even hotter. She had naturally wavy dark brown hair, almond-shaped hazel eyes, and a petite frame. She had once been mistaken for Mila Kunis by a group of guys at a bar and proudly gave out fake autographs. It wasn't that she was the most objectively beautiful. All her friends easily met the "typical" beauty standards of the day, but Alex just gave off a different vibe than the rest of her friends. She was uninhibited and just exuded sex. She had a way of making men think she was flirting with them when she was simply just talking to them, or just existing. She was also by far the most sexually experienced of her friends; college—and most of high school—had been fruitful for Alex.

Elyse was inspecting the suite, making sure it was up to par as she recounted the weekend itinerary to everyone out loud. "So, we'll hit the spa in a few hours, then there are a few really great restaurants on the strip we can choose from for tonight. Tomorrow we can do pool time most of the day, dinner, then the Thunder Down Under show starts at eight. Why don't we walk the strip before the spa? We have lots of time." The suggestion sounded like more of a direction than a question, as it always did coming from Elyse.

Rachel plopped down on the bed. It felt glorious to get off her swollen feet. Her baby belly had really popped over the last month, and she had never felt more out of place than being six months pregnant in Vegas carrying around a water-filled tumbler that read: "Bride's Bitches," with a penis straw in it. Maybe she could sneak out of Thunder Down Under and see Celine Dion instead, or better yet, have an early bedtime in a king-sized bed with 3000 thread count sheets. Rachel knew she'd be on the sidelines this weekend, watching her friends compete for center of attention—some subtly, some not so subtly. Luckily, Rachel was used to being on the sidelines—in fact ,that was where she was most comfortable. This weekend was about Alex, anyway.

"I may just chill here before the spa, maybe check out the gym or something, but the rest of you should go if you want," Leah said. She picked up on Rachel's desire to have some down time but also knew she wouldn't say anything if it went against what the group wanted.

"Yeah, I'll probably just hang back, too," Rachel said, just as Leah predicted. "If that's okay with you, Alex?"

Elyse looked slightly disappointed, but Alex quickly brushed it off. "Of course! Rest up, because it's gonna be a long night!" Alex said, as she downed a shot that no one quite knew where it came from. She caught a glimpse of the green missed call notification on her phone screen as she set her shot glass on the table. "Oh shoot! I missed a call from Andrew. Forgot to tell him when we landed."

Andrew and Alex had been together for almost three years, engaged for almost two. Andrew was the first guy who didn't think of Alex first and foremost as sexy. He saw the other parts of her. He was also the first guy who didn't seem intimidated by her looks. Before Andrew, she didn't think she had a vulnerable bone in her body, but their level of emotional intimacy was something Alex had never experienced before. She was an emotional intimacy virgin. Among the countless number of boyfriends, hook-ups, and hang-out partners, when she stopped and really thought about it, Andrew was her first love. Sure, she had said those three little words to a handful of other guys before, and even heard it said to her by more guys than that, but Andrew was her first partner to elicit any actual feeling behind those words.

He certainly wasn't the hottest guy she had dated, though. He was the type of guy who would never be identified if he went missing or was wanted by the police—average height, average build, medium complexion, dull brown hair and eyes. Or, maybe they were hazel? Whatever they were, they were forgettable. He wasn't unattractive by any means, but there was a big enough gap between the two of them, that people do a nearly undetectable double-take when they see them together.

He also wasn't the most successful; he was a mid-level account manager of a local sports media company. He was a pretty solid seven in most aspects of life. But he made her laugh, and it was the most fun, easy, and least dramatic relationship she had been in. Plus, the sex was amazing. Andrew didn't have the macho exterior, ridiculously good looks, or insane amount of money that her previous partners had, and without those crutches to rely on, he made up for it where he could—sex and jokes.

When he proposed just after a year of them dating, with no previous talk of marriage, Alex was completely taken by surprise but also didn't hesitate to say yes. Andrew felt like comfort, like family to her, and that's one thing that Alex never really had. And she didn't realize she wanted it so badly until she saw an opportunity to have it with Andrew.

"Did you guys finalize a date for your West Coast ceremony yet?" Leah asked, as she started to rummage through her overnight bag to find an outfit.

"It's not a *ceremony*," Alex hissed, immediately regretting how defensive she sounded.

Alex and Andrew were already legally married. The ceremony happened at the courthouse a few weeks earlier with just the two of them. They planned to have a more formal reception later in the fall when they could get to Seattle, where most of Andrew's family was. Normally, Alex wouldn't want her friends to have such an elaborate bachelorette party, but in a lot of ways this felt like THE celebration for Alex. The courthouse was perfect for just her and Andrew, and the West Coast celebration with Andrew's family would be non-weddingesque. No vows, no aisle, no first dance. But Andrew was close with his family, and they wanted to celebrate, so Alex agreed to a trendy venue with no more than 40 people. Plus, she had found a killer white blazer dress she looked amazing in—that was cut just a little too high on the legs and a little too low on the chest.

It wasn't that Alex was completely opposed to weddings. But whenever she started to envision hers, it would get complicated thinking about the things that seemed like no brainers to others. Who would walk her down the aisle? What kind of a speech would her mom give? Would her mom even give a speech? Could she find a way not to invite her stepdad, Dale? Trying to avoid messy family stuff just made the non-traditional route easier.

"It's just a very casual, very informal cocktail party thing with *his* side of the family" Alex softened her tone.

On the surface, Alex didn't have an overly dysfunctional family. Her dad left when she was just a toddler and hadn't once tried to contact or have any type of relationship with her. Her mom remarried quickly and was still with her stepdad. She had a stepsister from Dale's previous marriage, who was twelve years older, and a half-brother, who was fifteen years younger than her. But if anyone asked, Alex very much felt like an only child.

Alex sometimes felt guilty for feeling the way she did. It wasn't like her parents hit her, or they didn't have food on the table. But Dale was an angry guy who she always felt like she had to walk on eggshells around. It felt like his temper was this giant, tangible thing that her and her mom had to live their lives around. Even though Dale was the asshole, Alex found it hard not to resent her mom for not standing up to him. If anything, Cindy, her mom, was quick to throw Alex under the bus to ensure that Dale's anger wasn't directed toward her. Even if her resentment toward her mother wasn't fair, it was still there, and it took up a lot of space.

"And we landed on Thanksgiving weekend. Most of his family would be getting together anyway." Alex looked down at her phone to text Andrew that they had arrived safely, but mostly to avoid eye contact with Leah, and to avoid a conversation that would likely lead to the mention of her fucked-up family.

As soon as she was a teenager, Alex started spending as little time at home as possible, which often meant having sleepovers with boyfriends much sooner than any of her friends were generally allowed to do. When Alex went off to Providence College, she decided that she'd never let a man have that much power over her. She habitually broke up with any guy the second she thought she might actually care if they broke up with her first. That, or she just upfront refused to call anyone she was dating an actual relationship.

It probably didn't make sense that Alex felt more hatred toward Dale than she did her real dad, but it was hard to feel anything, let alone hate toward someone you didn't know. It was much easier to hate the man in front of her. The man who never physically hurt her but yelled constantly, called her names, and made her feel like she was an unwanted burden that he had to put up with to be with her mother. What made her the saddest was knowing that her biological dad was probably an even bigger asshole than Dale, so his behavior must have seemed more tolerable to her mom. Assholery really was all relative.

"That sounds like it will be so nice. What do you think of these shoes with this dress?" Leah responded, picking up on her friend's discomfort.

———

Later that afternoon, the girls all met at the spa, just as Elyse had planned.

"So, what are we thinking? Nice dinner then drinks in the suite?" Elyse asked Alex, eager to nail down a specific plan. Uncertainty wasn't Elyse's thing.

"Actually, Vibe was able to get us all on the list for Drai's, so why don't we go there after dinner? I mean, it's Vegas. We can have a hotel sleepover any other time," Alex replied.

Elyse narrowed her eyes, trying to look more annoyed than hurt.

Vibe, the PR firm that Alex worked for, had many nightlife clients. Even though the rest of the girls had drifted away from the nightclub scene, Alex loved that her job gave her the chance to keep her foot in the party door—where she felt most confident. She loved that she was using her brain and skills, even though to most it seemed as though she was just looking pretty and friendly in a black mini dress at most events. And even though that was the case, it didn't capture the hours of planning, coordination, expecting the unexpected, and Alex's most valuable skill, persuasion.

It was actually through Vibe that Alex met Andrew.

A few years ago, Alex noticed him first at the event she was working. His sports media company was hosting a party at an upscale lounge, and Alex had stepped in at the last minute to cover for her colleague who had been leading the event management but came down with a stomach bug the day of the party. Andrew stuck out to Alex, because he was the only sober one there. She had become so used to seeing professionals act completely unprofessional at these work events, so much so that most would not be caught dead showing their face at the office on Monday, and had become desensitized to it.

She knew that clients liked her, not necessarily Vibe. The after-hours conversations, where she could talk shop and be more than just a pretty face, were her favorite parts of her job. She was warm, charming but also smart and self-assured in those conversations. Alex had a way of making her clients feel like they were talking to an old friend, not hired help that they had just met that night.

What started out as a debrief about how the event went, often turned into clients sharing parts of their personal life—photos of their kids, their latest relationship or parenting struggles, or even the odd invite to use a beach house if she was ever in their area. Those were the conversations that had clients coming back again and specifically asking Alex to lead. She maintained her professionalism but very much saw it as part of her job to have a casual drink with the head honchos once the event was over. She never got too wild (not anymore) but just enough to lighten the mood.

That night they met, after Andrew had caught her eye, she was watching him shake hands with co-workers and party-goers. Trying to not be too impatient, she joined Andrew and his colleagues by the exit while they said their goodbyes.

"You throw one hell of a party," he had said to Alex once they were alone.

"Yes, I'd like to think I do. So, it was one hell of a party, but you've been all business," Alex had said, regretting it as soon as it left her mouth for sounding like too much of a pickup line.

"Eh, this stuff doesn't excite me. It was cool the first couple years, and now it's just another obligation of the job." Andrew shrugged. "We're actually hoping to do a similar event in the summer to launch an app we've been working on. We'd love to work with Vibe again."

Alex had smiled lightly, wishing he had said he'd love to work with her again, not just the company.

"Do you have a card?" He had asked.

Alex's smile grew as she grabbed one from her clutch, suspecting the ask was unnecessary since his company would already have all the required contact information.

"Just one complaint, though," Andrew had said.

"Oh yeah?" Alex had tilted her head with genuine surprise since the night had gone off without a hitch.

"Can we just get some fucking Bud Light next time? None of this Peroni, Stella, craft shit. The cheaper the beer the better, really," Andrew had said.

Alex had smiled coyly, with the intention of being flirty. "I know of a few places that happen to have some great shitty cheap beer."

Three minutes later, Alex was straddling Andrew as he lifted her up on the bar. Alex started unbuttoning his shirt as fast as she could, stopping for brief but sloppy kisses. The cleaning company they contracted to clean the venue after events would be there in five minutes. Luckily, Alex knew they were consistently at least fifteen minutes late.

"Whoa, whoa, what's the rush?" Andrew had said, pulling back.

Alex had stopped abruptly, almost shocked. She was used to being the one to stop a heated makeout session, not the one being stopped. It wasn't that she hadn't experienced rejection before, but it was usually just emotional rejection. Never sexual.

Andrew could sense her embarrassment. "You're not dying or something are you?" He had said, trying to ease the tension.

"No, I just...listen, I know you probably think I do this all the time, but I don't." At least not at work events. "And now you probably think even more that I do it all the time, because that's totally something that someone who does this all the time would say." She had started waving her hands around to make her point, as she often did when she was flustered.

"I don't care if you do this all the time. You just seem like the type that..." He had buttoned his shirt up as the cleaning staff knocked on the door right on time.

Shit. Alex ran over to let them in, desperate to get out of the current situation. "I should be going, thanks again..." Alex had rushed out as quickly as she could after letting the cleaning crew in the venue.

The whole cab ride home Alex didn't know whether to feel more embarrassed or angry, but she mostly just felt a little flutter of curiosity. Maybe she'd get to see him again for the summer event.

The next morning, Alex had woken up instantly feeling a pang of regret from her actions the night before. She rolled over and grabbed her phone and saw the familiar blue bubble of a text from an unfamiliar number:

6:30 a.m.—I know we didn't get much time to talk last night, but I'd love to take you out for a shitty cheap beer sometime...

Alex had looked at the time on her phone. It was 9:45 a.m. Sleeping in was another perk of her job. She smiled immediately realizing it was Andrew. Wow, he's an early morning guy, Alex had found herself thinking about him and started fully profiling this practical stranger, based on the small piece of information that, despite being up until two a.m., Andrew was already awake at 6:30.

She had immediately felt inferior and made a mental note to start waking up earlier to workout. She paused her racing thoughts and started to text back then sensed her own desperation and stopped. Then, thirty seconds later she did it anyway.

Alex: I don't know, I think I might be more of a Peroni girl.

Andrew: Fine, but you pay the difference.

Alex had laughed out loud at the response.

Their first date was amazing. She had changed her outfit six times before getting ready, and rather than each outfit getting progressively more revealing as it typically went, they went the opposite direction. Andrew made good on his promise and took her to a dingy pub where they split a pitcher of Bud Light, played darts, and talked and laughed until last call. In just a few hours, Andrew managed to get to know Alex on a deeper level than most people she had known for years.

Alex and Andrew didn't have sex until their sixth official date, which was only a week-and-a-half from the time they met, and a new record for Alex in her adult life.

———

While enjoying a sushi dinner at Yellowtail surrounded by her closest friends, Alex took it all in. She basked in the comfort of familiarity and being able to be completely herself, as well as the comfort of the three gin and tonics she already had by the time they finished appetizers.

"I still can't decide what pictures I'm going to use for thank you cards," Leah said, still on a high from her own wedding last month. "I love the ones of Mom and Dad walking me down the aisle, but I guess I should probably have the groom in the cards, too."

"That was so nice that you had both of them walk you down the aisle," Rachel said.

Leah's smile widened. "Well, Dad said Mom should also walk me down the aisle in case he was crying too hard to see."

Alex hated that her internal reaction to this conversation was a combination of cringing and jealousy.

Just as the waiter was passing by, Alex decided to order a round of shots for the table and get the bill.

"Oh god, I don't think I can do another shot," Elyse said, referring to the tequila they had downed in the hotel before dinner.

"When in Rome," Alex said. "Plus, we've gotta switch gears. I want to get to Drai's soon."

The girls were all dressed in their Vegas best. Elyse and Leah in their shortest skirts and highest heels, Brie in her dressiest

Birkenstocks, Rachel in maternity leggings, which she justified by pairing them with a ruffled top. Alex somehow managed to be simple and over-the-top sexy with black patent leggings, simple black strappy heels, and a cropped white camisole with an oversized black blazer that came off as soon as they got into Drai's. Her friends stared at her in envy. She had a way of always being on trend, without looking like she even tried. She had a way of going simple, when others went fancy, but made them wish they had gone simpler. Or, she'd throw in a funky accessory, or a statement piece, when others opted for basics, just to make sure she stood out a little.

Another round of shots, and then another. Alex was in full party mode, dancing seductively, knowing exactly which men were staring at her, and making sure they had the best view. She caught eyes with a couple of guys across the dance floor and gave them a flirty smile; one that most would interpret as an invitation to come over and dance, or maybe more. Some would say she was being promiscuous and teetering just on the borderline of inappropriate, since she was technically married.

But Andrew didn't care if other men stared, bought her a drink, or thought they might have a chance. He knew Alex was a flirt and nothing more. He knew how other men looked at her, and he knew that she knew how other men looked at her. He was never concerned about her physical fidelity; he was generally more concerned about emotional fidelity. His last relationship ended after his girlfriend at the time left him for her best friend's fiancé. They had always gotten along great and had often hung out as a foursome. It was one of those affairs that was hidden in plain sight and grew over time. A one night stand would've been less painful.

The rest of the girls watched uncomfortably. Brie hopped into the dancing mix and grabbed Alex's hands to create some space between her and the two guys who had started dancing very close to Alex.

"You wanna go grab another drink?" Brie yelled over the music while making a drinking motion with her hand.

Alex responded with a drunk nod.

Brie dragged her by her hand, like a toddler she didn't want to lose in the crowd, and led her to the brightly lit bar.

"Alex, what the fuck are you doing?" Elyse asked her as she approached the bar. "Are you looking to have the world's shortest marriage?"

"What does that even mean?" Alex asked, trying not to slur her words.

"Don't you think you were being a bit inappropriate back there?" Elyse asked.

"I was dancing. We're at a club. It's kinda the point," Alex replied, not trying to hide her annoyance.

"Yeah, with random guys sweating all over you," Elyse pointed out.

"They could've gotten worse fluids on me." Alex laughed at her own joke, but Elyse didn't seem impressed. "Oh my god, Elyse, it was just dancing. No one was anywhere close to crossing a boundary. Really glad Andrew isn't as uptight as you."

"I think Elyse was just watching out for you. Those guys seemed a bit creepy," Leah replied, trying to deescalate the situation.

"Oh yeah, they looked like the roofie-ing type for sure," Brie added, ignoring the fact that Alex was clearly welcoming their attention, creepy or not.

"Let's just get another drink." Alex shook her head, trying to move on from the conversation.

For the rest of the night, Alex stuck close with her girls and tried to be on her best behavior. Plus, she was very drunk and didn't feel like she had the physical coordination to be sexy at that point.

The next morning Alex woke up to a pounding head and a gift that room service had delivered— much too early. She opened a small, beautifully wrapped box that contained a watch she had been eyeing. The note read: *Hope you're having the best time. Love A.*

Alex smiled and couldn't wait to get home to her husband, who had spent the evening in sweats watching basketball and eating pizza in bed. Andrew already had his bachelor party a few weeks earlier. He and a few friends went to a pub for a few rounds, then another pub for a few more rounds, and he was back home before the clock struck midnight. It was comparatively boring, just how he wanted it. And just why Alex felt so loved and safe with him. After spending her childhood in chaos, and most of her twenties in tumultuous relationships, boring never felt so good.

She knew he'd be picking her up from the airport the next day, always at baggage claim, never in the parking garage, with her go-to coffee order in hand, because he was just that sweet.

Alex thought back to the night before, dancing with random guys—or more letting them dance with her. She didn't feel good about it, but she also didn't feel bad about it, because she knew she would never do anything to mess things up with Andrew. He was her husband. Her *family*.

Four

BRIE

FACEBOOK EVENT::
LET'S CELEBRATE BRIE'S PH.D.!

WHEN: FRIDAY, JULY 24TH, 2016 FROM 7 TO MIDNIGHT
EVENT BY: ELYSE MARSHALL
WHERE: FINNIGAN'S ON FIFTH

FACEBOOK WALL:
5 INVITED | 4 ATTENDING | 1 NO RESPONSE YET

Elyse: You sure you don't want something more formal, Brie?
Finnigan's doesn't do resos, so we may not get a table.

Alex: It's Brie's night, so she gets to choose.

Leah: I think Finnigan's will be fun…live band starts at 9!

Alex: Wait, Brie hasn't even confirmed, wtf Brie?

Brie: This is the party equivalent of "this meeting could've been an email."

Alex: ???

Brie: @Alex this FB event could've been a text :P

Rachel: Can't wait! Safe to assume I'll be driving you guys around?

Elyse: Ohhh maybe we should get a limo?

Brie: Only if it's one of those party buses with a stripper pole.

"Where the fuck is Brie?" Alex asked.

Elyse was wondering the same thing, but with less cursing. It was 7:50 p.m., and the rest of the girls were almost done with their first round of drinks, Rachel's fizzy water included.

"Speak of the devil," Leah said, as Brie walked through the pub door.

Brie was wearing a big smile and her signature flushed face after she had a couple of drinks. "Hey guys, sorry! Peter wanted to take me out for a drink first," Brie explained.

Peter was Brie's boyfriend, or partner, as they liked to refer to each other as. They met five years ago when Brie started grad school and was hired as his teaching assistant for an Intro to Sociology class. Luckily, their formal professional relationship only lasted a semester, although the girls were all fuzzy on the timeline of Brie and Peter's relationship. It ranged from one-and-a-half to three years depending on the context—and Brie's mood.

Brie's boyfriends were always the most mysterious to her friends, and despite being together for approximately two or so years, they didn't quite see the fit with Peter. But academia seemed like its own weird microcosm. Outside of academia, Brie would likely be considered too eclectic for most guys, but within it, she was probably too mainstream and too attractive. Any guys she had dated outside of her academic circle found her to be a bit too serious, a bit too argumentative, and as one of her exes had put it, "a bit too into the news." She found that with dating other academic types, they were at least on her level, intellectually, and were often just happy to have the attention of an attractive woman. This also meant that Brie sometimes had to compromise in the looks department.

The hottest guy in grad school would only be a six at best in the outside world. Brie was a natural beauty with shoulder-length, curly brown hair, dark blue eyes, and porcelain skin. She generally didn't fuss too much with high heels and makeup, because that wasn't her vibe, but also because she didn't have to.

Peter, while likely a great guy, had the personality of a doormat. Which is why Alex highly questioned whether Brie would've had any interest in Peter if he wasn't technically her superior. Not in a judgey way, just in a way that a younger version of Alex could very much relate to. Rachel, who worked in HR, still didn't understand how their relationship was considered permissible. But they didn't exactly hide it, either, so it must've been okay.

Leah tilted her head and asked excitedly, "So, what are you going to do now that you have a doctorate in Economics and Behavioral Studies?"

Brie straightened her back in her seat with a prideful grin. "The same thing I have been doing. Teaching, researching and finding conferences to attend in only the most exotic locations. Only now I get paid more and can have my own grad students to make miserable."

"Cheers to that!" Alex said, as all the girls raised their glasses.

"Umm wait, what is that I see Brie?" Elyse asked, staring at a small marquise cut diamond on Brie's right ring finger. The ring stuck out like a sore thumb on Brie. She rarely wore jewelry, and if she did it was usually something funky or vintage.

Brie, who was known for being outspoken, uncharacteristically retreated. She slumped her shoulders and averted her gaze, dreading the conversation to come.

"Tell me a forty-something tenured professor making well over six figures did not buy you a promise ring," Elyse said, with a straight face.

"Jesus, Elyse, you get a new piece of jewelry every other week and no one grills you," Brie replied, sounding more defensive than she intended.

Leah smiled warmly at her clearly uncomfortable friend. "I think what Elyse meant to ask was, are there strings attached to this ring? What did he say when he gave it to you?"

Brie explained, more so to herself than to her friends. "Sometimes a ring is just a ring. Besides, diamonds are like the dumbest fucking things someone can buy. From a depreciation perspective. He was just being nice and wanted to say he's proud of me. That's all."

"You know I'm not trying to be an asshole. I just want the deets!" Elyse said, as apologetically as she was capable of. "I need to know if I need to plan another bridal shower. Maybe a bachelorette, a rehearsal luncheon?"

"I can guarantee you won't need to plan a luncheon for me any time in the foreseeable future," Brie said matter-of-factly. "You didn't forget to plan the traditional doctorate orgy though, did you?"

Alex, who was somehow on her third drink, while the others were on their second, laughed out loud, which made the other girls follow suit.

"So, how did you leave things?" Leah shifted in the worn leather booth, grabbing for one of the sweet potato fries in the communal basket the girls were sharing.

"Well, he mentioned us moving in together again. I mean, he's said it in passing once or twice before, but he asked directly what I thought about moving into his place," Brie said, less than enthusiastically.

Elyse's eyes widened. "Aaaaaand?"

"I told him I'm not interested in giving up my place," Brie replied.

"Okay, but that's not exactly a no, either," Alex pointed out.

Elyse jumped in, "You guys could keep both places, or would he move into yours? I mean, you've been together a couple of years, and at this stage of the game, what's the point of waiting—"

"What stage of the game, Elyse?" Leah asked, cutting her off.

"Uh, we're in our late twenties..." Elyse said with a hint of panic.

Rachel, true to form, hadn't gotten a word in yet, but she continued to look on intently, knowing Elyse's comment would get a rise out of the rest of the group.

"The horror!" Alex said, raising her eyebrows in feigned distress.

"I told him we could talk more about it when I get back from Peru," Brie said, trying to change the subject.

For the next two weeks, Brie and her mom would be traveling through Argentina and Peru. As much as Brie loved her girlfriends, her mom was her true best friend. If Brie seemed a bit difficult to figure out, she made a lot more sense once meeting her mom, Dora.

Also an academic, Dora raised Brie as a single parent, but she never felt she was missing out. Dora was progressive and passionate about politics and social issues. She took Brie to protests from the time she was a toddler and considered activism a civic duty more people should carry. Knowing no other way, Brie always found her friends' moms growing up to be shallow and boring. They only seemed interested in recipes, diets, and coupons. It always gave Brie a subtle sense of superiority that she had the cool, albeit weird, mom. She vowed early on that she'd never become one of those simple, complacent, suburban housewives.

Dora treated Brie as more of a peer than her daughter and never tried to shield her from anything. She encouraged her daughter to go on birth control in junior high, because it seemed like the feminist thing to do. Conversations about the birds and the bees were more about female erogenous zones than the nuts and bolts of it all, or general deterrence. She didn't try to stop Brie when she tried to grow her own weed in a terracotta pot in her bedroom in high school. Probably because she knew it would never live. It was an unlikely mother-daughter relationship, but the most important relationship Brie had in her life.

"Oh my god, so jealous. What an amazing trip. I could never do two weeks with my mom, though. I'd go crazy," Elyse said, scrunching her nose.

"Yeah, but Dora's not a regular mom. She's a cool mom," Leah chimed in.

Dora had spent enough time with the rest of the girls over the last decade that they all felt a special connection with her. It was not uncommon for Dora to pop into a party or meet Brie and the girls for a drink. She even attended a concert or two with them over the years.

Brie's features relaxed as the conversation shifted from Peter to traveling with her mom. "Dora's not a regular anything, that's for sure."

"So, what do you think you'll say to Peter when you get back?" Alex asked, leaning closer.

Brie shrugged her shoulders. "I don't know, probably that it's important not to become subservient to a man, and the data is clear that women who make compromises that put men's financial needs above their own, things like home ownership, have long-term detrimental consequences to their financial status and growth."

"So, a bunch of feminist mumbo jumbo?" Alex asked.

Brie raised her glass. "With a sprinkle of academic BS."

"Brie, have you ever thought that maybe Peter isn't it? Like if you're this hesitant, maybe something else is going on?" Rachel asked, finally finding the chance to get a word in.

This question coming from anyone else would've been interpreted as offensive, but Rachel knew her friend well, and nothing about Rachel was offensive.

"I think it's more about me than him. I wouldn't want to move in with anyone right now, and I'm definitely not giving up my apartment. Besides, I've kinda been thinking of post-doc programs. Like taking a sabbatical and doing some research overseas would be my dream."

Brie always liked having her Ph.D. as an excuse to put things off, and she didn't realize until now just how quickly she was already looking for something to replace it.

Her extended studies made it easier to avoid the inevitable inappropriate questions people liked to ask women her age. Like when do you think Peter will propose? How many kids do you want? Not that she necessarily had insecurities about those things, and she had no problem telling anyone who asked those questions right where they could go.

Even though she was the odd woman out in her group of friends, her friendships were genuine, and she had no issue celebrating the engagements, the weddings, the babies, all the conventional stuff that her friends wanted, but she didn't. While others in Brie's position might feel left behind, she felt ahead of the game. Almost like she had outsmarted societal expectations by refusing to meet them. And now with her Ph.D. completed, Brie felt like she could finally get her real life started. Not the cookie-cutter one the rest of her friends were living, but one with even more travel, more adventures, more doing what she wanted, and when she wanted—as long as it aligned with academic semesters.

Living a less conventional lifestyle felt natural to Brie, because that's what was modeled for her growing up. She didn't know who her dad was, but her family always felt complete with just her and her mom. Her mom lived an independent, adventurous life, and Brie was looking forward to doing the same.

Five

RACHEL

A BABY IS BREWING!
PLEASE JOIN US FOR A TEA PARTY TO SHOWER RACHEL
AND BABY WITH LOVE
SUNDAY, AUGUST 19TH, 2016 AT 2 P.M.
46 DERRY STREET
PROVIDENCE, RHODE ISLAND
CONTACT ELYSE MARSHALL FOR REGISTRY DETAILS

It seemed like every other baby shower guest included a tube of nipple cream with their gift. Or, some sort of equally mortifying gift—peri spray, breast pads, ready-to-freeze padsicles, that reminded Rachel of the havoc that would be wreaked on her body in eight weeks—seven, if she was lucky. Being pregnant was a wallflower's worst nightmare. Not only were all eyes on you, but all of sudden it was somehow normal for the most intimate parts of you, the ones that would be stretched, torn, swollen and leaking, to be an appropriate topic of discussion.

Leah picked up one of the many tubes strewn about the pile of opened gifts. "God, you think you got enough nipple cream, Rach?"

The girls had spent the afternoon at Rachel's baby shower "awwwwwing" every thirty seconds over all the tiny, adorable, and impractical gifts. They stuck around after the rest of the guests left to help clean up and were now helping themselves to the leftover cupcakes that Elyse had to order in pink and blue, because Rachel was choosing not to find out the sex of the baby, yet. The fact that Rachel had access to information that she could use for planning purposes and was willfully ignoring it baffled Elyse.

This intimate, casual setting with her closest friends was much more Rachel's speed than being the center of attention. Even in this comfortable setting, Rachel still didn't say much when they were all together. She was meek, and some of the other girls did enough talking for everyone so getting a word in could be difficult. But Rachel was also the one who everyone went to privately. Groups may not have been her strong suit, but those deep one-on-one conversations were where Rachel thrived.

She tried not to notice that it was rarely reciprocated from her friends, though. It wasn't so much that the rest of the girls weren't concerned about Rachel's feelings. It was more that Rachel wasn't as concerned about her own feelings. Any attempt from the others to offer a supportive ear or shoulder to cry on was usually quickly deflected by Rachel and quickly turned into a conversation about the other. She was proud of the way she was able to connect with each of her friends, even though she often felt very different than them.

While the rest of the girls did everything they could to stand out, Rachel did everything she could to fade into the background.

Most of them chased the latest trends in hair, makeup and fashion, while Rachel replaced clothing only out of need, only wore the odd bit of mascara and lip gloss, and had been wearing her mousy brown hair, sans highlights, just past her shoulders since she was a teenager. Her beauty was understated, and she easily gave off the girl next door vibes. Rachel was happy to settle into an entry-level job in human resources. She wasn't passionate about it, but it was a logical choice that offered a good enough salary and some stability.

Despite her meekness, Rachel always had a boyfriend throughout most of her adult life, even though she tended to date down. Rachel wasn't sure why. Probably because it was the safe choice. The most attractive guy Rachel had dated actually ended up becoming her husband. Sean was an X-ray technician at Miriam Hospital and liked to brew his own beer. The biggest surprise about Sean wasn't his half-sleeve of tattoos that covered his left arm, or his man bun—it was that Rachel had met him through a dating app that none of her friends knew she was on.

At first sight, Sean and Rachel look like an odd couple. Not from an attractiveness perspective but from an energy perspective. Sean was a weird mix of angsty and bohemian, and Rachel gave off sweet librarian vibes. Despite his look, Sean was gentle and soft-spoken, like Rachel. However, somehow their personalities meshed. Elyse tried to imagine them having a conversation—just the two of them. The silence in their house must've been maddening, she thought.

"So..." Alex paused to swallow the last bite of her cupcake. "Do you have any guesses about the sex, any mother's intuition? We started a betting pool and figured you might want in."

Rachel wrinkled her nose. "Oh gosh, I really don't know. Am I supposed to have mother's intuition already?"

Brie let out an exaggerated exhale. "You're asking the wrong crowd."

"More importantly, what's your first drink going to be?" Alex asked, before she gulped down the last of her mimosa.

"Sean's brewing a porter. Dark beers are supposed to be good for lactation so probably that," Rachel replied with a shrug.

"So, what are the hospital visiting rules? Are you going to be one of those bitches who doesn't let anyone see the baby until they're practically walking? Or, oh god—" Elyse began, clutching her chest, "please tell me you're not doing a home birth, or something like that?"

Rachel grinned. "Of course not. Just a good old regular medicated birth in a terrible sterile hospital. No playlist or anything. I'm going to have Sean and my mom in the delivery room. Once we're settled, Sean will text you guys, and you can come if you want."

"You know we'll be there the second we get that text," Leah said.

Rachel smiled. "Can you guys do me a favor? I know it will be different, and I won't be able to do as much, but can you guys still invite me out, even though I'll probably have to say no ninety percent of the time?"

"Whoa, you didn't get the memo? Babies are an automatic dismissal from the friend group. Sorry, Rach," Brie teased.

Rachel smiled. She rarely asked anything of her friends and never had any tension with any of them. That was probably because she rarely made her needs or wants known. She would gladly put her thoughts and feelings aside if it meant keeping the peace.

Throughout most of her life she had questioned if her friendships were really about a genuine connection, or if she was just an easy person to have around, because she would generally do whatever the others wanted. She was the perfect non-threatening "sidekick," and happily let her friends shine in the spotlight. In the pictures of all the girls over the last ten years, Rachel was always in the background, never front and center. She knew others thought of her as a doormat, and honestly, she thought the same thing sometimes.

It would be easy to assume that Rachel was jealous of her friends, who comparatively had nicer clothes, better jobs, and more Instagram followers, but there was something about the fussiness of their lives that never appealed to her. Rachel liked simplicity and was more than happy with the mundane, routine parts of life. The parts that others found boring and made them restless. These were the parts that made Rachel feel comfortable. And she would take comfort over excitement any day.

As much as she had enjoyed her college years, she couldn't wait to get out and get away from the 24/7 partying. Sure, she enjoyed a drink or two, but she just wanted to settle into an average, kind of boring life. With the right person, that sounded like an absolute dream, and Rachel was confident that she found that person in Sean.

Being the first of her friends to have a baby was simultaneously very like Rachel, and very unlike Rachel at the same time. She wasn't competitive and didn't necessarily see having a baby as an achievement, something to check off a list. She was rarely the first to do many things. Being the first usually came with attention and pressure, two things she'd avoid at all costs. But at the same time, becoming a mother seemed like it would open the door to the next part of her life. The part where no one expected her to be exciting. Besides, Rachel was already a little motherly anyway, so she might as well have made it official.

"Don't be silly, you'll still be invited to everything, and we better get a billion baby pics in the group chat," Leah reassured her, squeezing her hand.

"Thankfully, the events and parties are starting to slow down. This summer has been so packed. After our beach weekend, I can't believe I have a weekend free," Elyse said, raising her brows.

Between celebrating major milestones, throwing in a couple other bachelorette and work parties, and a weekend beach trip, the girls had spent practically every weekend together this summer. And it was all culminating in their annual girls' beach trip.

It started six years ago at the Providence College library. They were all procrastinating from studying for their finals— their *final* finals of college, and decided they needed to let off some steam and congratulate themselves for making it through their four years of college.

Brie booked them the cheapest beachfront rental she could find, which was a dingy one-bedroom that luckily had a pull-out couch in the living room. It was tiny, shabby and had questionable standards for cleanliness. But the setting didn't matter so much as the quality time they spent together. And it was nothing that a few bottles of wine couldn't help them ignore. Even Elyse temporarily lowered her standards to enjoy the fun.

That first year had become a core memory for all of them, and they made sure to return every year. It didn't matter what else they had going on, the annual girls' beach trip was what they looked forward to the most. And fortunately, as the years went on, the rental properties got nicer, cleaner, and had the appropriate number of beds.

"What are you going to do with all your free time now that your unofficial job as our personal party planner is coming to an end?" Alex asked Elyse, referencing the fact that whether she's asked or not, Elyse seemed to find herself menu planning, color coordinating, and invite list-checking every event.

"I'll get started on Leah's birthday. It's only a couple of months away," Elyse said matter-of-factly.

"Twenty-fucking-nine. Don't remind me," Leah groaned.

"I can't believe we'll all be turning thirty soon!" Rachel said.

Alex threw her head back. "Ugh, depressing, don't remind me."

"What!? Everyone says your thirties are the best. Like, you just stop caring what other people think," Brie said.

"Well, in that case, sign me up. I could go for being a bit more carefree," Alex said.

"Who cares, it's just a number," Brie protested. "It's also such bullshit that it's hyped up. I feel like this can somehow be blamed on capitalism, or the patriarchy or something."

"No, Brie's right. Everyone says your thirties are the best. You're more established and confident but still young enough to enjoy it. Your thirties are basically the new twenties, anyway. Just with bigger bank accounts and less casual sex," Elyse said earnestly.

"Well, here's to the best decade just around the corner," Leah said, raising her tea cup.

Part Two
Dirty Thirties

Winter 2023

Six

ELYSE

THE GIRLS GROUP CHAT:

Elyse: We're all still good for dinner tonight, right?

Leah: Wouldn't miss it!

Rachel: Brie, do you want me to pick you up?

Brie: Only if you're bringing the mini-van

Alex: Ah, I really don't know if I can make it. My sleep's been shit
and there's a couple of big work events coming up

Elyse: Bullshit, you're coming Alex. I already made sure Andrew
forces you out the door. We've been planning this for 3 months...
no excuses ladies!!

Elyse: See you all @ 8 p.m. @ Il Cibo

Elyse opened her medicine cabinet and glanced at the organized shelves consisting of mostly beauty products with pretty packaging, the odd cold medication, and Mark's nose hair trimmer. As she was scanning her products, she quickly glanced over the prenatal vitamins and instinctively grabbed her $150 bottle of retinol serum.

"You were up early babe," Mark said, as he hugged Elyse from behind.

She jumped ever so slightly, as though she had been caught in the act. Like he somehow knew she was prioritizing a toxic chemical that would keep her looking young over nourishing her body with the perfect mix of nutrients for a fetus that didn't exist.

"Yeah, I was just on the spin bike. You know I like to get the endorphins flowing early when I have a big meeting. If I land this client, my bonus this year should easily pay for the kitchen renovations we want," she said excitedly, unscrewing the top of the serum.

"You. The renovations *you* want," Mark said teasingly with a light squeeze. "You'll do great, sweetie. You always do."

"You're running a bit behind, aren't you?" Elyse suggested, as she glanced at the time on her phone.

"It's only seven," Mark replied, as he grabbed the nose hair trimmer from the open cabinet.

"Yeah, but you know that if your official start time is nine, then the unofficial start time is more like eight fifteen," Elyse said, referring to the many unwritten rules of working in the highly competitive financial industry, especially when partner opportunities were coming up at both of their firms.

Mark wasn't fazed by any of the "unwritten rules" and the hyper-competitiveness of his profession. He was happy to stroll into the office at 8:57, while his other mid-career colleagues clenched their jaws and found ways to turn even the most mundane tasks into a competition.

Being a partner was never something Mark was striving for. Maybe at one time that was what he thought he wanted, but the longer he'd been in the game, the less it appealed to him. He valued his own time too much. The ability to do so was one of the many luxuries that came with growing up with money. Elyse had the opposite experience. The longer she had been working as an investment banker, the more she wanted to climb the corporate ladder to the very top.

Elyse pumped a generous amount of retinol into her palm. "Don't forget I have dinner with the girls tonight, and I'm likely going straight from work."

"Oh right! I guess it's pizza night for me then. Say hi to everyone for me," Mark said, as he gave her a kiss on the cheek, placing his trimmer back in the cabinet. "Are you going to drive?"

Elyse knew that was Mark's way of asking if she was going to have more than two drinks. Not because he was concerned that she would drive drunk, but because Mark was fucking obsessed with them getting pregnant in the next few months, and he was very attentive to everything Elyse put into and onto her body. Fortunately, he hadn't read up on retinol—yet.

They hadn't officially started trying, but Mark was convinced this month would be it, just as he had thought so many other times over the last seven years.

He had been ecstatic when they had a pregnancy scare during their first Christmas after moving into their house in 2016. The holiday cheer and booze got the best of Elyse, and they had one drunken night where they were less cautious than normal. Even though they hadn't officially discussed trying yet, Mark was excited at the thought of an unplanned pregnancy. Elyse knew her body like clockwork and wasn't concerned as she knew she was nowhere near ovulating.

The first few years, Elyse was able to delay having a baby easily. Mark wasn't as obsessed and would only bring it up a few times a year. There was always a vacation, or a work thing, or a holiday that Elyse could respond with, "Let's wait until we get past this."

Eventually, Elyse had to start being a bit more honest.

She wanted to be more established at work, and she knew there was no way she could recover from a maternity leave—no matter how short it was—in the first five years at the firm. That would be career suicide.

Mark understood, because he knew it was true. But ever since Elyse turned thirty-five a few months ago, and Mark had apparently heard somewhere that being thirty-five is the antithesis of fertility, he'd forced several conversations about when they would start trying, looking for actual timelines and pressing her when she gave vague responses.

It wasn't that Elyse didn't want a baby; she just wanted other things more. And it turned out that those other things seemed to be in direct conflict with a baby. It broke her heart that she knew Mark wanted to be a father so badly. It also simultaneously terrified her that if she kept him waiting much longer, he may just find someone else who wanted the same things.

Despite her ambivalence to babies, she loved Mark, and when she thought of having a baby as a favor to him, like a really big, life-altering, body-and-career-destroying favor, having a baby seemed more digestible. So, that's how Elyse thought of it—she would be doing Mark a favor, for better or for worse.

"Yes, I'm driving. I should be home by elevenish. Don't watch Housewives without me," Elyse said, rubbing the retinol into her wrinkle-free forehead.

Seven

ALEX

ALEX PUT THE Zoloft bottle back in her top drawer and looked up at the mirror. She saw dark circles, a fuller face than she wanted, and brows that were in desperate need of repair.

She swallowed her pill with a handful of tap water and looked down at the baby monitor. She could see Lola was starting to stir, and she got that mixed feeling of excitement and dread—excited to see her baby, but not wanting her peaceful alone time to end. It was hard to come by these days.

Andrew was also starting to stir, as though he was almost in sync with his daughter.

Lola was fourteen months and was a spitting image of her mom. Dark hair, hazel eyes, long lashes.

Alex quickly grabbed a pair of black trousers, a basic black tee, and gray blazer. She hated her new practical, boring mom wardrobe, but it was a solid ten-to-fifteen pounds she needed to lose, before she could fit back into her mini dresses. But the reality was, she wouldn't be needing them anymore.

Before getting pregnant, Alex had been Vibe's go-to employee to work all the big events, and with all the big clients. She continued to be that person well into her second trimester. But somewhere between picking nursery colors and researching swaddles, Alex found herself on more breakfast events, an important luncheon or two, and most demeaning of all, a bookstore opening. But it was all temporary, she told herself.

She was pregnant, and she wouldn't be pregnant forever, and she didn't mind the change in pace and schedule as she moved further along in her pregnancy.

But since her return to work, Alex was back on the breakfast, luncheon, and bookstore-types circuit. And newer, younger, skinnier women were running the events at restaurant openings, lounges, and wineries.

Alex originally planned to only take a few months off work after having Lola, but the overwhelm of having a newborn made her push that back to six months. And after six months, the thought of starting solids and changing nap schedules made Alex push it back to nine months. Luckily, Vibe was understanding, until they weren't, and gently gave Alex the choice of coming back now, or never.

She had most of the normal ups and downs of being a first-time mother that Leah and Rachel had told her about. The late-night feedings, the googling of poop colors, feeling like you need an Excel spreadsheet to manage breastfeeding, feeling like a terrible, guilty but better-rested, quitter when you finally succumb to formula, the lack of sleep, the lack of control, the lack of time.

So much of it seemed like it was the norm. She kept finding herself thinking things like, once Lola's sleeping through the night, once her naps are longer, once she drops a nap, once she's crawling, once she's eating, once she gets over this sleep regression, once I'm back to work and she's settled in daycare, that's when I'll relax, unclench, live in the moment a little. But the once's would come and go, and Alex still didn't feel any better.

The worst feeling was the guilt of not being as happy as she should, because she had a beautiful, perfect daughter who deserved a mom who could be that happy. That maternal instinct that Rachel and Leah always referred to just never kicked in for Alex, all the cries sounded the same, and they all sent her into a panic and spiral of worst-case scenarios.

The decision to get help, rather than continue to bury her increasingly intrusive thoughts was extremely difficult at first. But when she thought of the possibility of her little girl— her perfect, innocent little girl, having any of the same spiraling, relentlessly negative thoughts that Alex had lived with for so long she practically didn't realize that it was possible not to, the decision was easy. She likely never would've made the decision to seek treatment for herself, but Lola deserves more.

So, Alex sucked it up, swallowed her pride, and casually mentioned to her doctor at Lola's one-year appointment that she had been feeling a tad off for a while. She came home with a prescription for Zoloft, which she couldn't bring herself to fill for two weeks. It was hard to not feel like a failure for taking the "easy" way out, but she reminded herself what her doctor told her—no one wants to go on medication for anxiety, but sometimes it's *necessary*.

The following week, Alex was going to her first therapy session, because she knew that the meds would only do so much. Plus, Alex wasn't convinced it was *postpartum* anxiety, so much as it was anxiety that's always been there, just waiting to really take hold when she was in her most vulnerable state. She had always been high-functioning enough that her anxiety was not only disregarded but often rewarded. Almost as though she was high-functioning *because* of it and not despite it. But when she had to start existing for not just herself, but also a tiny, helpless human she was responsible for, that's when she really got knocked down a few rungs on the functioning ladder. The whole experience shook Alex, because she thought she was tougher than this.

Brie was the only one who knew she was taking medication and was actually the one who convinced her to find a therapist. "Nothing to be ashamed of. I go to therapy, too. Very casually, but I still go," Brie had told her.

Alex couldn't tell if she was just being nice, or if she actually did go, or if she was interpreting her conversations with the psych professors in the staff lounge as *therapy*.

"Hey, my sweet girl!" Alex said in her highest-pitched voice, causing Lola to smile brightly.

Andrew had gotten Lola out of her crib while Alex got ready for work, as he typically did. Lola reached for Alex, and she instinctively grabbed her, feeling her weight, as if it always was supposed to be there.

"Excited for dinner with the girls tonight?" Andrew asked from the doorway.

It killed Alex that everything Andrew said, as loving and perfect as it was, had a concerned parent tone to it.

"Yeah, it should be fun," Alex said, looking at Lola, not Andrew.

"I was thinking maybe we could try to grab dinner, or even lunch sometime soon. I'm sure Brie or Rachel would babysit, and we could always go once Lola's down for the night," Andrew suggested, preemptively trying to find solutions to all the reasons he knew Alex would say no.

"Uh, yeah maybe that could work," Alex said insincerely.

She hadn't spent a night away from Lola yet, hadn't missed one bedtime, or one bathtime. Not that it was intentional—she didn't expect it to be this way—but she just didn't trust anyone but herself to care for Lola. Plus, her options were limited. Andrew's family lived on the other side of the country, her girlfriends all had busy lives, and her mom was, well, she was her mom. She still managed to have the odd night out; it just had to begin after Lola was in bed.

Alex handed Lola back to Andrew, took a quick look in the mirror, and then grabbed her work bag. She did a double-take and decided to put a bit of coral lip gloss on. And in that thin coat of gloss, she felt just the slightest remnants of her previous self.

Eight

LEAH

"MOOOOOOMMY, Mooooooommy, Mooooooommy." Leah ignored the toddler whines coming through the baby monitor, while she injected the first dose of fertility medication into her stomach. The irony was not lost on her.

She and Scott welcomed Oliver two-and-a-half years ago. Leah got pregnant the second they officially decided to start trying, which was after a buzzed conversation in a Tuscan vineyard. She knew she was lucky, but she also figured when it came time for baby number two, there wouldn't be any issues. The only timing she would need to plan around would be any vacations they wanted to take before hunkering down into the blur that is postpartum.

They had only been trying for nine months, but given Leah's newly acquired "advanced maternal age" of thirty-five, her OB/GYN wanted to start earlier on fertility drugs to stimulate ovulation as soon as possible.

She was doing her best to be optimistic. She already had an easy time getting pregnant with Oliver and had a smooth pregnancy, so surely it shouldn't have taken that much intervention for baby number two, she thought.

Scott was indifferent at best. Having one kid was busy enough, and he could see why people only opted for one, or just ran out of time, or forgot to have a second. Leah wasn't deterred by the chaos she knew she would be doubling by having another baby, but her vision of a complete family had at least two kids. She wanted Oliver to have a sibling, and if you're going to have a kid, you might as well have two, she thought. It wasn't the most sound logic, but Leah believed it.

They had never officially—mutually—landed on trying for baby number two. There was no vineyard conversation, but when trying the normal way wasn't cutting it, decisions had to be made. Leah knew Scott would be fine to have just Oliver, and he had already shown how much he was willing to pour everything he had into being his dad. But she also knew, as great of a father as Scott was, putting in any extra effort wasn't his strong suit. He was the path of least resistance type. He'd be fine to chalk it up to "not meant to be" and move on.

Leah also knew that getting what she wanted would probably be the path of least resistance, despite the elaborate process that was required of her. Really all Scott had to do was ejaculate at the right time. Leah was happy to do the heavy lifting for the rest of the process, which meant drugs, injections, bloating, and some other unpleasant symptoms.

Leah finished up with her injection and said to Scott, "First one done!"

"Niee," he said nonchalantly, as he passed Oliver off to her.

"First what, Mommy?" Oliver asked with the genuine curiosity that only a toddler can have.

"First big bear hug of the morning!" she said, as she engulfed Oliver in her arms, sparing him the complexities of the situation. "Why don't you run downstairs and play with your trains? Mommy will be right down to get you some toast."

"With peanut butter!?" Oliver asked excitedly.

"You know it!" By the time Leah finished her response, Oliver was already halfway down the stairs, singing a song about trains as he went.

"So, babe you remember that I have dinner with the girls tonight, right?" Leah asked, as she perused through her side of the closet.

"Yeah of course. And you remember that I'm away for the hockey tournament on the thirtieth, right?" Scott said, as he did the same on his side of the closet.

"Yup," Leah replied, just as she realized that date was sticking out as being significant for some reason. "Shit, the thirtieth?" Leah thought out loud as she remembered what that significance was.

"Yeah, why?" Scott replied.

"That's when I'll be ovulating," Leah said.

She had never been so preoccupied with dates, calendars, and timing as she had in the last nine months.

Scott stared blankly at her, waiting to read her next thought before he spoke. After she gave no indication of what the solution should be, he said, "You don't really want me to cancel this tournament, do you? I go every year, and it's for charity," Scott said, realizing where her train of thought was going.

Leah felt an immediate sense of dread and guilt. Scott was a homebody and devoted to his family. He only had a few big outings every year that he looked forward to, and this tournament was one of them. The few outings made it possible for Leah to have plenty of evenings to herself and dinners with her friends, so she always encouraged Scott to go when he had the chance.

"Of course I don't want you to cancel it. But I can't exactly cancel my ovulation, either. And I just injected about three hundred dollars-worth of drugs into myself to make sure that it's going to happen," Leah reminded him with raised eyebrows. There were a few seconds of awkward silence before Leah spoke again. "How far is it again?"

"It's in Cooperstown so about four hours," Scott replied skeptically.

"What's your game schedule?" Leah asked.

Scott knew where she was going with this. "Leah, this isn't exactly reasonable. I can't drive eight hours in the middle of a tournament to have sex with you," Scott responded.

"Twenty-five-year-old Scott would've jumped at that opportunity, you know," Leah said, crossing her arms and trying to lighten the mood.

Leah's joke broke the tension, and Scott grinned. Leah's well-timed humor was one of the things he loved most about her.

"We'll figure something out," Scott said gently. "And if not, there's always next month."

This was a phrase that Leah was starting to hear more often, and she hated it.

She pursed her lips then said dryly, "Right, always next month."

It was her go-to response when she didn't want to feel like she was agreeing with Scott but also didn't want to fully get into it with him.

She heard a cup of milk spill on the hardwood floors and snapped out of it. She made her way downstairs to clean up her toddler's spilled milk, which he was crying over.

———

The following Saturday, Leah left Oliver at her parents' house for the afternoon while she drove two hours in the pouring rain. Scott did the same between games, missing a beer-filled lunch with his teammates. Meeting halfway at a hotel was the most logical solution to Leah. Maybe it would even be kind of fun and sexy, she thought. But, it wasn't.

It was the most awkward and uncomfortable she had felt being intimate with her husband. It was sex, purely out of obligation, in a hotel room rented solely for that purpose. Not because they were on vacation. Not because they finally had some kid-free time and had a nice date night.

But Leah felt good about this one. It seemed like the chances of getting pregnant should directly correlate with the amount of effort put in. If that was the case, this definitely had to be her month.

Nine

RACHEL

"HENRY, THAT'S MINE!!"

"NOOOOOOO, Julia, my turn."

The high-pitched barking of Sadie, their ten-pound terrier, almost drowned out the early morning bickering that had become a routine to Rachel.

While the kids screamed and the dog yapped, Rachel mindlessly slathered some sun butter and jam between two slices of bread and threw a variety of packaged snacks into her kids' lunch boxes—regular lunch boxes, not the fancy forty-dollar bento style boxes that most of the other kids had. Not because Rachel couldn't afford it, but because she thought it was absurd.

"Julia, let your brother have a quick turn with the iPad," Rachel instructed, yelling over her shoulder.

The kids were using Rachel's iPad to play games. Even though it was technically hers, she never used it, so instead, she loaded it with kids' games and YouTube with as many safety filters that she could find.

"We have to be out the door in ten minutes anyway, and you both still need to brush your teeth."

Julia rolled her green eyes, which were a spitting image of her mother's. Julia was in the first grade and was mostly sweet, with just occasional glimpses of second-grader sass shining through. But she tried not to be too hard on Julia because, well, Henry was annoying. Obviously, Rachel didn't think her own kid was that annoying, but she was his mother and not his older sister. Henry was four, and like most youngest children, could be a real shithead sometimes, but he also got away with probably a lot more than he should, because he was really cute.

"Is Daddy going to be at supper tonight? He told me we could have pizza for supper," Henry asked without even looking up.

Rachel glanced at the eyesore that was the brightly colored family calendar that took up most of the refrigerator's surface.

"Check the calendar, Henry. See it's Friday, and there's a red dot. That means it's Daddy's working nights, sorry bud. But he'll be home all weekend. We can get pizza then," Rachel reassured him as she zipped up all of the lunch boxes.

Sean was still working as an X-ray technician at the hospital, which meant he was still doing shift work. It also meant that Rachel was the default parent. The one to do all the drops-offs, pick-ups, appointments, and the one who took time away from work when there was an in-service day, a snowstorm, or when someone was sick.

After having Henry, Rachel cut back her work hours to accommodate the chaos that was coordinating two different drop-offs and pick-ups every day. This also meant that she proportionately cut back on her income, paid vacation days, and pension. The irony of her working in human resources and accommodating employees' lifestyles, except for her own, was not lost on her. And despite her and Sean having relatively equal careers and income, hers was the one put on the backburner to accommodate his. But if Rachel was being honest with herself, her kids had become her career, if not her identity.

Despite being a competent professional, Rachel felt more comfortable in the role of being a mom than any other. Maybe all those years of listening empathetically to the countless reasons why people can't just come to work, while also firmly upholding corporate policies, had been good practice for parenting.

However, the biggest pressure Rachel felt wasn't about her stagnant career; it was that she didn't care about her stagnant career. Although she felt like it was some sort of betrayal to feminism, Rachel (mostly) happily took on the role of "stay-at-home mom," while trying to squeeze in thirty-two hours of work a week. And although she knew it was regressive, she felt like it made things easier on her relationship.

She had witnessed so many of her female friends' and co-workers' relationships, and marriages deteriorate because of their ambition. These women were trying to be one-hundred percent career-focused, bringing in equal if not more income than their partners. But also trying to be domestically superior to all their friends, while maintaining the physique of a teenager and spending a small fortune on every age-defying product or procedure that money could buy. Trying to be the Pinterest mom, while also not letting it become her identity. It all took a toll, and Rachel saw how the resentment built and built. For some, it would come and go in waves, and for others, it was a slow and steady path to divorce.

Resentment is the antithesis of sex, which luckily for her and Sean, was still a central part of their relationship. They had made it through two rounds of the sometimes months-long pregnancy and postpartum droughts and were pleasantly surprised to find out that they do still enjoy each other's company, emotionally and physically.

"Why is there a balloon on today?" Julia asked, looking at the calendar.

"Mommy's going out with her friends tonight," Rachel said. "I'll be here for supper, but Grandma is going to come to put you guys to bed."

"Ohhhhh, are you going to get dressed up?" Julia asked excitedly.

Unlike Rachel, Julia loved to stand out. She often left the house wearing sparkles, tutus, and multiple hair accessories. She couldn't handle not having her fingernails painted at least one shade of pink at all times.

"Maybe a bit. We're not going anywhere fancy," Rachel replied, feeling the need to defend her bland fashion choices to her six-year-old daughter.

"Mommy, you should wear a dress. You never wear dresses. Or makeup," Julia reminded her.

Rachel slipped on her practical black work flats. "Okay, time to get going."

Then, feeling the judgment of her six-year-old, traded them in for her slightly fancier black wedges, with the half-inch heels that had barely been worn.

Ten

BRIE

THE SOUND OF a flushing toilet stirred Brie awake.

"Sorry babe, didn't mean to wake you," the raspy voice of Brie's latest love interest said.

She glanced at her phone. It was 10:45 a.m. After texting with the girls earlier that morning, Brie drifted back to sleep, while the rest of them commuted in rush hour traffic to their respective offices. It was one of the many perks of being a college professor that got to pick her class times.

"It's fine, I should get up, anyway. I have a one o'clock lecture I haven't prepared for, yet. It's a bad look when the professor hasn't even done the readings."

Brad was a 26-year-old post-doc fellow that she had been seeing for a few months. A week after Brie returned from her Peru trip, she ended things with Peter. He was a nice enough guy, but a bit boring, and Brie didn't see herself with him—or really anyone long-term. That was the confusing thing about knowing she didn't want to get married ever, but she also wasn't going to swear-off relationships altogether. She assumed if she met the right guy she'd be okay with some sort of long-term dating relationship. Since breaking up with Peter, she'd been in a string of non-serious six-month encounters that she refused to label as relationships, the latest of which was Brad.

The thing about Brie's boyfriends was even though she got older, they seemed to stay the same age. She had shifted quickly from dating older men, to exclusively dating younger men. This helped avoid any potential awkward conversations about where the relationship was going. The older guys took themselves too seriously, anyway.

"Hmmmm, that probably means you have at least fifteen minutes to spare," Brad said, as he began to kiss her neck. This was another pro of dating younger men, most of the time.

Brie let herself indulge for just a moment then heard the clanging of pots and pans downstairs and jerked away. "You should probably get going. I forgot I need to take my mom to an appointment before class," Brie lied.

Brad rolled over, giving Brie space to get up. "I can't believe your mom lives here, and I still haven't met her, yet," he said.

"Well, ya know, she prefers to keep a low profile," Brie said, rushing Brad out the door off her bedroom deck. Having an exit off her bedroom once seemed like an unnecessary quirk of the house she rented, but it had proved to be quite useful now that her mom was living with her.

Once Brad was gone, Brie quickly ran down to the kitchen to see what her mom was doing.

"Hey, Mom," Brie said nervously, never knowing which version of her mom would respond.

She found Dora smoking an unlit cigarette, a habit she had given up thirty years ago. Brie had removed all the lighters and matches from the house after a few close calls. Plus, Dora didn't seem to notice or mind that the cigarette wasn't actually lit.

Brie's mom moved in with her last year. She could tell her friends thought it was odd, but she figured that they likely chalked it up to the fact that her and her mom always had an unconventional mother-daughter relationship. Brie wasn't ready to tell them that the real reason Dora had moved in was because her mom couldn't be left alone. Brie typically didn't keep much in, but the right moment to let her friends know that it felt like her world was closing in on her just never presented itself.

It began as little mistakes and forgetfulness that Brie could easily pass off as her mom being quirky and flaky. But after a few too many phone calls not knowing why she called, a couple of incidents leaving the stove on, and the tipping point, when she started to refer to Brie as Jan, her sister who she hadn't seen in more than a decade, Brie couldn't deny it anymore. And her family doctor confirmed what Brie already knew, that Dora was experiencing early-onset dementia at the age of sixty.

It crushed her to see her mother become someone she didn't even recognize. But she mostly avoided that crushing feeling by focusing on all the logistics that it took to try to keep Dora from endangering herself. It was a full-time job. So between that and her actual full-time job, Brie just didn't have the time to feel, only to do.

When Brie realized that Dora couldn't safely live on her own, Brie promptly gave up her beloved apartment in College Hill and found a small house to rent in Mount Hope. This was another move her friends didn't understand since Brie had loved her old eclectic apartment and vehemently avoided the suburbs, but they mostly just assumed it was Brie being impulsive and quirky.

Brie took one hesitant step into the kitchen. "Okay, Mom, I'm going to shower. Do you want me to make you some toast first?"

"You are such a cunt, Jan," Dora replied.

It wasn't going to be a good day. Brie ignored the comment and proceeded to put bread in the toaster.

"I'll be here for the next couple of hours working, but then I'm going to campus for the rest of the afternoon. My cell number is on the big pink paper on the fridge, and Tanya is home next door. She will probably come by at some point to say hi. I'm also going to dinner tonight, so Cheryl will come hangout later." Brie relayed all this information to her mother, even though she knew it probably didn't mean much to her.

Tanya was Brie's elderly neighbor, who was nosey but meant well and was also a warm body who could check in on her mom during the few hours a day Brie actually left the house. Cheryl was a respite worker who was unfazed by the name-calling that had been escalating, and her mom's latest trick of undressing spontaneously. Between Cheryl, Tanya, an automatic stove timer, a fall alert pendant that Dora refused to wear, and every other electronic gadget she could find, Brie had created a mini forcefield around her mom so she could feel somewhat okay when she left the house. She was able to move a couple of her courses online and held virtual office hours as much as possible.

"Who are you going to dinner with, Sweetie?" Dora asked. And she was back, Brie wondering how long she would stay.

"Elyse, Rachel, Alex and Leah," Brie replied.

"Oh my goodness, say hi for me. I feel like I haven't seen the girls in so long," Dora replied coherently.

These moments of normalcy were more and more fleeting, and that made them more painful than happy. They just served as a reminder of the woman who was slipping away. To see someone who prided herself on her independence become so dependent was jarring. What Brie missed most of all were the adventures that her and Dora would go on. She was always planning a little getaway, a road trip, and impromptu Airbnb rental in a different part of the city. Brie hadn't realized that her mom was her main source of entertainment until she was no longer able to plan it.

"I will, Mom," Brie replied.

Eleven

IL CIBO

SINCE THEY GRADUATED from college, the girls had always planned an annual beach weekend, just the five of them. It was the highlight of their summers and was the breeding ground for some of their favorite memories, best belly laughs, and worst hangovers.

Over the last few years, the annual girls' beach weekend had evolved into a dinner at a local restaurant that wasn't too loud and where parking was easy. Dinner was easier than any overnights let alone an entire weekend, which now seemed impossible to coordinate with work hours, kids' birthday parties, ovulation calendars, and baby sleep schedules. And somewhere along the lines it got pushed up to February rather than the summer, which had quickly become the most hectic time of year.

A couple of hours chatting over mediocre, overpriced food located in a strip mall wasn't quite the same as three nights at the beach, but it still provided their worst hangovers. Not because they went crazy, but because they were in their mid-thirties and having more than two drinks in one sitting required several days of preparation—and several days of recovery. But in the last few years, every time they met for dinner, they agreed that they would get back to the beach the following year.

"Can I get a glass of the sauvignon blanc?" Alex asked the waitress who she thought looked like she was barely old enough to work, let alone drink.

"I'll just have a club soda. I'm not really supposed to be drinking right now," Leah said to the girls, alluding to her fertility treatments.

A few minutes later, Elyse walked in uncharacteristically late, just as the rest of the girls were being served their drinks.

Elyse had some extra pep in her step as she approached their table. "Better save some room for champagne, on me!" she said enthusiastically. "Guess what?"

"You're pregnant?" Leah blurted out with intense excitement and just a hint of resentment.

"No," Elyse's shoulders slumped slightly, already feeling the air had been let out of her important news. She took a seat at the end of the booth and set her Chloe bag on the sticky pub table, ignoring the disappointment she felt that the most exciting thing her friend thought could happen to her was to get pregnant.

"I made partner!" She declared with a beaming smile as she bounced slightly in the booth.

"Oh my god, that's amazing Elyse!" Brie said, clapping her hands together.

"So proud of you, Elyse!" Leah squeezed her friend's shoulder, trying to hide her sense of relief—and her feeling of guilt for that sense of relief—that Elyse wasn't pregnant.

"What did Mark say?" Alex asked.

Elyse hid behind the rim of her glass. "Um, I haven't actually told him, yet. I came straight from the office."

Brie raised her eyebrows. "Whaaaat? Go call him! He'll be so excited for you."

"Uh, I'd rather tell him in person," Elyse lied, keeping her eyes on her drink.

She was dreading telling Mark this news, because she knew a baby timeline conversation was sure to follow.

Rachel immediately picked up on the lie. The rest of the girls didn't know the struggles that she and Mark were having, but during one of Rachel's many nightly therapy sessions she usually ended up having with each of her friends, Elyse confided in Rachel that tensions were high with all the baby talk.

"Speaking of celebrations, Henry is finally fully potty trained," Rachel said, trying to change the subject for Elyse's sake.

"That's great!" Leah said so quickly it bordered on dismissive.

Rachel knew this comment wouldn't get a lot of traction, because the only people who actually care about the potty training status of a toddler were their parents.

"So, Leah, how have you been feeling? How is everything going?" Rachel followed up, in further pursuit to take the focus off Elyse's marital strain.

"Okay, I guess. Hormonal. Bloated. Mostly just nervous. All this anticipation is killing me. Luckily, Oliver keeps me distracted most of the time," Leah replied with a one shoulder shrug.

"Maybe you just need some of Brie's boyfriend's twenty-six-year-old sperm," Elyse quipped. It came out so much more judgmental than she had intended.

Brie, unfazed, playfully shook her head, while Leah gave a half-hearted smirk.

The little anecdotes, suggestions, and well-meaning jokes that her family and friends provided in response to her fertility struggles were becoming less cute as more and more time passed. But Leah also knew they came from a good place, and that people made those comments mostly because they felt awkward not saying anything at all.

"Is your boyfriend actually twenty-six, Brie?" Leah asked, happy to now have the attention off of her.

Brie gripped her beer glass a little tighter. "I wouldn't call him my *boyfriend*. Just a guy I have a connection with," Brie responded.

"So, you're just sleeping together then?" Elyse asked, again sounding much more judgmental than she intended.

"Would that make it better for you?" Brie responded, unbothered.

"You don't find it awkward with your mom living there?" Elyse asked.

"Something tells me Dora isn't much of a cock block," Leah interjected. She was the only one who knew about Brie's mom having "some health issues," as Brie had told her, and she got the sense that Brie didn't want to get into it any further.

Searching for a distraction from Brie's current living situation, Leah turned toward Alex. "So, Alex, how is it being back at work? Are you and Lola all settled into your new routines?"

She immediately regretted putting Alex on the spot. Leah could tell she was struggling. When she looked at Alex, it was like being transported back to the early postpartum days. They were rough, but they did end. She could see in Alex's eyes that she was still in the newborn phase of overwhelm, lack of confidence, and lack of identity. But Lola wasn't a newborn, and Alex was still a shell of herself. Leah had been so wrapped up in her own issues that she had barely checked in on Alex these last couple of months. She made a mental note to grab a coffee with her soon.

"Uh, it's been okay I guess. A bit of an adjustment. Lola seems to like her daycare, though, so that's good." Alex slumped her shoulders slightly, like she was trying to make herself smaller.

"Oh my god, did you guys see Jessica's Facebook post?" Brie asked, referring to one of their college friends they had mostly lost contact with. "She's definitely had some work done." Brie normally wouldn't make such shallow, anti-feminist comments, but she was the only one who knew about Alex starting medication and therapy for her postpartum anxiety and figured she didn't want to talk about it in such a public place.

She looked around at her friends who all seemed half-guarded and tight-lipped. Everyone was *fine*. She was *fine*. She thought of the stuff she was going through with her mom, and how Leah was the only one who knew, and how likely it was that everyone else was having some big or little struggle that they were keeping to themselves, or downplaying the issue. She wasn't sure when or how it happened, but somewhere between graduating and now, they were bearing the weight of their burdens alone, rather than sharing it with each other. The most minor of inconveniences used to be immediately shared via text then promptly followed up with a dinner or drinks, or dinner *and* drinks. It certainly wasn't an erosion of their connection and trust with one another. That was still intact. But when you let things fester, it just gets easier to keep letting them do so, and before you know it, you and your closest friends are *fine*.

So, instead of putting someone else in an uncomfortable position to talk about their current life struggles, Brie figured the safest bet would be to take the pressure off everybody by finding a common ground, which was shit-talking some of their old college "friends," who they had only creeped on via Facebook rather than having any actual conversations with them.

The rest of the dinner flew by with mostly surface-level chit-chat and a few good laughs. And of course the obligatory "we need to do this more often" and the "let's start looking at dates for the beach next year" promises; and the "next year should be easier" and the "this year has just been so hectic" comments.

As they paid their respective bills, feeling like their metaphorical cups were just a little bit fuller, they said their goodbyes and promised each other that they'd *do this more often.*

As they made their way to their cars, Rachel looked at Elyse dreading the fight she knew she and Mark were going to have. Elyse looked at Leah feeling simultaneous sympathy and jealousy. Sympathy for her friend who was struggling to have the one thing she'd been trying to avoid, and jealousy of Leah's certainty about having another baby and being selfless enough to do what it takes to make it happen. Leah looked at Brie, knowing she was dying to get home to her mom. Brie gave Alex an extra squeeze during their hug goodbye, knowing that just getting out tonight was really difficult for her. And Alex didn't think of anyone but herself, not in a selfish way, but just because she didn't have the capacity to take on other people's struggles, in addition to her own right now.

So, there they all were, dealing with their own unexpected struggles but mostly worrying about the others'.

Spring 2023

Twelve

ELYSE

"SORRY, I'M LATE!" Elyse said, as she sat down in the booth across from Mark. He always let her have the booth seat.

Elyse and Mark had a regularly scheduled date night every other Wednesday. It was one of those things that they'd been doing so long that they never considered not doing it. They would always meet up at a restaurant directly from their respective offices. It was a little something that broke the week up and always made Wednesdays fly by with excited anticipation. At least it used to.

In the earlier days of their relationship, Elyse would be counting down the minutes on the clock before she could leave work. But now it felt like the only reason they were doing it was because they always had. And instead of counting down the clock, Elyse found herself wanting to slow it down.

It was Mark's turn to pick the restaurant, but he inevitably always picked something that Elyse wanted—Italian or sushi, even though he usually preferred Thai or pub food. He chose Italian this time, which worked out nicely since he could at least pick away at a bread basket while Elyse kept him waiting.

"The meeting went late, and I had so many follow-up questions and chit-chat. You know how it goes..." Elyse explained pridefully, ignoring the annoyed expression on Mark's face.

"I've been waiting twenty minutes. You could've at least sent a text," Mark said matter-of-factly, holding his hands out.

Elyse sunk down a little farther in the booth, almost as though she was trying to make herself smaller. "Sorry, babe," was all she could say.

She didn't have the fight in her to retort and defend herself, like she normally would have. So, instead, she had just gotten used to saying "sorry, babe" a lot.

Elyse had been in the role of partner for three months now, and aside from her crumbling marriage, she was the happiest, most confident and fulfilled she had been in her entire life.

After she told Mark about making partner, they had the biggest fight of their relationship. But it didn't start out as a fight. Mark tried his best to seem genuinely happy and proud of his wife, but when he found out that Elyse accepted it without even so much as a discussion with him about how that would impact the timeline for babies, things escalated quickly. Elyse had been doing a mental play-by-play daily for the last three months, trying to find all the ways that she was right and Mark was wrong. Going over it in her head made it more vivid, or maybe she had just replayed it so many times that what was said, and what wasn't said, was tweaked ever so slightly every time she recounted the scene.

"I just want a straight answer, and you've never been able to give it to me. If this is never going to happen, then just tell me now," Mark had said to her.

"I'm not saying never. I'm just saying I don't know when," Elyse had explained.

"You're delusional, Elyse. You keep saying that. You've been saying that for like eight years. At least have enough respect for me to be honest," Mark had challenged her. Mark challenging her was something she never had to deal with too much before now.

"Well, what if the answer was never, Mark?" Elyse had asked, equally as frustrated as he was.

Elyse wasn't really sure that the answer was *never*. It was a comment that came more as a reflex. Not because she wanted Mark to seriously entertain the possibility that she never wanted to have a baby, but because Elyse hated being backed into a corner.

Mark was right about her needing to give him a straight answer, but he also wasn't being completely honest. If this was truly a make-or-break decision, if he was willing to leave Elyse if she wasn't willing to have a baby, she had the right to know that as well.

Then, there was silence.

"Well?" Elyse had asked, forcing a response.

"I don't know," was Mark's three-word reply.

Elyse can still picture the look on Mark's face when he said *I don't know*. His eyes and lips had shifted down slightly, he had recoiled, and he lowered his tone. It seemed like such a blatant lie. At least that's how she remembered it.

"I think you do *know*," Elyse had said and left the room without another word.

She expected Mark to follow her out of the room to continue the fight, but he never did. This was how more and more of their arguments had been ending—or not ending. Just one of them throwing in the towel out of pure exhaustion, or because they had already said the same things to each other over and over again.

Once she realized Mark wasn't coming to apologize, or even look for an apology himself, Elyse did the best thing she knew how to distract herself. She took her phone out of her pocket and started going through her work emails. There were only a couple of unread ones. Elyse never left the office without ensuring her inbox was at zero. So, in the absence of any real work to do, she started sending unimportant emails—a reminder to her assistant about an upcoming meeting, a question for her colleague about a report that definitely could've waited until the morning, meeting forwards that she likely had already sent.

That night, she slept in the guest bedroom; the one that Mark had planned on turning into a nursery.

Elyse was not a good fighter. Or, maybe she was a great one, depending on how you looked at it. Getting the last word was more important than finding solutions. When Mark pushed her on anything, especially baby stuff, she would just push back harder.

It was one of those fights they couldn't tell if they were still in and the adrenaline had just worn off, or if all the subsequent bickering was a spur of new fights, or simply flare-ups from the original fight. No real solutions came from them, though. They both understood each other's perspectives but weren't willing to change their own. The fight hadn't really ended, but they at least seemed to have agreed on some sort of cease fire for the time being. At least for Wednesday date nights, anyway.

"I'll have the panzanella salad, dressing on the side," Elyse instructed the waiter.

Mark couldn't help but resent the fact that he gave up his restaurant choice so Elyse could order a salad at an Italian restaurant. He made a mental note that next time he'd choose the greasiest pub he could find, and she would have no choice but to just eat a fucking carb for once.

"Can I have the spaghetti bolognese," Mark asked, pointing to it on the oversized menu.

Just order off the kids' menu, why don't you, Elyse thought to herself.

"So, are you still up for brunch with Sarah, James, and the kids this weekend?" Mark asked, referring to the plans they had made with Mark's sister, brother-in-law, and nieces.

It wasn't really a question so much as it was a diversion tactic to avoid a more contentious conversation. This was a pattern they had gotten into. Bringing up easy, neutral topics—small talk almost to fill the silence. The silence that would inevitably lead to another argument, or just a lot more silence.

"Yeah, sure," Elyse lied. She knew with the kids coming, they would be going somewhere that had crayons at the table. It felt like a waste to be spending her childless years going to restaurants that had grilled cheese on the menu.

"And you're still good with going for a run Sunday afternoon?" Elyse asked, knowing the answer would be yes, since they almost always went for a run on Sundays, weather-permitting.

Mark would likely never go if she didn't force him, though. He'd probably spend his Sunday sitting around in sweats watching TV if left to his own devices. It wasn't that Mark was lazy. He and Elyse just had very different ideas of what relaxing on the weekend looked like. Even though he'd prefer to sleep in a bit and take things easy, he almost always obliged Elyse. At this point in their marriage, it was mostly out of habit. But the more he and Elyse disagreed about having children, the more he thought about the other things they disagreed on—like how to spend a Sunday afternoon. It was like this one big disagreement had unearthed a bunch of little disagreements that Mark hadn't been aware of until now.

Elyse was getting annoyed that Mark hadn't asked any questions about her work presentation. Mark was getting annoyed that he could tell all Elyse wanted to talk about was her work presentation. Mark knew that Elyse was a star performer at most things she committed to, and even still she had a way of overexaggerating her own excellence.

Whenever she recalled how amazing something she did was—the work presentation, a recipe she made, a joke she told that everyone howled at—he wondered how other people in the room really experienced it. The longer they were together, the more Mark questioned Elyse's delusions of her own grandeur. He also couldn't help but think her sense of self-importance was getting in the way of them having a baby. Like if she didn't think she would somehow be the only professional, career-focused woman to have a baby, or the firm would crumble without her, maybe if she could just put her ego aside temporarily, she would be more open to a baby right now.

After a mostly silent dinner that should've felt awkward but didn't, because they had both gotten so used to the tension, Elyse and Mark returned to their picture-perfect home.

Thirteen

ALEX

"HOW ARE YOU doing with the trousers?" The sales lady at the department store asked.

"I think I'll need fours in the gray ones and navy ones," Alex said with pride.

Whether it was the medication, the therapy she had already started to slack on, the extra ten pounds she had finally lost, or just the passage of time, Alex was starting to feel much more like her old self. She was able to be more in the moment and just generally felt lighter. It also helped that Andrew basically kicked her out of the house at least one evening a week to get some time to herself while he handled the dinner, bath, and bedtime marathon with Lola. She usually used this time to take herself shopping, get a massage, or one of her favorite things to do, see a movie alone.

After taking the extra long way home to buy herself more alone time, Alex walked through the door shortly after ten in the evening.

"Have you been talking to your mom lately?" Andrew asked immediately, as he met her at the door.

It wasn't the greeting Alex had expected. "Uh, no, not really. I don't know, we text here and there. Why?"

"She called me tonight and said she has been trying to get a hold of you for weeks," Andrew told her, gently looking for an explanation.

"I mean, I may have missed a call or two, but nothing that extreme," Alex lied.

Her mother had texted or called almost every day for the last few weeks, and Alex ignored every single one of them. Alex hated talking about her family dynamics and downplaying the situation to Andrew made it easier for her to pretend like she wasn't actively avoiding speaking with her mother. The lack of contact with her mother was another factor she attributed to her improving mental health.

It had seemed like her mom had become more interested in Alex's life once Lola came along; the exact timing that Alex wanted even less to do with her. Up until Lola was born, Cindy's interest in her daughter's life was apathetic at best. When Alex and Andrew eloped, all she got was a congrats text. Cindy of course couldn't make the West Coast celebration with Andrew's family, but that made Alex more relieved than disappointed.

"She sounded pretty upset. I ended up inviting her to dinner on Sunday," Andrew said, cautiously. Alex felt her lightness dissipate quickly. "I normally would've asked you first, but she practically invited herself. She kept talking about how she'd have to come over for dinner sometime, and it was getting awkward."

Alex's expression remained unimpressed. "Is she coming alone at least?" She asked, referring to her stepdad, Dale, although Alex liked to think of him more as her mother's husband than an actual father figure.

"She didn't say," Andrew replied. There was a brief silence before Andrew continued. "You know you could call her and find out, right?" Andrew suggested and immediately regretted it. Alex looked at Andrew like he had just suggested they commit a felony, but that didn't stop him from talking. "Babe, I know this isn't my place, and I know you guys have an odd relationship, but she seems like she wants to try, and maybe it would even be nice for Lola to have some time with her grandmother."

Andrew knew he was treading on thin ice, but Alex was so closed off when it came to discussing her mother, and he never quite felt like he knew that part of her life, other than she hated talking about it. Andrew was a supportive and caring partner, but he also had a very normal upbringing with parents who seemed more like actors playing the role of perfect parents on a TV show.

"Yeah, I guess," Alex said, less in agreement and more in defeat, as she propped her elbow on the sofa's armrest and let her head fall into her hand.

Thinking about dinner with her mom overwhelmed Alex. Thinking about her mom in general overwhelmed her. It was just too much feeling, too many emotions—anger, guilt, pity, ambivalence, shame. And most of all, resentment. A lot of resentment. Even though Alex had only been a mother a fraction of the time that her mom had, this new perspective made it even more difficult for Alex to empathize with her mother. Her mother's pattern of constantly putting her kids' needs behind others' needs, mostly behind the verbally abusive Dale, was even more difficult to understand now that Alex is a mother herself.

Whatever her feelings were toward her mother, they had been amplified since she had Lola. She knew it was unfair, but there was a part of her that felt like her postpartum struggles were somehow her mother's fault, like she didn't have the genes for being a good mother, because she hadn't seen good mothering modeled to her growing up. It seemed both nature and nurture were working against her in the mothering department.

As a mother, she had gotten slightly more confident but mostly just more comfortable with not knowing what she was doing. What she had now were not "motherly instincts." It was carefully curated, hard-earned knowledge, gained through many tears, some obsessive pattern-tracking, and an unhealthy amount of Googling.

Before slipping into bed, Alex popped Lola's nursery door open just to get a quick peek of her daughter and a whiff of her post-bath lavender-scented hair. It was one of those things she often did without even thinking about. An outsider looking in would likely see that and think *what a great mom*, but Alex didn't see all the little day-to-day things that she did to show her love and dedication to her daughter. She was too focused on the stuff she felt she was screwing up, or worrying about screwing up to see all of the good. The good stuff was her blindspot.

———

Alex gave herself a quick glance in the mirror. She was dressed up, more than usual, in a black midi skirt and cream mock-neck blouse. She made sure to keep it relatively conservative, since her mom wasn't shy when it came to making comments about her fashion sense, often referencing her "promiscuous" style that she had back in high school, and for most of her twenties.

As she made her way to the front door, she caught a glimpse of one of Lola's stray blocks and quickly picked it up and chucked it down the basement stairs. Out of sight out of mind. Why she was so concerned about her mom's impression of her looks, her house, her life in general, she didn't know. Her mom was hardly the epitome of domesticated bliss. She was more the sit back in her robe and chain smoke while her drunk husband berates her kids kind of mom. A never once been to a parent-teacher meeting, couldn't tell you the name of her friends kind of mom. And yet, Alex still wanted to impress her. Or, maybe this was Alex's adult version of rebelling against her mother—by trying to be the exact opposite of her. By showing her that she was better than her mom, in spite of her. Either way, it was probably unhealthy.

"Alex, how are you, sweetie?" Her mom greeted her with a big hug, as though they were best friends.

Alex could feel her body instantly tense up, as if it were physically trying to reject the hug. "Hi, mom," Alex said awkwardly.

Cindy glanced down at Lola, who clung to Alex's leg, and immediately scooped her up. Alex instantly reached out to take her back but caught herself before it was noticeable. Seeing her mom embrace her daughter, a very normal, mundane, joyful experience for most other moms, made Alex feel immediate discomfort. Who was her mother to just go over and scoop her granddaughter up like that? The granddaughter that she could probably count on one hand the number of times she had seen in her seventeen-month life.

What's worse was that Lola, who was normally timid around new people, seemed to like this practical stranger named Grandma and immediately let out a big smile and numerous coos and laughs. It wasn't normal or healthy to feel betrayed by a toddler, Alex had to remind herself.

"Hi, Cindy, let me take your coat," Andrew intervened, thankfully.

"Oh, come here, give me a hug! And aren't you just as handsome as ever," Cindy said, pulling Andrew in.

Seriously, who was this woman?

Cindy finally let go of Andrew and turned her attention back to Lola. "I can't believe how much she's grown since the last time I saw her!"

Alex started doing the math in her head. It was five months ago, which was basically a third of Lola's life.

Thankfully, Cindy had come alone. It was Dale's night that he played darts with his friends at a bar. Knowing this, Alex specifically suggested they have dinner that night. They didn't explicitly acknowledge it, but Cindy knew that Alex didn't want to be around Dale. Normally, she would've pushed back, told Alex she was being petty and selfish, but she knew Dale equally didn't want to be around Alex, so it ended up working out in everybody's interest.

Feeling the need to rush through this evening as quickly as possible, Alex chimed in, "Dinner is almost ready, so we might as well sit down at the table now." She led the way to the dining room. "I thought we'd keep it simple and have some sausage penne, with salad and garlic bread." That was a lie. This type of meal qualified as a *fancy* meal in her house.

"What, no frozen pizza and french fries?" Cindy asked smugly, referencing the fact that Alex ate like a college student until she was in her late twenties.

Andrew could see Alex stewing. "I'll open a bottle of wine," he said, trying to break the short but awkward silence.

As the evening waned on slowly, Alex felt like she wasn't actually at the dinner, but more like she was having an out-of-body experience and watching some other family that wasn't hers.

Thankfully, Andrew could make conversation with a pole, and there was nothing like watching a toddler eat pasta to distract from the awkwardness.

Dinner was tolerable, but as Andrew got up to start clearing the plates, things headed downhill fast.

Whether it was a build-up and release of the last hour and fifteen minutes, or her mom sensed that Alex was just starting to unclench, or the bottle-and-a-half of wine they had gone through, the mood shifted quickly once Cindy brought up Dale.

"Oh, and Dale sends his best," Cindy said. "It's his dart night, otherwise he would've been here."

Bold of you to think he would've been allowed through the front door, Alex thought to herself. Alex barely acknowledged the comment, but the mere mention of Dale elicited an internal visceral response from her. The mood continued downhill from there.

"Oh, honey, is Lola still in diapers?" Cindy asked, spotting Lola's clearly full diaper, bulging under her leggings. "I think I had you potty trained before you were even walking."

That would never happen with Cindy, Alex thought to herself.

Alex gave a fake look at the time. "Sorry, Mom, I really should get Lola in the bath. Bedtime is seven, and it's already a quarter to," she said, looking to wrap the evening up before it got worse.

"Oh, but she only gets to see her grandmother so often..." Cindy rebutted. And whose fault was that, Alex thought. "Ya know, you don't need to be so rigid. If they're on too much of a schedule, then they get fussy and won't be as adaptable. At least that's what I always found," Cindy proclaimed.

Alex thought her head was going to explode from the bombardment of parenting advice and critique from Cindy. Alex wasn't sure if it was that Cindy was actually making more annoying little comments about her parenting, or if she had been making them this whole time, and Alex was just not interpreting them as annoying until now. If there was a threshold for annoying Cindy comments, it had been reached. No, surpassed.

"Kids are just way too coddled these days," Cindy continued. "You guys practically put yourselves to bed and look how independent you are now."

"I think that's called borderline neglect, Mom. Especially when the reason you're skipping bedtime is so you can pick up your drunk husband from getting into a fight at a dive bar at six in the evening...on a Tuesday," Alex said with a biting tone. She had heard enough from her mother.

Andrew caught the looks on both Alex and Cindy's faces and quickly grabbed Lola. "I'm going to get Lola's bath started," he said, trying to get out of there as quickly as possible.

Ignoring Andrew, Alex asked, "Why did you even reach out, Mom?" before Cindy could respond to her neglect comment.

"Do I really need a reason to see my daughter and her family?" Cindy replied, sounding more angry than hurt.

"Yes, you do, apparently. Because you've barely done it over the last seventeen months. Actually, make that thirty-five years," Alex retorted from her seat across the table, though it wasn't far enough.

"You know, Alex, most daughters would be happy to have a grandparent around during this time. Or, hell, they might even reach out to their mothers so they don't have to invite themselves over," Cindy's slight smile oozed with smugness.

"Oh, come on, Mom. Don't act like this is normal behavior," Alex challenged her.

One thing she found more unacceptable than her mother's parenting style was her mother's ability to pretend like it was somehow normal.

"Well, I've just been so busy, and Dale has a lot of stuff going on right now. I guess I just felt bad for you. I know Andrew's parents are on the other side of the country, and I just want to make sure you're doing okay. It takes a village, you know," Cindy explained in a patronizing tone.

Oh, hell no. Her neglectful mother did not just imply that Alex needed help, because she couldn't handle her own kid. Who was Alex's village growing up? Her abusively drunk stepdad, stoner step-sister who came and went, or the series of older teenage boys that her mom didn't give a shit about Alex hanging around with when she was much too young?

"How thoughtful of you, Mom," Alex said tersely.

"We really should get together more, though, and you know if you and Andrew need to get away, I can always come for an overnight. Date nights are important, you know," Cindy said, again in a patronizing tone.

Over my dead body, Alex thought.

Just then, Cindy's phone vibrated. Alex glanced down and saw the message was from Dale, as noted by the heart emojis bookending his name.

"I should get going. Dale needs me to pick him up from darts. Tell Andrew thanks for a wonderful evening. Let's do this again sometime." And with that, Cindy was out the door the second Dale needed her.

Alex shut the door behind her and poured herself another glass of wine. If she wasn't already completely numb to these interactions with her mother, then surely a glass of malbec would do it.

Fourteen

LEAH

"B-24." Leah glanced down at the paper ticket in her hand as she heard the clerk announce the number.

It looked like she had been holding onto it for a week, not the last fifteen minutes. But holding her ticket with a death grip between her thumb and index finger had become one of the many nervous little habits she had developed over the last few months while waiting for appointments. So many appointments. The individual appointments were usually innocuous—a needle here, a speculum there, an ultrasound every now and then—but they all reminded her of the reason she had to go to them, and with each one, Leah felt like she was getting one step closer to the root cause of her fertility issues. It simultaneously filled her with hope and terrified her that there may not be a solution to whatever the issue may be.

B-32. She would be here for at least another forty-five minutes. She started mentally calculating the amount of time she had spent at the blood collection clinic, not because the information was particularly helpful or interesting, but because she needed a distraction for the rest of her wait. Unfortunately for her, her engineering brain did the math in no time at all.

She pulled out her phone and opened her messages, looking for another distraction. She glanced over her most recent ones, which were from Scott, her mom, Rachel, The Girls group chat, Elyse, Alex, Oliver's Daycare, then Brie. She knew Rachel would be her best bet for a quick reply this time of day.

Leah: Hey, you on lunch?

She saw the three dots appear instantly.

Rachel: Just finishing up. Have to go into an interview in 15 mins. What's up?

Rachel could always sense when there was a deeper emotional need behind a text.

Leah: Just at my second home...the blood clinic 👎

Rachel: Ah, that's rough 🖤 You want to grab a coffee tomorrow? I can meet you after I drop the kids off?

Leah hesitated. Rachel was so generous with her time. Too generous. Rachel, without being asked, volunteered to take a PTO day to watch Oliver overnight when she heard of Leah's upcoming egg retrieval.

Leah: Sure, I'd love that.

She felt relief and guilt for the amount she emotionally dumped on Rachel throughout this process. She tried to talk to Scott only about the logistics of IVF and not the overwhelming emotions of it all.

Scott was a tasks' guy, not a feelings guy. Not that he was insensitive, just more aloof than anything. But after another three months of unsuccessful attempts, Leah was on a mission to get pregnant and knew that the best way to keep Scott on board was to give him specific tasks, dates, reminders rather than try to share the emotional weight of this whole process.

Leah often wondered if Scott even recognized the gravity of the situation. She also tried not to dwell too much on these thoughts. She knew Scott wasn't as resilient as her, and if she made this situation any harder for him he'd be looking for the first exit off the IVF highway. He already seemed to think that providing a sperm sample was an unreasonable request, but Leah thought that seemed like a relative breeze compared to everything her body had already been through, and what was to come.

Between texting with Rachel, checking work emails, and scrolling through Instagram, the rest of her wait flew by. After going through the familiar motions at the blood collection clinic, Leah sat in her car for a few minutes before she headed back to work.

Her phone buzzed. Glancing down, she saw a text from Scott.

Scott: Hope you're having a good day babe. Love you.

Leah gave a half-smile. Half because it was a cute text, one that she often received from Scott mid-morning when he's procrastinating at work. But only half, because she also knew that he had absolutely no idea that she had to go to the clinic this morning. She wondered what it was like to be so blissfully unaware. It was probably pretty nice, she decided. She tried not to be so hard on him, because to be fair, all the appointments were Leah's, and even she could barely keep them all straight herself.

The IVF process was confusing enough for her, so she didn't expect Scott to be an expert. She was constantly getting bloodwork to check her hormone levels, but this particular test was important. If her hormone levels were where they needed to be, she could do an egg retrieval in just a couple of weeks. If they weren't, she'd be waiting another month.

As she drove away from the clinic, Leah couldn't help but feel cautiously hopeful. With no underlying issues or clear causes, IVF seemed like a sure bet. A *very expensive* sure bet that she was grateful she and Scott could afford. Between living relatively frugal lifestyles, both making six figures as engineers, and having good health insurance, a round of IVF luckily wasn't going to bankrupt them.

Leah refused to think of herself as infertile. She already had a child, so there was just no way that she could be. It happened before, so it can happen again. Even if assistance—expensive, physically and emotionally draining assistance—was required. But it was all a small price to pay in Leah's eyes.

———

Two Weeks Later

"How's she feeling?" Rachel asked as she handed Oliver over to Scott.

"Sore, but she seems to be doing okay. You can come up to see her if you want," Scott answered.

Scott looked exhausted. Leah's egg retrieval was the day before, and despite Rachel taking Oliver off his hands, having a whole day where he was in charge without Leah available to guide him, Scott could barely put one foot in front of another. Maybe it was a symptom of them having been together for so long, basically since they were kids. But during that time, Leah grew up and Scott never really had to, because Leah figured everything out for the both of them.

"No no, that's okay. I know Oliver is anxious to get some snuggles," Rachel replied.

"Moooommmmmy," Oliver shouted.

"Hey buddy, remember, only gentle hugs and no jumping on the bed," Scott instructed.

Oliver excitedly ran up the stairs to Leah's room.

"Thanks so much for taking him overnight, Rach, really," Scott said sincerely.

"No problem at all. He had a blast. He was Henry's shadow the whole time. I swear three is easier than one or two," Rachel immediately bit her lip, recognizing her misstep.

She quickly realized Scott didn't pick up at all on what could've been seen as an insensitive comment, and she was glad she said it in front of him and not Leah.

"Anyway, I'll let you get back to Leah and Oliver. Tell Leah I'll call her later tonight if she's up for it," Rachel said.

"Thanks again, Rach. Leah's really lucky to have a friend like you." Scott thanked her as she made her way back to her car.

———

Five Days Later

THE GIRLS GROUP CHAT:

Leah: We got three. Three embryos that are high-quality enough for transfer!

Rachel: Amazing! So happy for you guys. One step closer!

Brie: You going to stuff them all in there at once?

Elyse: Congrats!! You must be thrilled. Keep us updated!

Alex: <3

Leah: Haha Brie. I think I am actually going to transfer two, to increase the chances. And twins wouldn't be the worst thing in the world :)

Fifteen

BRIE

"THIS IS THE third time this week you've canceled on me. You realize I have a job that I'm supposed to go to, right?" Brie scowled, as though the woman on the other end of the phone call could see her.

"Like I've already told you, we don't have the staff. Your mother requires very advanced care, and she's already been both physically and verbally aggressive with our staff," the care coordinator, whose name Brie had already forgotten despite talking to her several times a week, replied, equally as irritated.

"What about Jill? She was really good with mom. Can you send her?" Brie asked, sounding more desperate than annoyed, as she anxiously doodled on a notepad in her home office.

"Ms. Lawrence, that's not how this service works. We have thousands of clients. Your mother isn't the only one. And quite frankly, with your mom's track record, you need to take what you can get," the care coordinator replied, not even trying to sugar coat the truth that Dora was "difficult."

Even on her best days, Dora was resistant to receive any care and was uncooperative with staff. On her bad days, which she was having more and more of, she was verbally abusive to staff and had even started kicking and hitting them. Brie had lost track of how many incident reports she had signed over the last couple of months.

"Fine. Can you at least make sure someone is here on Thursday?" Brie replied in defeat.

"We'll do the best we can."

Brie ended the call and let out an audible sigh of exasperation, going over her options in her head. She had to cancel her office hours last week and really didn't want to make a habit of it. But with Dora's behavior escalating much quicker than she anticipated, it looked like that was going to be the case. Cheryl, her respite worker, still came twelve hours a week and had even done the odd overnight shift, but she had other clients and a life of her own, and Brie knew that Dora was probably one of her more challenging clients. Tanya, the neighbor, wasn't an option anymore. With Dora's propensity to call names and kick, Brie knew it was too much of a liability with Tanya being elderly and frail herself. So that left her with the municipal homecare agency that sent someone different half of the time and canceled the other half.

Brie was drowning, and she knew it. And she had pretty much isolated herself. She had the odd coffee date with Rachel, but other than that, she didn't have much of a social life. She had also cut ties with Brad, telling him she just didn't see a future with him, which was technically true, anyway. The only things saving her at work were her overzealous grad students, and the fact that her professor ratings were high, especially this year when her grading was more than generous. Students generally didn't complain when they got a higher grade than they deserved.

Luckily, Cheryl had an open day, and when Brie called her sounding desperate and offering to pay her double what she normally does, Brie was able to keep her office hours.

As Brie was getting her things together to head to campus, she heard her phone ring. "Hey Cheryl, where are you?" Brie answered her phone after only half a ring.

"I'm stuck in traffic. I-95 is a mess today. I'd say I'm going to be another fifteen or twenty minutes," Cheryl responded.

"Shit, shit, shit. I'm just on my way out the door," Brie said, throwing her head back.

"I'll be there as soon as I can," Cheryl said, sounding stressed.

Brie did the traffic math in her head. Her drive to campus was usually only six or seven minutes but finding a parking spot usually added another few minutes onto it. Add in what was probably going to be another few minutes walking from said parking spot, and she concluded she was likely already late for her office hours. She glanced at Dora out of the corner of her eye and saw her mother sitting on her favorite recliner, where she had been for the last forty-five minutes, fully entranced by a Woodstock documentary.

"Okay, Dora is just watching TV right now. She seems content. Can you let me know when you get here?" Brie asked.

"Will do," Cheryl responded.

———

Forty-five minutes later and twenty minutes into her office hours, Brie finally got a call she had been dreading for months. She had gotten side-tracked with students and hadn't realized how much time had passed. When she finally looked at the clock and the incoming call from Cheryl, her stomach dropped.

After taking more like half an hour to get to Brie's house, Cheryl finally arrived to an open garage door and no Dora.

"Fuck, I'll be right there," Brie said rushing out of her office, leaving behind a very confused freshman.

As she sped home, Brie's mind was racing. She had triple-checked the oven, as she always did. She made sure the door was locked from the inside, and there was a clear path to the bathroom, and the TV remote was in reach. Since Dora had moved in, identifying potential safety hazards had become second nature to Brie. She had a mental checklist she went over every time she left the house, but somehow managed to forget to close the garage door in her rush to get to campus.

By the time Brie arrived back home, Cheryl had already called several neighbors, a couple of nearby shops, and the police who did not seem to think this was an urgent matter.

"What did the police say?" Brie asked frantically.

"That they can't issue a warning until it's been twelve hours," Cheryl responded, equally as frantic.

"Twelve hours will be three in the fucking morning. We're supposed to get frost tonight," Brie said, as the image of Dora in her thin long-sleeve and open-toe slippers flashed in her mind.

It was technically spring, but it was also the Northeast so temperatures below freezing late at night and early in the morning weren't that uncommon in Providence.

"I know, Brie, I know," Cheryl responded with a sigh. "They said that with a lot of these cases, the best bet is to alert the neighbors and wait for her to come home on her own."

"She's not a fucking dog, Jesus," Brie said, outraged. "Cheryl, you stay here. I'm going out to look for her."

Brie drove, somewhat aimlessly, trying to remember all the usual routes she would go with Dora. There weren't many. There was the grocery store, the pharmacy, her doctor's office across town, a Starbucks that wasn't the closest one to them, but the one Dora preferred to go to because she thought one of the baristas was hot.

Five minutes of speeding later, Brie entered the Starbucks on Angell street and saw Duncan, the hot barista, was working. He recognized her, giving a familiar smile.

"Have you seen my mom?" Brie asked, like a lost, scared child.

"Uh, no, sorry, I haven't," Duncan responded, with his brows drawn together.

"Can you please call me right away if she comes in?" Brie could feel her voice starting to crack, as she shakily wrote her phone number down on a napkin.

"Of course. I'll let the evening shift know as well. Is everything okay?" Duncan asked empathetically.

Brie opened her mouth, not knowing how to respond to Duncan.

"Brie?"

The familiar voice had Brie turning around to see the familiar face. It was Elyse.

"Hi..." Brie responded.

Elyse saw the fear in Brie's eyes, and tears started to well within them. "Did you drive here?" Elyse asked calmly.

Brie nodded.

"Okay, come with me. I'll drive. Should we take you home? What's going on?" Elyse replied, worried for her clearly distraught friend.

"Dora is gone," Brie explained.

"What do you mean, gone?" Elyse asked.

"She left the house, and I don't know where she is." Brie could see the confusion on Elyse's face, wondering why she would be worried about an adult woman leaving her house.

Brie realized just how little she had shared with one of her closest friends, as Elyse clearly didn't know what was going on. She had been so caught up in just surviving the day-to-day management of her mother's situation, that she hadn't taken the time or emotional energy to share this with the people who were there to support her. Maybe it was because the rest of the girls seemed like they had enough of their own emotional baggage to carry, and she didn't want to add to the weight of it. Or, maybe it was because talking about it out loud—really talking about it, not just skirting around the issue—would make it so much more real. Or, maybe it was both.

"She has dementia, Elyse. And it's been pretty bad lately. She basically can't be left alone. Obviously," Brie finally admitted, throwing her hands up.

"Oh, Brie..." Elyse said in her empathetic tone that she reserved for very rare occasions. In true Elyse fashion, she quickly jumped into problem-solving mode. "Okay, here's what we're going to do. You're going to get in my car, and I'll drive wherever you want to go to check for her. And while I drive, you can get on the phone and contact whoever you need to contact."

Brie was glad that of all the people she would have run into at that Starbucks it was Elyse. She may not have been the warmest and fuzziest of her friends, but she was probably the most useful in a situation like this.

———

After two hours of driving around, multiple calls to every location that Dora had been in the last six months, and checking some parks and trails, Brie finally got a call from Cheryl saying that Dora was home.

Before Brie could ask any specifics, Cheryl said, "She is okay. Long story. I'll let you know when you get back home."

It turned out that Dora had jumped on a city bus and took it downtown to the art gallery. She hadn't been there in forever, but she used to frequent the art gallery with one of her girlfriends twenty or so years ago. It was by luck that one of the long-time staff members recognized her, and when she seemed kookier than usual and disoriented, she had called 9-1-1.

When Dora had settled back in, and Cheryl finally left two hours later than she was supposed to, Elyse ordered her and Brie Thai food and opened a bottle of wine.

"How come you haven't told us about this Brie? Jesus, we're here to help each other," Elyse said in the gentlest, yet slightly scolding tone, as she took her first bite of Pad Thai.

"I don't know...I just...it's all happened so fast. And I was managing fine, until I wasn't, and I just...I guess I just don't want to believe it," Brie shared. "She's not getting better. I knew that she technically wouldn't, but I didn't think I'd lose her this fast. I thought I'd have more time, more good days with her," she said, dropping her chopsticks and trying to hold back tears.

"Oh, Brie, you know you can't do this all on your own. And you know Dora would also hate seeing you tied down like this," Elyse said. *Tied down* seemed like a harsh way to put it, but Brie knew that it was true, that Elyse was right. "What options have you looked into?"

Brie knew where this was going. "I can't put her in a nursing home, Elyse."

"You know there are some really nice ones out there. And nothing a little extra cash can't do to make it even nicer," Elyse said.

"But she's my mom. It's not just that she's my mom. She's my person, my whole family. I don't have anyone else," Brie said, dropping her head into her hands, as if she was just realizing it for the first time.

Elyse reached out and placed her hand on Brie's shoulder. "Of course you do," she replied, referring to their close-knit group of friends.

"No, I just...I never worried about having like a traditional family, because I saw how independent and cool my mom was, and now here she is needing someone to change her diaper, and it's just all such a mind fuck. And when she's gone, I'm going to be alone."

Brie didn't like to admit that one of the hardest parts of this wasn't watching her mom decline. It was the purely selfish thought of what Brie would do when her mom was gone, which beyond physically, she pretty much already was.

"Brie. Look at me. You'll never be alone. You have all of us. Plus, you're thirty-five. That's still plenty of time to meet someone and start a family if that's what you want. Is that what you want?" Elyse asked gently. She was mindful that she was asking Brie the question that she hated to be asked herself.

"No, I don't want a new family. I'd never settle down just for the sake of not being alone. I just want my mom. Dora was amazing." Brie had already gotten used to talking about her mom in the past tense. "She just did her own thing and literally never cared what anyone else thought. Growing up with her, it never even occurred to me that I needed a husband. She made it seem like guys were just these people to have fun with, if that's what you wanted, and nothing more. You know that beyond the sixth grade, I've never actually cried over a guy? Anyway, it's just so weird, because my mom was so amazing by herself that it made me not really want a husband and kids. My mom was such a good mom that it made me never want to be a mom. How fucked up is that?"

"Did you ever stop and think that maybe your mom wasn't alone? That she had you just as much as you had her?" Elyse asked. "And have you ever thought that maybe your mom was faking it a bit? Maybe she was lonely here and there, and maybe she did want a traditional family, but it just wasn't in the cards for her?" Being profound wasn't really Elyse's thing, but every now and then she'd hit one of her friends with a life-altering question they never thought to ask themselves.

Brie looked like she had the wind knocked out of her, and Elyse immediately regretted saying it. What was supposed to be a comfort to Brie, she realized had just possibly changed her entire perspective on the most important person in her life.

"You know, Elyse. I never even asked her. I never asked her if she actually wanted those things. I had all this time to ask her, and I never did. And now I can't." Brie shook her head gently and pursed her lips together to keep them from quivering.

Elyse grabbed Brie's hand in between both of hers. "Brie, this next little while is going to suck. There is no getting around it. But you know you are going to be okay, right? Even if you're not okay for a little while." The only way Elyse knew how to deliver encouragement was with a side of no nonsense.

Brie nodded. "You know you'd make a really great mom, Elyse," Brie said, knowing Elyse would appreciate the irony of the situation.

"I know. But don't tell Mark that," Elyse replied with a small smirk.

"Things still shaky?" Brie asked, happy to have the conversation shift to someone else's drama.

"That's one way to put it. I've been in this terrible limbo for eight years, thinking I'll eventually find myself wanting children, or the time will finally feel right, and it's just not coming. But I'm also not ready to rule it out, either," Elyse confided in Brie. "And poor Mark. Let's be real, if the roles were reversed, and he was keeping me waiting with no clear timeline, I'd likely be long gone by now," Elyse said matter-of-factly, staring at her lap.

Elyse had her faults just like anyone else, but lacking self-awareness wasn't one of them.

"You think Mark would be open to adopting a thirty-five-year-old orphan?" Brie asked.

Elyse laughed, and Brie joined her. Not because either of their situations were funny, but because sometimes you just had to laugh at yourself to lighten the load of all the heavy stuff life throws at you.

Sixteen

RACHEL

"SO, THIS NEW gluten-free, dairy-free, keto diet I've been doing has me feeling amazing! It's only been a couple of weeks, but I can tell already that it's going to be the one that sticks. Like I can't tell you how incredible I feel. You've gotta try it, Rach," Paula said.

Rachel nodded supportively as she bit into her turkey and cheese sub.

Paula was Rachel's chatty coworker from the finance department. They had nothing in common, but their lunch breaks were at the same time, and so they were acquaintances that had become best friends for the last ten years that Rachel had worked at her company—between 12:15 and 1:15 p.m. anyway.

"Thanks again for taking care of that grievance meeting, Rach," Lina, Rachel's new director, said as she walked into the lunchroom.

Rachel swallowed her bite and said, "Of course, anytime."

"I really appreciate it! You're a lifesaver. I'm still trying to learn all the logistics of this organization," Lina responded with a slight exasperation. "Anyway, enjoy the rest of your lunch, and I'll see you later this afternoon," Lina said, walking out of the lunchroom before Rachel could respond.

"Doesn't it drive you crazy?" Paula asked.

"What?" Rachel responded.

"That you've been here way longer than her and know way more than her and have basically been doing her job, even though she's your boss and gets paid way more than you," Paula pointed out, stabbing at her lettuce.

"She's only a few months in. She's still getting her feet wet. Plus, I don't mind helping," Rachel justified to Paula but also to herself.

"Mmmmm, I don't know, Rach. I'd be careful. It seems like she knows she can dump stuff on you to get done, and then be able to take the credit. I have no idea why you didn't apply for the director role when it was open. You were basically already doing the job," Paula said.

This had been brought to Rachel's attention multiple times. Most of her colleagues had expected her to apply for the role when it came up a few months ago. While she had watched most of her friends and coworkers get promoted and make strategic career moves over the last decade, Rachel had been in the same HR advisor role since she had started with the company. She had hired and trained so many others that had since moved on to new roles, new organizations, and new, higher salary ranges. Rachel knew most people would see this as a failure on her part, but it made things easier for her family, which made things easier for her.

"Yeah, I know, but I wouldn't have been able to work compressed hours as the director. Plus, Lina has good experience in other sectors. She brings a lot to the table," Rachel defended Lina, even though she wasn't sure she believed it. But overselling others while underselling herself came naturally to Rachel, almost like it was a reflex.

"Well, you know, as the director of HR, you probably could've changed that compressed hours policy. It's only a few more hours a week, surely you could've found a way to make it work," Paula pointed out.

"No, with the kids in different locations for daycare and school drop-off and pick-up, it's just too chaotic. And as long as Sean is doing shift work, it's just way easier this way," Rachel explained. "Besides, I can always apply next time. I'm in no rush. I've got decades of work ahead of me. Believe me, I'm familiar with the pension plan."

"Well, that part is certainly true," Paula agreed. "But how often is the director position going to come up? Lina is basically your age, and if she can make the salary she's making while dumping most of the hard work on you, then she's not going to be leaving anytime soon."

"We'll see when the kids are a little bit older. How is your marathon training going?" Rachel asked, hoping to steer the conversation in a different direction.

"Seriously, Rach. You know you could do it, right? You've gotta have more confidence in yourself!" Paula insisted, ignoring Rachel's attempt to change the subject.

"It's not a can or can't thing. It's just that I don't know about the timing and circumstances. We just have to do what's best for us. That's *all*," Rachel said in what she thought was a firm voice to try to end the conversation.

Rachel also used "us" and "we" way more than "me" and "I." Her family unit was more her identity than she was as an individual.

Rachel had gotten used to having to justify her decisions, or lack thereof. People often mistook Rachel's meekness and lack of ambition as a lack of confidence, when the opposite was true. Rachel was confident. So much so that she didn't feel the need, or the intense pressure, to show everyone what she was capable of. It wasn't that she didn't believe she could do the job of her director. It wasn't that she couldn't obsess more about diet and exercise, and maybe have a more involved beauty routine. It wasn't that she didn't think she could have more hobbies outside of her kids, and maybe post more on social media and really put herself out there. It wasn't that she didn't believe she could "do it all," like she was supposed to. She just didn't want to kill herself in the process like so many women her age seemed to not only do, but do so as though the self-inflicted suffering was a badge of honor they could display on their perfectly filtered Instagram pages.

But saying these things out loud would make her a bad feminist, or a bad millennial, or just a bad person. So, instead she just didn't say anything and let people think of her as poor, reserved Rachel. It was just easier that way, in her opinion.

In order to truly shut the conversation down with Paula, she did what every thirty-something-year-old did when they wanted out of a social situation. She picked up her phone.

In the ten minutes that Rachel was eating her lunch and defending her life to chatty Paula, she had missed texts from Leah, Alex, and Brie. Leah was likely in a waiting room somewhere looking to be distracted. Alex was likely sending a screenshot of a text exchange with her mom, wanting Rachel to share her outrage, and Brie was probably looking for some sort of practical advice about the HR implications on her job, as she struggled more and more to keep up with caregiving for Dora and working full time.

Rachel excused herself from the lunch table and made her way back to her cubicle where she would spend the next forty minutes texting back and forth with her friends.

Summer 2023

Seventeen

ELYSE

"AND HOW DOES what Mark said make you feel, Elyse?" Laura asked.

"Annoyed, mostly." Not just at Mark but also at Laura, their couples' therapist.

After getting nowhere for five months, Mark asked, or more or less threatened Elyse that therapy was the only solution. He insisted that their issues were deeper than having a baby, and they needed to start communicating differently. It was the last thing Elyse wanted to do. But she figured that since she hadn't delivered on her last favor for Mark, she should probably follow through on this one. She didn't believe in therapy, at least not for herself. It was probably fine for other people, but she didn't like the idea of having a stranger tell her what to do. Elyse didn't have any prior experience to back up that opinion, but, like most of her opinions, she assumed she was right.

"Why don't you elaborate, Elyse?" Laura pushed in her obnoxious tone that teetered between soothing and condescending.

"I know I seem like the selfish one in this scenario, but I'm also being realistic. It's always on me to be the practical, realistic one," Elyse explained.

"Remember what I said about using terms like *always* and *never*," Laura interjected, heavier on the condescending tone this time.

Fuck you, Laura, Elyse thought so loudly she was sure Laura could hear her inner monologue.

"What I'm trying to say is that I think Mark can sometimes be unrealistic. He tends to romanticize things, and then I'm the one who has to deal with the realities of things," Elyse said.

"Tell Markus, not me," Laura instructed.

This woman hated her. Elyse could tell.

"Markus," Elyse emphasized his name, turning toward him, "I think a baby would be the exact scenario I just described. I'm the one who has to physically deal with having a baby. It's easy to pin it on me as being selfish, but I don't think that's a fair judgment, since you're not being asked to sacrifice anything, and I'd be the one sacrificing my body, my career... my sanity."

"And that's time for today," Laura said before Mark could respond. "Great progress. Thank you to both of you for showing up for yourselves and each other."

Elyse mentally rolled her eyes at Laura and gave her a smug smile.

"Thanks Laura, we'll see you in a couple of weeks," Mark said with genuine appreciation.

"See you then," Elyse said, already halfway out of the door, while Mark was just beginning to stand up.

She couldn't bring herself to say "thank you." Elyse hated lying, and of all the things she felt toward Laura, thankful was not one of them.

After a silent elevator ride, Mark and Elyse gave each other a quick peck and went opposite directions, back to their respective offices, as though the last fifty minutes didn't just happen.

———

"When did you become so ambivalent toward kids?" Mark asked, finally breaking the silence of another takeout dinner in front of the TV. "You love your friends' kids, and you're great with them."

Normally on the evening after a therapy session, Elyse would ask Mark to watch a movie, or do something with family or friends. Anything to avoid having their therapy session follow them home.

"This has nothing to do with how I feel about kids. It has everything to do with how fucking hard I've worked, and I'm not about to let that all go. And if we're talking about being selfish, I think it's pretty selfish for you to ask me to do that."

The floodgates had been opened. Elyse was always the one to escalate an argument. She wasn't sure if it was a defense mechanism or just her competitive nature shining through. Like she could see where Mark's thoughts were going and needed to add all her counterarguments before Mark could even get his thoughts out.

"Just because your career has been handed to you, and you half-ass it doesn't mean I also have that luxury." Elyse knew she overstepped with her last comment. To her surprise, that one rolled right off Mark's back. *Was that really how complacent he'd become with his career? Must be nice.* "I've only been partner for a few months. You know I can't take time off now," she continued, while Mark just calmly took it all in.

His lack of reaction infuriated Elyse even more. But Mark had gotten used to Elyse's fighting style and knew it was better to let her get all of her points and insults out upfront before chiming in. He also knew that staying as calm and non-reactionary as he generally did, made her even angrier and was mostly why he did it.

"So, I'll take time off. I'll take paternity leave. I'll wake up at night to do feedings, change diapers…" Mark trailed off, before Elyse cut him off.

"You know I have to be on my A-game, especially this first year. I can't be running meetings while puking in trash cans, and I can't take time away for all the appointments. You have to be at the doctor like every other day when you're pregnant."

"You're being so stubborn. You're not even trying to find a solution here. It's like you don't want to find a solution," Mark replied.

"No, Mark, I'm being realistic. I'm the one this would be happening to. I'll be the one trying to run a goddamn firm with chapped nipples and no fucking sleep, not you," Elyse said in a tone that shut down any further comments from Mark.

There was a long silence. Seconds that felt like hours. Neither of them looked mad. Just exhausted from having the same fight over and over and over again.

"I'm worried I'll resent you for never even trying to have a family," Mark finally broke the silence.

"And I'm worried I'll resent you for making me have one," Elyse responded.

That would be the end of their fight for that evening. They had gotten so used to arguing that they intuitively knew when the fight was over, or really when it was time to pause it. Elyse had gotten the last word in as she always did, and they had both finally said the thing that made them realize they couldn't come to a compromise in this situation. And instead of taking the next step when coming to that realization, they stopped, because they weren't ready to have that part of the fight—the last part—just yet.

Eighteen

ALEX

ANDREW: GOOD LUCK AT WORK TODAY BABE.
ANDREW: NOT THAT YOU NEED IT :)

ALEX SMILED AS she read the texts from Andrew, who was already on his way to work for an early meeting. She had a big client presentation that day; one that, if landed, would mean her biggest bonus to date and likely an extra vacation this year. After a rocky transition, Alex was starting to find her feet again professionally. Yes, the schedule and the clientele were a bit different but so was her mindset. She actually felt better, like she had been promoted out of her mini dresses, not held back.

Things in general had been going well for Alex. Since the dinner with her mother, Alex had seen Cindy four times over the course of a few months. This was a new record since Alex moved out and went off to college. After debriefing with Andrew, spending a solid two therapy sessions on the topic and many texts with Rachel, Alex decided that having a bit more of her mom around wouldn't be the worst thing in the world. More so for Lola than for her. Maybe being a somewhat involved grandmother was her way to make up for being a completely uninvolved mother to Alex. Luckily, Dale hadn't entered the equation. That was a clear boundary for Alex. No way in hell she wanted to see that man, let alone have her daughter be in the same room as him. But that was a bridge they hadn't needed to cross, yet. It worked out that Dale likely disliked Alex as much as she disliked him.

Alex looked back up from her phone and caught a glimpse of Lola covered in oatmeal. Why did she give her oatmeal on the morning she was on her own and had to be at work by 8:45 a.m., sharp?

"Oh my, let's get you cleaned up!" She said playfully, as Lola wiped an oatmeal-covered hand through her hair.

Fifteen minutes later, with them both in fresh, oatmeal-free outfits, Alex pulled out of the driveway. She went through the motions of daycare drop-off: hung Lola's belongings by her cubby, helped her get her indoor shoes on, and gave her a hug and a kiss.

As she hopped back in her car and pulled onto the highway headed toward her office, the image of the whiteboard outside of Lola's classroom popped into her head. She must've seen it when she was there, but it didn't register in her brain until just now. It was Show and Share day.

"Shit. Shit, fuck, shit," Alex said out loud to herself.

She forgot. She sent Lola empty-handed on Show and Share day. She looked at the time. No way could she pull off at the next exit, make it home, back to daycare, and get to the office on time for the client meeting.

She couldn't believe she forgot the stuffy that Lola had picked out the night before. She had specifically put it on the entryway table by the keys so she wouldn't forget it.

She frantically dialed her coworker Pam. "Any way we can push the client meeting by fifteen minutes?" She asked as soon as Pam picked up the phone.

"Hi, Alex. I really don't think so. Not at this point."

"Shit. I think I'm going to be late. Like fifteen, twenty minutes," Alex replied.

"Oh, that shouldn't be a big deal. You know how the beginning of these things go. Mostly just chit-chat," Pam reassured her.

Alex knew that was true, but she loved the chit-chat. She was good at chit-chatting. She had won more clients over with her chit-chats than with her boring powerpoint presentations and graphs.

"I just, I forgot my laptop, and I made a few tweaks to the presentation, so I need the version on my laptop," she heard herself lie.

It must've been that she knew how ridiculous it seemed to potentially sacrifice a million-dollar client to pick up a stuffy for her toddler, who likely wasn't even aware of what Show and Share day was.

She made the decision in the nick of time to get off at the next quickly approaching exit and head back home. No way in hell was Lola going to be the kid with the mom who forgets her toy for Show and Share. That was something Kng Cindy would do, and Alex was not Cindy. But fuck, this client was huge. Landing them would allow her to buy all the stuffies in the world for Lola. But would that even matter to her if her mom can't even remember to pack it?

Alex felt herself spiraling. Listening to her own inner dialogue was exhausting. Jesus, how does a toddler's stuffed animal and a million-dollar client take up the same amount of brain space in her head?

Exactly eleven minutes later, Alex pulled back into Lola's daycare and sprinted inside, stuffy in tow. She opened the classroom door and the first face she saw was Lola's. It lit up the second she saw her mom, and Alex felt a huge sense of relief.

"Oh, we just finished with Show and Share a few minutes ago," Carrie, Lola's daycare teacher, said as she took the stuffy from Alex and handed it to Lola. "But that's okay, Lola, why don't you show everyone what you brought?"

"I–I missed it?" Alex said.

"Oh, no worries. Lola can share now. It's no biggie," Carrie said casually.

"Oh, okay," Alex replied. The juxtaposition of her frantic state with Carrie's calmness was so stark that it brought Alex back down to reality.

"Okay, bye sweetie. Love you." Alex waved goodbye to Lola, who didn't even notice her exit. She was too busy with a group of kids around her, looking at her stuffy.

Alex hopped back in her car and sped off. She held the tears back in her eyes as she made her way to the office. She had made it back to daycare, but she hadn't prevented that dreaded moment that Lola would've had to say, in her toddler gibberish, that she didn't have anything for Show and Share.

Growing up, Alex had become a pro at coming up with all the reasons that she wasn't properly prepared or equipped for something—no toys for show and tell, unsigned permission slips, no themed outfits for winter carnival. But that was different, right? This was just one time, and she was busy and distracted, and it was nothing at all like Cindy. No, no, that couldn't have been the case with her mother. Her mother just didn't care. She couldn't be bothered. Or, maybe she was distracted, too? But with what?

An incoming call on her Bluetooth snapped Alex out of it.

"Hey, Pam. I'll be there in ten. Please, please send my apologies," Alex said, forcing the stuffy debacle to the back of her head.

"No worries, they were a few minutes late anyway. Just getting coffee and AV set up now," Pam updated.

"Okay, see you soon!" Alex said as she ended the call.

Well, she had somehow managed to still let Lola down and be late for a huge client. Maybe this was that work-life balance that everyone talks about—screwing up equally at home and work.

Alex made it to the office just as everyone else was finishing their coffees and niceties. She paused for just a moment before entering the boardroom and adjusting her posture and facial expression, trying to mentally shift from a woman who was crying over a stuffy minutes ago, to the self-assured professional that she was, or at least pretended to be.

The presentation went off without a hitch. She apologized again at the end for being late and assured the clients how valuable their time and consideration were to her. The clients didn't care, and Alex tried to fight the instinctual urge to tell herself that her presentation probably didn't actually Kally sway their decision. She heard her therapist's voice in her head, which was starting to sound a lot like her own voice. *No, Alex. Stop downplaying yourself. You did a great job and it's okay to think that. You are a strong, smart, capable woman, and you deserve to feel proud of yourself.* These little internal pep talks seemed silly, but when your brain is conditioned to constantly tell yourself the opposite, they are necessary, and surprisingly a lot of hard work.

———

As she pulled into the daycare parking lot for the third time that day, Alex caught a glimpse of Lola in her classroom window. All happy and covered in paint and what looked like spaghetti sauce. She was playing with blocks in a circle with other toddlers.

"She had a great day today, only napped an hour, though," Carrie reported, as Alex got Lola's coat and shoes on.

That was it, no mention of the stuffy or Show and Share. No inkling that Lola was showing signs of distress because of an absent-minded mother.

As she buckled Lola in her car seat, her work phone vibrated. It was a text from Pam.

Pam: Sorry to message so late but thought you'd want to know that we landed it! You killed it today by the way!

So, there she was with her happy well-adjusted toddler, landing big clients, and still somehow feeling like a major fuckup. In her moment of weakness, she wanted to call her mom. Maybe not her mom but *a* mom. This was usually when she would reach out to Rachel. It surprised her how much she yearned for that feeling. How much she felt like she needed a mom even now. Especially now. Despite getting through her teens and twenties without any amount of parental guidance, and now being in her mid-thirties with what most would consider to be an accomplished career, she never felt like she needed a mother more than she did now.

———

Later that evening, once Lola had gone down for the night, Andrew insisted on opening a bottle of Alex's favorite—and overpriced—sparkling wine to celebrate her landing the client.

"Cheers to you, my incredible, smart, sexy wife," Andrew said, raising a glass. God, was he actually this perfect?

"Babe, you really didn't have to go out of your way to pick up the fancy wine," Alex replied.

"Don't worry, it's on you, anyway," he joked, referring to the large bonus Alex would now be getting.

Andrew's humor always brought a smile to Alex's face and made her feel just a little bit lighter.

"Well, I knew you could do it. Did you really have any doubt?" He asked, before taking a sip of wine.

"No," Alex shook her head so quickly and instinctively it caught her off guard.

She was so confident in her professional life that she really didn't have any doubts about how this would go with the client. Of course she questioned if the presentation was executed perfectly and just how much the tardiness would come into play, but she realized at that moment that she had never once doubted her ability to get the outcome she was looking for.

It was the exact opposite of how she felt as a parent. She wasn't confident. She questioned every little decision, and it was exhausting. Everyone says that raising kids is hard, but she thought it was the big things that made it hard—potty training, curfews, test scores, behavioral issues, not every little minute detail of everyday life. It was like every interaction with Lola was an opportunity to do it better than how she was raised, and more importantly, it was an opportunity to screw it up. She just wasn't good at this whole parenting thing. She objectively knew she wasn't terrible, but she still just wasn't *good* at it in her mind. Alex wasn't used to being just okay at something. She had worked hard and perfected faking it until she made it, so that she could have a level of stability and control over her life that she didn't have growing up.

It wasn't that Alex thought she was good at everything; she had just made sure she was good at the things that mattered, and somehow the things she wasn't good at, like cooking and parallel parking, just didn't matter. Downplaying her weaknesses was one way she never had to accept mediocrity. But parenting was different. It mattered. It mattered so much it hurt. And yet, she wasn't good at it. But she couldn't just brush it off as unimportant like she did with cooking and parallel parking.

The spiral of negative thoughts felt like a crushing weight. Since starting therapy, Alex was more mindful of her pattern of negative thinking. She might have been mindful of her negative thoughts but not yet in control of them, which in some ways, felt worse than when she wasn't so damn mindful. She felt tears beginning to well in her eyes.

Andrew noted the quick shift in Alex's mood and tilted his head to try to meet her watery eyes. "Whoa, babe, what's wrong?"

She snapped back to the conversation with Andrew. "I forgot Lola's stuffy for Show and Share today," Alex explained.

Andrew was silent, mostly out of confusion. "And?" he asked, breaking the brief silence.

"And I had to turn around and go back home and get it, so I was late for the client meeting. I got it to her, but it was just as it was ending and...and I almost missed it. She almost didn't have a toy for Show and Share—"

"Well, you must've really wowed them if you kept them waiting, and they still signed on right away," Andrew interrupted.

"No, no that's not the point. I forgot the stuffy. What kind of mother forgets this stuff? I bet you Rachel has never done anything like that," Alex said.

"Alex, she's not even two. She doesn't even know what Show and Share is. If her biggest problem in life is that you forgot her stuffy, I'd say the kid has it pretty good, wouldn't you?" Andrew said, trying to talk some sense into Alex.

Alex shrugged her shoulders. "Yeah I know," she agreed, even though she wasn't convinced.

She hated that she didn't have a barometer for good parenting. She knew Andrew was probably right and she was overreacting, but what was the tipping point? How many times does forgetting about Show and Share, or some equally minor offense, add up to bad parenting? When does the accumulation of all these little mistakes add up to years of therapy for Lola? Is this rationalization what Cindy would do? Did Cindy just excuse all the little things, to the point where excusing the big things was also okay? Alex made a mental note to save these questions for her next therapy session, because there was no way she was going to find the answer here herself.

———

Later that night as Alex went through the motions of her nighttime routine—taking off her makeup, examining her face in detail for fine lines, and applying several different products that promised eternal youth and beauty—she couldn't get her newly acquired epiphany out of her head: that she wasn't good at the thing that mattered most to her in the world. And it seemed like simply trying harder, a technique that worked for all of her professional problems, didn't work with parenting. Maybe it made things worse. Kind of like how they say if you're in quicksand, the harder you try to get free, the farther you'll sink.

As she climbed into bed, still feeling the weight of the emotions from the day and still questioning why she couldn't just be better at this whole parenting thing, she felt her phone vibrate.

Cindy: I need some pics of Lola...you never send any. You'll regret it one day if you don't take more ya know.

And there was her answer. As if the universe was giving her a direct answer to her question. Cindy.

She ignored Cindy's text and instead zoned out on her phone for forty-five minutes, followed by a quick ten minutes of work emails to justify the forty-five minutes of scrolling.

"So, what do you think about being a family of three?" Alex asked Andrew as he joined her in bed.

Alex felt a desperate need to feel like she was doing something proactive to quell her inferior parenting and the discomfort it caused her. So, in the last hour she had decided that the best way to do that was to not expose any more children to it.

"It's amazing..." Andrew started.

"No no, what do you think about *staying* a family of three?" Alex explained, as Andrew had clearly misinterpreted her question.

They hadn't yet discussed having another child, but she was pretty sure Andrew was expecting that they would.

"Well..." He paused cautiously as he shifted closer toward her under their duvet. "I think I'd be happy to have one or two more. I mean one is probably more realistic at my age. I'd also be happy to just have Lola. Not just. She's amazing and perfect obviously. Just like her mom. How do you feel about it?"

"I mean, yeah, I just think one and done. I mean it will just be so much easier. We can travel more and have more money to provide Lola with everything she could ever want or need," Alex justified, leaving out the part about her parenting insecurities.

She felt both relieved and hurt that Andrew was on board. Maybe he also thought she wasn't a good enough parent. Instead of just being thankful for a supportive partner, Alex took the path of least resistance, which for her, was to give in to her negative self-talk. To really let it run wild. To assume the worst. To think that Andrew was agreeable only because he, too, thought Alex wasn't a good parent, or that she wouldn't be able to handle any more kids after watching her struggle so much in the early days of having Lola. She had to tell her inner voice to shut up, but it was just so freaking loud sometimes.

"Plus, you're right. You are over forty, you know?" She teased.

Andrew smirked and pulled Alex into his arms.

Andrew's a loving and supportive partner. If there was anyone she could open up to about all of her parenting insecurities and deep-seated fear of screwing up Lola beyond repair, it was him. But Alex liked to try to sort out her feelings herself first before she burdened anyone else with them. Because that's what *her* feelings were—a burden.

During one of her many late-night Googling sessions, Alex learned that this tendency to keep her feelings to herself was likely the result of never having her feelings validated as a kid. When she discovered that article on Psychology Today at two in the morning, she made a mental note to ask Lola about her feelings more. Sure, she was only aware of like three emotions at this point in her life, but Alex wanted to give Lola all the tools to make sure she didn't turn out like her. Her next Google search was for *toddler books about feelings.*

A stack of them had arrived at her front door two days later, and they currently sit on her bedside table, full of creases, dog-eared pages, hand written notes in the margins and other signs of frequent use. Because even if her genetics and childhood environment didn't equip her with the tools to be a good mother, surely she could study her way to competent parenting.

Nineteen

LEAH

"YOU'RE GOING TO be late, babe," Leah heard Scott call from the bathroom.

She rolled over from under her cozy duvet to face the en suite doorway. "I called in sick."

Scott gave her a skeptical glance from behind his toothbrush. "But, are you sick?"

He really didn't know how to read a room. Leah gave him a very loud and clear answer with only her eyes.

Scott sighed. "Does Oliver need a packed lunch today?" He asked with a slightly annoyed tone.

"Jesus, Scott, just figure it out. I've managed to pack lunches every day for the last two years without a manual," Leah snapped at him.

Scott just stared at her. He wasn't used to Leah snapping at him, and he wasn't used to defending himself, either, so silence with a blank stare had been his standard response to Leah's snarky comments that had increased substantially over the last few months.

"I'm sorry," Leah said genuinely as she sat up in bed.

A few months had passed since Leah learned the devastating news that the transfer of two out of her three embryos was unsuccessful. After waiting the longest two weeks of her life to take a pregnancy test, seeing the negative result shattered Leah. She spent hours staring at the multiple pregnancy tests she had taken, trying to will a second pink line into existence. She even held onto them for an extra couple of weeks and would periodically re-check them, as though it was possible that she could have missed the second pink line that she was desperate to see.

Ever since, she had been moody, sad, and withdrawn. She was still going through the motions of it all: all the follow-ups, the blood work, the appreciative nods when doctors said, "these things happen," or "it's so common," and "don't worry you've got another embryo left." But the process was hard enough when she actually had some hope, excitement even. Without that, the process was terrible, all-consuming and soul-crushing.

Scott was sweet at first, and he also seemed genuinely sad that IVF hadn't worked. Or, maybe it was just because Leah was so sad. For the first couple of weeks after finding out she wasn't pregnant, it felt like she and Scott were actually grieving *together*. It was the most in sync she had felt with Scott since they had started trying for a second baby, and that connection felt like a very thin silver lining to living through her worst-case scenario.

But the thing with grief is that everyone has a different timeline for theirs. Leah was still very much in the midst of hers, whereas Scott promptly snapped out of his after a couple of weeks. Leah realized that the period of grief immediately after was miniscule compared to the grief she felt when everyone, Scott included, had seemingly moved on. The only thing worse than grief was being alone in it.

Scott's sweetness faded to irritation and then exasperation when he realized they weren't done. That Leah was still dead set on doing everything she could to have a second baby. It was like the more Scott resisted, the harder Leah would push. And the harder Leah would push, the more Scott resisted. The argument they had a few weeks after Leah's negative pregnancy test was one that Leah replayed in head daily. And every time she replayed it in her head, the more annoyed and determined to have another baby she got.

"At what point do we decide that enough is enough? You can't keep putting yourself through this," Scott had said to her.

Leah couldn't help but think that what he really meant to say was *you can't keep putting me through this.*

"Scott, we can't spend as much time and money on this as we have to not explore further options and figure out if there are any other issues. We still have options, and we still have an embryo. I'm not giving up that easily," she had told him.

"I'm sorry, babe. I just want you to know that you don't have to keep doing this," he had told her, with an expression that he probably thought conveyed love and concern, but all Leah could see in his face was disingenuity and condescension. Leah hated that look.

Every attempt Scott made to take the pressure off of her felt like a veiled attempt to get her to stop. It was so like Scott to try to get her to be the one to make the decision to stop, even though that's what *he* really wanted, not her. His lack of directness, which sometimes hovered into cowardice, or even borderline manipulation, was one of the few things that really bothered her about him.

"What makes you think for a second that I don't want to keep doing this?" Leah had responded, accusingly.

"I didn't say you didn't want it. I just meant that you don't have to...I mean if you feel like you need a break..." The vision of Scott struggling to find the right words so as not to upset her was vivid in her memory.

"I'm fine, Scott. Slowing this process down will make me feel worse, not better," she had said, making it clear what their next steps would be.

Scott had nodded slowly and wrapped his arms around her. A giant embrace from his tall, broad frame always made Leah feel better. Scott also knew this and tended to use this approach to end an uncomfortable conversation he didn't want to be having with Leah. And Leah knew that too, but she still accepted the hug because she really needed it at that moment.

What Scott didn't know was that Leah was not slowing down. In fact, she was speeding up. Waiting for the medical system and being tied to twenty-eight-day cycles drove her crazy. So, she had gone full tilt into everything else she could do day-to-day. If there was a tea or a supplement said to boost fertility, she was now taking it.

One day she'd read something about cutting out carbs, the next she'd hear of someone who got pregnant after increasing their carbs and lowering protein. One second she was hearing that eating plant-based was the key, and the next she was hearing that nightshades are bad, whatever those were. Her diet was all over the place. The best one she heard, the one that she had yet to successfully try, was to relax more and stress less.

The truth was that Leah knew most of this was marketing bullshit preying on desperate women to confuse, scare, and try to make a buck off them. But she ignored the logical side of her brain, and instead was fully invested. She didn't actually expect any of it to help her get pregnant; she just had to do something to make her feel like she had some control in the situation.

Scott finished brushing his teeth and walked over to give Leah a kiss on the top of her head, as a way of letting her know he accepted her apology.

Leah let out a small sigh. "Thank you," she practically whispered.

Scott continued kissing her head then moved on to her temple, then behind her ear. Not in a sexy way, but because he knew how ticklish Leah was and that she would have to laugh. And she did. *Damn him for always turning the mood silly. But also, thank God for him always turning the mood silly.*

Even though her frustration with Scott seemed justified, she knew her snapping at him wasn't. She was so used to being described as laid back and rational, but with the combination of hormones and the stress of uncertainty, Leah felt like she was practically a different person. She always got especially worked up right before a medical appointment. She had to double check her calendar to see what this week's appointment was. There had been so many injections, blood draws, and pelvic exams that they all melded together. This week was her OB/GYN appointment to talk about genetic testing of their remaining embryo.

Leah hated these appointments. She'd take the physical discomfort of a speculum scraping her cervix over the emotional discomfort of discussing the remaining embryo any day. Having one embryo left should've given her hope, but instead, it caused stress and anxiety. The feeling of any sense of control over her situation was quickly slipping away, just like her options. All of her eggs were in one basket. Except it was just the one egg—an embryo, and instead of a basket it was a tank of liquid nitrogen at the fertility clinic.

After saying goodbye to Scott and Oliver, Leah settled back in her bed and turned on the TV. She knew she was sulking, but she didn't care. And then she got a text from Elyse.

Elyse: Hey, I'm in your neck of the woods for a meeting. Are you free around 1? If so, we should grab lunch!

Leah: Hey! Yeah, sure I'd love that.

Leah decided to leave out the part that she wasn't actually at her office and had plans to stay in jammies most of the day, but Elyse was the last person she wanted to tell that to. An excuse to get out was likely just what she needed rather than wallowing in self-pity.

A few hours later, dressed in business casual so Elyse wouldn't question her whereabouts, Leah showed up at their favorite café ten minutes early. She ordered her usual decaf iced green tea with lemon while longing for an actual cup of coffee.

Fifteen minutes later, Elyse joined her in their usual spot by a window.

"Hey! How are you?" Elyse asked, as Leah got up to hug her friend.

Elyse looked a million times more put together than Leah, but Elyse usually looked a million times more put together than most people, so she tried not to let it bother her.

"Good," Leah said, very unconvincingly, as they sat across from each other. "What about you?"

"Amazing! Work has been great. I really think I was meant for the partner life," Elyse said enthusiastically. She was never one to downplay her own triumphs.

Leah smiled at her friend warmly. She could always count on Elyse to take up all the space in a room, or in a conversation. Sure, it could sometimes be a bit much, but then there were times like this, when it was just what Leah needed to distract herself.

After listening to Elyse go on about her work in painstaking detail for twenty minutes, Leah asked, "What else is new? How is Mark doing?"

"He's good," Elyse answered in a much too high-pitched voice. After a brief pause, Elyse told Leah what she already knew. "Things are the same. We're just at this stalemate. It's like he can't understand that just because I don't want kids now doesn't mean I don't want them at all. I don't get how he can't see that this is just really bad timing for us, with me making partner and all. We actually started therapy a few weeks ago," Elyse said with a grimace, as she balanced the menu between her hands.

"Oh wow." Leah raised her eyebrows, trying not to seem too shocked that Elyse would go to such lengths. She knew Elyse wasn't a fan of therapy.

"I know. Clearly, it wasn't my choice." Elyse pointed out the obvious.

"Do you feel like it's helping?" Leah asked.

"No," Elyse said without hesitation. "I'm pretty sure our therapist hates me, but the feeling is mutual."

"So, what do you want out of it, if you don't mind me asking?" Leah asked gently as she tilted her chin downward.

"I think I want to be a dad more than a mom, to be honest. Like yes, I do want a kid, maybe two. But I just don't want to be the one sacrificing everything. And all the equality mumbo jumbo is bullshit. All the women I went to school with or worked with who got pregnant in the first five-to-ten years, well let's just say they're not partners of their firms, or even close to being one," Elyse said.

"And what about the ones who don't have kids?" Leah asked.

Elyse thought for a moment before speaking. "Well, of the people I know, one is recently divorced, one should probably be divorced given she's been sleeping with her coworker for well over a year, and the other I'm pretty sure is an alcoholic." Elyse let out a breathy laugh, reflecting on the depressing nature of the situation.

"Well, I'm sure if there's anyone who could be partner, have a kid, and not have a drinking problem, it'd be you. Plus, you know Mark would likely breastfeed for you if he could," Leah joked, causing Elyse to chuckle.

"I'm sorry. I'm being an asshole. I know babies are a touchy subject," Elyse said, lowering her menu and placing folded hands on top.

Leah gently shook her head. "Don't apologize. I think our situations are probably more similar than they are different."

Leah could feel the presence of the waiter approaching their table, as if he could tell that they were having a serious conversation and was waiting for an appropriate time to interrupt it. They quickly recited their orders—salmon salad with goat cheese and balsamic dressing on the side for Elyse, and avocado toast with poached eggs for Leah—before handing their menus back to the waiter.

"So, what's next for you guys?" Elyse asked.

"Well, we still have an embryo frozen, but I don't really want to transfer it before knowing the likelihood of success. I've got some follow-up appointments in the next couple of weeks. My doctor thinks getting pregnant naturally is still a possibility. So basically, we have no answers and a very expensive embryo that scares the shit out of me," Leah said.

"This is going to sound like a dumb question, but how do you know? Like how can you be so sure that it's what you want?" Elyse asked.

Even though all of her friends were in different parenting, or intentionally non-parenting situations, what she was most jealous of was their certainty in their decisions. Rachel knew she wanted two kids and timed them almost exactly two years apart. Brie had been adamant about being childless by choice since she was a teenager and felt she was somehow burning down the patriarchy while doing it. Alex had recently come to the conclusion that she and Andrew were one and done, and Leah wanted at least two, if not three. For the rest of her friends, the decisions were about the minute details—when, how many, names, nursery themes. But the actual decision of whether or not to be a parent was an easy one for the rest of them. Elyse didn't like to admit jealousy, but this was one topic where she could. Even greater than her feeling of jealousy, was her feeling of frustration with herself for not being able to make this decision.

"I don't think you're supposed to fully know one-hundred percent. I think with your first you're pretty much just pretending to be adults, like you're just playing house or something, and then after you have the kid is when it actually dawns on you that you made a really big decision. And in terms of having a second," Leah's eyes moved upward and her lips thinned, as though she was just having this realization for the first time, "well for me anyway, knowing it might not happen has made me that much more sure that it's what I want."

"Well, I truly hope it all works out for you guys. Don't tell the rest of the girls I said this, but Oliver is definitely the cutest kid out of the bunch, so you guys should definitely make some more babies," Elyse said, trying to lighten the mood.

"Secret's safe with me," Leah replied with a wink.

Twenty

BRIE

THE THICK AIR hit Brie like a ton of bricks as she unlocked the door to Dora's apartment. It was one of the hottest days of the summer, and air conditioning was a luxury that Dora could absolutely afford but chose not to because it seemed frivolous. It was one of the many choices Dora made out of silent protest that made her life more difficult than it needed to be and helped absolutely no one else in the process.

Despite living with Brie for the past eight months, Dora had kept her apartment. They both genuinely thought her staying with Brie would be a temporary thing, and somehow Dora would go back to living on her own in her funky, three-story walk-up apartment. Looking back, Brie now realized how dumb it was to think that.

Now that her class schedule had slowed down for the summer, she didn't have as many distractions as she wanted to. The ones that helped her cope day-to-day. She was left with no other choice than to start focusing on the longer-term logistics and decisions regarding her mom.

Decisions. It seemed all Brie did these days was make decisions, now that Dora's doctor had officially declared her incompetent. Now it was up to Brie to make what seemed like unfathomable, huge, life-altering decisions that she realized she would've normally turned to Dora for advice for. Despite being a free spirit, Brie had relied heavily on Dora's guidance throughout her life. She hadn't realized how much so until now. Even though Brie felt like she knew her mom inside and out, she found it impossible to make decisions on someone else's behalf. Brie wasn't sure if this was a universal thing, or a Dora thing. It was probably easier to make decisions for someone who was a bit more rational than Dora was—is.

One of those decisions was what to do with Dora's apartment. Once it became clear that there was no way she would be living alone again, it didn't make sense to pay two rents. And as Brie had been told several times by doctors, nurses, social workers and the countless other staff she interacted with on a daily basis to coordinate her mom's care, the fewer assets Dora had in her name the better.

Having a lower net worth would avoid being charged extra for future care needs and the less she would get dinged for when it came to "government assistance." That was a tough one for Brie. Any way to pull one over on the government would be strongly supported by Dora, but she was also a huge fan of publicly funded services. It was one of her many contradictions.

Brie found the thermostat and turned the dial. There was initial resistance, reflective of just how long it had been since the dial had been moved.

"Sorry, Dora," Brie said aloud.

If Brie's summer project was to clear out Dora's apartment and terminate the lease, she was at least going to be comfortable doing it.

Trying to figure out where to start was overwhelming. Brie decided specifically to avoid the closet. Dora's wardrobe was so eclectic. Fun, boho, curated. It seemed like every piece had a story behind it. It was connected to some trip, or experience, gifted or borrowed from someone special, and rarely ever purchased from a mass producer. Her wardrobe was too "her," and Brie figured it would be too difficult to start with something that was so blatantly Dora. She also wanted to avoid the bedroom for as long as possible for obvious reasons. Dora's openness with sexuality never bothered Brie like it would've most daughters growing up, but now that Dora was no longer Dora, no longer "competent," it felt weird to think of her in that way or recognize that was once a part, a very important part, of her life.

So, Brie started with the safe, boring choice—the entryway nook that Dora used as her "office." Brie already had most of the important required legal documents. And Dora being semi-retired for the last five years meant that Brie was mostly just hoping to shred and dispose of her mom's documents, maybe keep a few books on her bookshelf and donate the rest.

She decided to torture herself and start with a dusty box on the bottom of the bookshelf labeled photos. Most of them were of Dora in her glory days. There were lots of pictures with big groups of friends, and lots of different men. You could never tell if they were love interests, casual acquaintances, or often in Dora's case, both.

Brie had already accepted that she may never know who her father was. And to be fair, she didn't think Dora truly knew, either.

There was obviously a short list. Dora had never explicitly tried to stop her from finding out; she just didn't really know herself and never seemed to be bothered by that fact. After a brief stint as an angsty teenager when Brie felt betrayed by not knowing, she had accepted that she likely would never know but also that it didn't matter. The other fifty percent of her genetics didn't bother her, because she knew deep down, she was all Dora.

Brie moved onto the next box, realizing she hadn't actually done anything with the contents of the previous box. This box was labeled "Brie." It was like stepping into a different era of Dora. Instead of photos of Dora drinking on the beach with friends, this box was filled with pictures of Brie as a little girl. Brie had seen most of them before, but there were some hidden gems in there as well, like a photo of Brie with their family dog that they had for just a few short weeks. Brie remembered Dora changing her mind, because the domestication of dogs felt unnatural and unethical. Ever since that experience, Brie had always silently judged people who had pets.

In the present moment, Brie realized that Dora probably just didn't want to have to do all the work to care for a puppy in an apartment. Funny how that had never occurred to her until now. After combing through photos of herself and many terribly made arts and crafts that Brie couldn't believe Dora had held onto, and she subsequently chucked in the garbage, she moved onto the next box. It was mostly a lot of old bank statements, some of them not even open.

Brie's breath was taken away when she saw Dora's handwriting. Something she hadn't seen in a while. Something so mundane that she'd never really thought about, until she realized that Dora hadn't written anything on her own in months. The envelope, which had a return to sender stamp on it, was addressed to Mary in San Juan, Puerto Rico. Mary was Dora's old college pen pal who she wrote to sporadically over the course of many years. Brie ripped it open and started reading it.

Hola Mary!

I'm writing to you from a birthday cake-filled coma, or maybe it's just exhaustion?

Today was Brie's first birthday. We made it! It was a wonderful day, but it was a lonely day. That must be why I felt compelled to sit down and write to you. For some reason, there's something about her turning one that makes me feel like my single mother status has been finalized. I guess that's my fault though, since I haven't exactly done much over the last year, or when I was pregnant, to track down her dad. There are a few possibilities, and my gut tells me I know who he actually is, but it's such a weird situation to try to navigate. And who has time to track down one-nights stands when you've got a baby to take care of?

It's funny. I've gone to so many marches and protests about abortion, donated to planned parenthood, all that. It would have been the logical thing to do, to terminate my pregnancy, but I just couldn't do it. And now I have this amazing little girl, but oh my god, you have no idea how tough it is being a single mother. It's hard in every way. Time is no longer my own. I guess that's what I get for being such a "free spirit" all these years. Financially it's hard. Obviously, child support isn't really an option here. At least being a research assistant at Providence College has been great, because they let me bring Brie along, and I can study and get my tuition for half-price. I know things could be a lot worse, but everything feels like an uphill battle now.

One of my professors complimented me last week. How admirable it was that I was such a modern woman who does it all. A single working mom, who also studies full time, and doesn't take a penny from a man (not that it's really an option for me, and also I'm not sure why that is admirable). It was a nice compliment, but I felt like a fraud accepting it. Like if only my professor knew that I would just love to meet a nice rich man that could take care of me and Brie. Is that really so bad? That's also what my parents wish, too, I think. I just want to be taken care of sometimes you know?

Anyway, thanks for listening to my rant. How are you? How are your courses this semester? Any love interests? If so, for the love of god, use protection!

Adios!

Love, Dora

The handwriting was unquestionably Dora, but the sentiments expressed were not. This was not the Dora that Brie knew.

Brie realized she never actually thought of Dora as a single mother. She obviously knew that she was, but she had never once heard Dora refer to herself as that. She just thought of her as this independent, self-sufficient badass, who also happened to be her mom. Not that the two are mutually exclusive. It had always just been them, and Dora never acted like anything was missing. Maybe to protect Brie, so she didn't feel like she was missing out, or maybe it was more to protect herself?

Who was the real Dora? Was she the one that Brie knew her whole life? The one who had never once visibly expressed self-doubt? The one who made Brie feel like their life was full? Or, was she the Dora in this letter? Were they really different people? Brie felt a lot of things at that moment. Mostly confused but also a deep sense of shame, because realizing that Dora was maybe just a little bit more conventional, a bit more vulnerable, and was independent out of necessity, not by choice, disappointed Brie. It was like she had been lied to her entire life. What a shitty thought, Brie considered.

She slipped the letter into the back pocket of her jean shorts and decided to move on from the office to something more emotionally neutral, like the kitchen cupboards. She put her ear buds in, blasted some Fleetwood Mac, and started chucking everything from the kitchen cupboards without thinking twice. It was a lot of wasted food that Dora probably would've wanted Brie to give to a homeless person, but Brie was adamant that she was actually getting something done while she was there, so she could reduce the number of visits she would need to make over the next few weeks. After spending an hour and a half going through three boxes, just to have her entire perception of her mother blown up, it felt good to rip through the kitchen, staring at empty cupboards only twenty minutes later.

After filling three garbage bags, and likely to Dora's dismay, ignoring what was recyclable and what wasn't, Brie glanced at her phone and realized it was time to pick Dora up from her adult day program. Another thing that Brie hated but also desperately needed to get Dora out of the house two days a week.

———

Later that week, on the other day that Dora was at her adult day program, Brie met up with Alex on her lunch break. They opted for grab-and-go bagel sandwiches from the café in the bottom of Alex's office building and walked the two blocks to enjoy them on a park bench overlooking the Providence River.

"How's the apartment purging going?" Alex asked, biting into her smoked salmon and cream cheese on a pumpernickel bagel.

"Well, I'm here having lunch with you instead," Brie deadpanned.

"I'm sorry. It must be so tough to have to go through all her things," Alex said, stating the obvious, because she didn't know what else to say.

"I have my moments. It's weird going through her stuff. It's like she's gone, which I mean mentally she is. But then I go pick her up, or go home to her, and she's there. Like I forget that she's still actually....around." Brie couldn't bring herself to use the words *alive* and *dead*, because it felt too morbid.

"When I was there earlier in the week, I found this letter..." Brie went on to detail the contents of the letter to Alex. "I don't know why, but it's really shaken me. It was like a completely different person wrote it. Like who was this woman?"

Alex set her bagel down on its wrapper in her lap and shifted on the bench to face Brie. "I mean, your mom and Dora from the letter can still be the same person. Maybe just in different phases of life? Or just slightly different shades of Dora. We all have different versions of ourselves when you think about it."

Brie leaned her elbow on the back of the bench and let her head fall into her hand. "Yea, I guess. I just wish I knew which one she truly was? Like deep, *deep* down."

"It probably depended on the day. And the audience. God knows there's a version of Alex that I'd rather not have Lola know about. Even if Dora had a side she didn't show you, it doesn't change how close you guys were, and how much of an impact she's had on you," Alex said, trying to comfort Brie. She wasn't used to seeing her friend struggle like this.

"I know. I guess, I just hate that I feel like maybe I didn't know her as well as I thought I did," Brie admitted.

"Well, at least you probably don't have any latent trauma about your mom forgetting your Show and Share toy," Alex said, referring to Lola's stuffy debacle she had already filled Brie in on.

Brie chuckled supportively. "Well, no I don't recall Dora forgetting a Show and Share toy, but that sounds like something that encourages capitalism, so she probably would've written a strongly worded letter and tried to get Show and Share shut down instead."

Alex laughed. "God, it's almost like there are endless ways to permanently mess up your kid or something."

"Speak for yourself. I'm the most well-adjusted person I know," Brie said sarcastically.

Twenty-One

RACHEL

"SO, WE'RE THINKING the theme for the Back-to-School Fall Fair could be either barnyard fun or apple harvest. If we do barnyard fun, I have a petting zoo hook-up," Christina, the head of the PTA, declared proudly. "What do you think about that, Rachel?"

Christina singled her out, probably because she was the only one who hadn't nodded enthusiastically at Christina's ideas. The ideas themselves were fine; Rachel just didn't idolize Christina like the other PTA moms did.

School had barely been out for two weeks, but the planning for the annual Back-to-School Fall Fair had already begun. As if parents didn't already have enough shit to worry about the first week of school, the fair added themed dress-up days and bake sales to the mix. With both Henry and Julia attending the same school starting in the fall, Rachel thought she should get more involved in the school activities. So, her lunch breaks for the next six weeks would be spent in an elementary school gymnasium.

"I think barnyard fun sounds great. The kids will love it," Rachel gave the answer that she knew Christina wanted to hear, not what she actually thought, which was that apple harvest would be so much easier and likely involve less poop than farm animals.

"Okay, so it looks like barnyard fun it is!" Christina said enthusiastically. "Next order of business, let's try to work out the volunteer schedule quickly so we can get out of here on time. Rachel has to get back to the office," Christina made a point to let everyone know.

Rachel was the only working mom on the PTA, a notable difference that the other moms like to point out frequently.

"So, most of the activities that require volunteers are on Friday, so I'm going to be there all day. Diane, why don't you take the nine-to-eleven shift. Krista, you can take the eleven-to-one shift, and Rachel can you do one to three?" Christina asked while staring down at her laptop, without bothering to wait for any agreement.

"Uh, actually, I was kind of hoping I could do the lunchtime hours," Rachel piped up. "It's just that I'm working that day. So, I'm going to try to just take a bit of a long lunch, so that's really the only time I'm able to...sorry," Rachel apologized unnecessarily.

There was a brief but very awkward silence.

"Oh, yes. Yes, of course," Christina said. "Krista, you can switch with Rachel then."

Krista, another mom who reveled in elementary school politics, nodded in agreement, not that Christina had really given her an option.

"Okay, that's all for today. Thanks ladies! And please grab some donuts and coffee in the back. I won't eat them," Christina emphasized the last sentence, hoping to convey her superiority for avoiding pastries.

Rachel ignored the humble brag and made her way to the back of the gym to grab a few donuts to take home to Sean and the kids.

"So good to see you again, Rach," Krista said as she poured herself some coffee. "Really, no almond milk for the coffee? Jesus. I didn't realize anyone actually still consumed dairy."

"You, too, Krista. I should really be on my—"

"Oh, right, you have to go back to work after this," Krista cut in a patronizing tone.

It's 1:10 on a Tuesday, Krista, where else would I be? Rachel thought to herself but just gave a sympathetic nod instead.

"Rachel, I don't know how you do it! Working full time and kids, and then to volunteer for this. It really is important, though! Not like the rest of the uptight power suit moms who act like they're too good for it. It's so refreshing to see someone who works but still prioritizes what really matters, you know?" Krista said.

"Well, I'm technically not full time. I reduced my hours, so I have a bit more flexibility." Rachel could hear how she undersold herself and deflected the compliment, if it even was one.

"You really must join us for lunch after one of these meetings. It's where the real fun stuff gets discussed," Krista said with a wink.

Rachel didn't even know what to make of that.

The truth was, Rachel just didn't mesh with the stay-at-home moms, but she felt equally out of place with the hustling and bustling mom crowd, too. Getting into the minutiae of whether or not it was ethical to provide non-organic snacks at the fall fair is where the PTA moms lost her. She quickly blocked out the voice that judged these moms. The voice that said, "You know, if you also had to work you may not have the time to navel gaze over the most trivial details of your kids' snacks that they probably don't even eat." But she almost never let herself have those thoughts. No, she wouldn't be that mom.

She knew she was being judged by the career moms for not being career-oriented enough. She also knew she was being judged by the stay-at-home moms for not caring enough about the nutritional integrity of her kids' food. Not that she would've changed much about what she fed her kids, even if she did stay at home. It was funny that being a mom was so much of her identity, and yet she couldn't seem to find others like her.

When she settled back into her cubicle at work, she got a text from Sean.

Sean: Mandated overtime so going to miss bedtime tonight

Sean: Sorry

Sean: Give the kids extra hugs for me

Rachel: Will do

Once or twice a month Sean would get mandated to stay an extra couple of hours after his regularly scheduled shift. When he worked days, it meant getting home after nine at night and missing the kids' bedtime. When he worked nights, it meant getting home after nine in the morning and missing the morning rush to get out the door. Rachel firmly believed there was a special place in hell for whoever invented the twelve-hour shift, both from an HR perspective and a tired mom and wife of a shift worker perspective.

Sean hated when it happened, but he never truly needed to worry about anything, because Rachel had his back. She had the whole family's back. Some would say that the household wouldn't function without Rachel. It was an immense pressure, but one that Rachel didn't know what she would do without.

Sean: Thanks babe, you're the best. Love you

Rachel: Love you too.

Fall 2023

Twenty-Two

ELYSE

"I'LL HAVE A decaf almond milk latte with one-and-a-half pumps of sugar-free hazelnut, extra hot, extra foam, no whip," Elyse said to the barista.

She almost purposefully recited her elaborate order as fast as she could. As though it was a test to see if the college student taking her order could keep up. Elyse did this a lot without even realizing it. Giving little tests to the people around her, as though they needed to live up to her standard. It wasn't her most endearing quality, but Elyse loved it when someone gave her a challenge. It was an opportunity to prove herself, which she always did. So, it never occurred to her that maybe others would not also like those opportunities as well.

Elyse grabbed her coffee cup and took a sip. The barista had gotten the order right, but she saw the spelling of her name on the cup written "Alese," and she was probably much more annoyed than she should've been.

She strolled through the airport until she found her gate. She was one of the first passengers at the gate, but she liked to get to the airport early so she could grab a seat looking directly out the window and sip on her latte. She also wanted an excuse to go straight to the airport from the office, so she had booked the earliest Friday afternoon flight she could. It was conveniently scheduled so she wouldn't have to see Mark all weekend. She didn't like to think of it as avoiding her husband, so much as it was avoiding fighting with her husband.

She'd be spending the weekend at a Women in Financial Leadership conference. She had attended once early in her career, mostly as a token move to pad her résumé and try to make connections, but it had since fallen off her radar. To be honest, Elyse wasn't sure if conferences like those actually helped or hindered women in the workplace. She had always found that silently working harder and being twice as competent compared to her male counterparts was the ultimate equalizer. But the conference was in Florida this year, and one of the keynote speakers was Jackie Andrews, a big name in the investment banking world, and someone who Elyse liked to think she could be a younger version of.

She had already tracked down Jackie's assistant and managed to book a pre-conference cocktail hour with Jackie that evening. It never occurred to Elyse that maybe Jackie wouldn't be interested in using what little spare time she had over the weekend to have one-to-one meetings with overzealous conference-goers. But, after some initial pushback from Jackie's assistant—which was met with even more of Elyse's unrelenting persistence, she squeezed Elyse into Jackie's calendar. Elyse was confident that Jackie would be impressed with her tenacity and not annoyed with her for filling up a spare hour. So many people hated networking, but Elyse loved it.

It was another opportunity to prove herself—to whom and for what was irrelevant.

———

After an uneventful flight, Elyse settled into her hotel room, had a shower to wash the plane air off of her, and ordered herself a mini pizza from room service. She had to fill up now because after cocktails with Jackie, she'd be attending a conference welcome dinner. She had already perused the menu and knew she'd be having some sort of thirty-dollar salad, not because that was what she wanted, but because that's what women like her ordered, especially when she would be surrounded by other women like her: women in power suits, eating their sad, overpriced power salads.

After eating her room service pizza in bed and watching reality TV, Elyse put on her meticulously pre-planned outfit that would work for cocktails with Jackie and the welcome dinner. Black wide-legged trousers, an oatmeal cashmere long sleeve with a black oversized blazer. It could work as a standalone outfit, or the blazer could easily double as a jacket if she got there and others were dressed more casually. This was the typical level of planning ahead Elyse put into everything. She'd been doing this for so long that she didn't even recognize some might think it was over the top.

She finished her look by taking out her thin ten-karat gold huggie hoop earrings and replacing them with slightly thicker, eighteen-karat gold huggie hoop earrings. The ones that Mark had obediently bought her for Christmas, after she had already put them on hold at the jewelry store.

———

"Right this way," the hostess walked Elyse to the small table in an alcove located toward the back of the restaurant but on the opposite side of the bathroom and tucked away from the kitchen—just as Elyse had requested. Even though there was a perfectly acceptable bar at the hotel where the conference was taking place, Elyse had set up their reservation at a cocktail bar a block away. She didn't want any other conference-goers to spot Jackie and intrude on their conversation.

She was ten minutes early, but to her horror, Jackie was already seated there, halfway through what looked like a scotch and soda, aggressively typing on her phone. Elyse quickly looked her up and down and saw that she was wearing a black oxford shirt tucked into dark jeans with a pair of loafers, that if they weren't obviously Prada, would probably be considered ugly.

Shit, she thought to herself. She quickly took her blazer off so she'd be dressed more casually to match Jackie's aesthetic.

Jackie looked up as Elyse approached the table. "You must be Elyse," she said matter-of-factly. As though it was more of a command than a question.

The next forty-five minutes flew by. Elyse was impressed with Jackie and also with herself for how naturally she was able to keep the conversation flowing with a complete stranger. Of course, this was because she had already thought of several different topics and questions to ask. Some because she actually wanted to know what Jackie thought, and some because she wanted Jackie to be impressed with her.

As the waiter was bringing their second round of drinks, Jackie's phone vibrated.

"Sorry, I need to take this," Jackie said, excusing herself from the table.

A few minutes later she returned, setting her phone down beside her plate. Elyse caught a glimpse of her wallpaper. It was a young woman, probably in her early twenties, Elyse guessed, and a young man, likely a year or two older. They were clearly brother and sister, since they had the exact same sharp cheekbones and icy blue eyes as Jackie.

"Sorry about that. It was my daughter. She's doing her grad school applications, so everything is an emergency to her right now," Jackie explained with a slightly annoyed but caring tone.

Jackie Andrews had kids. Two of them. Elyse had never thought to ask. She started doing the math. Jackie was likely late forties, early fifties. Her daughter is applying to grad schools, so probably twenty-two, twenty-three-ish. So, Jackie must've been late twenties, maybe thirty when she had kids.

Elyse felt an almost immediate sense of panic. Had she missed the boat? She thought career women like her waited longer to have kids, like late thirties, not twenties. Shit, should she have already had kids by now? Interesting strategy, she thought. Have kids, *then* establish your career. It was like it had never even occurred to her that was an option. She had been taking the opposite approach this whole time. And God knows having kids and establishing a career were not simultaneous activities.

"Oh, I didn't realize you had kids," Elyse said, raising her brows.

"Oh, yeah. I have two. Aubrey and Riley," Jackie replied with a nod.

Interesting, Elyse thought. Two androgynous name choices. Elyse didn't ask who was who. She always thought if she had a girl she'd give her a classically feminine name, like Elizabeth or Mary...Elyse cut off her train of thought to respond to Jackie once she realized the gap in conversation.

"Oh, ummm, I guess you just have never mentioned you have kids in your talks or articles. So, I guess I—"

"You just assumed I didn't have any," Jackie said, finishing Elyse's sentence, unbothered. "I prefer to keep business and personal life separate. It's another one of those things that if men mention they have kids, they are praised for it, and if women like us mention it, we're considered a liability. In the workplace, anyway."

"How did you do it? Have a family and the career you wanted?" Elyse asked, going majorly off her script of pre-selected topics to discuss with Jackie. But she was genuinely interested.

Jackie seemed genuinely eager to share as she leaned in closer and raised her eyebrows, as though she was about to give a masterclass in working motherhood. "The truth is, I didn't for a long time. Things are great now. But my kids aren't exactly kids anymore. I was miserable the first five, six, seven years, because I couldn't work like I wanted to. I mean, as a mother, you're really not supposed to say that, but it's the truth," Jackie replied.

The only thing Elyse loved more than dishing out some brutal honesty was hearing it come from someone else.

"Then things got a little easier. I hit a stride with work once the kids were in school. I probably did miss a few too many basketball games and piano recitals. And of course, when I did show up, I got the stares from the other moms. I stuck out like a sore thumb in my corporate outfits while the rest of them acted like their athleisure was somehow superior to my Prada suit. But whatever." She waved a hand flippantly. "And yes, I had some guilt about missing stuff, but I also had the ability to pull my kids out of school at a whim and take them on vacations, and give them experiences that most of their friends would never have. I'm not talking Disney shit. We did that, too, but safaris in South Africa. We hiked Machu Picchu for Christmas last year, and my kids have seen the Galápagos Islands. So, I'd say that I more than made up for my career in a lot of ways."

"Wow, talk about doing it all," Elyse said, genuinely impressed but also somewhat uneasy.

"No, that's the point. You can't do it all. You do have to choose which is your priority. I know that's not a popular opinion. But yeah, you have to choose, and then find ways to make up for the second choice," Jackie said, glancing at her phone while emphasizing *second*.

Elyse couldn't think of a time she had ever heard a mother refer to her kids as her *second* choice.

"It's probably harder today than it was twenty years ago, though," Jackie continued. "There wasn't as much of this mommy martyrdom bullshit back then, as there seems to be now. Like if you're not suffering, you're not doing a good job. Like your kids are going to be messed up if you're not overly involved in every aspect of their lives. Your kids don't have to be your whole life for you to be a good parent. And the reality is my success has allowed me to be a better parent in other ways. I mean I've worked hard, so why not unapologetically use that money to outsource the shit you don't want to do. Hire a night nurse, get someone else to cook, clean, and pay for the expensive sleepaway camps." Jackie was clearly passionate about this topic, or maybe she had just gotten so used to defending her choices. "So yeah, I missed some stuff. I didn't make anything for bake sales. I don't have any amazing recipes that I'm passing down to future generations. But my kids had a wonderful childhood that I provided for them, and now they're pretty independent self-sufficient adults who work hard and will undoubtedly be successful. And that's the goal, right?" Jackie asked, rhetorically.

Elyse gave a small smile and nodded, unsure whether she agreed with Jackie, who didn't mention anything about whether or not her kids are actually *happy*.

Jackie swigged back the last sip of her scotch and soda and continued. "You're never in balance day-to-day, but I guess when I look back over the last twenty-three years, it's probably averaged out. But I guess that depends on who you ask."

Elyse let Jackie ramble on, but she had stopped actually listening. She was still trying to process all the information that Jackie had spewed in the last few minutes. You actually *can't do it all.* Kids are her second choice after her career, but she's still a good mom and basically makes up for it in other, mostly materialistic ways. Was that actually possible? Sure, Elyse was as materialistic as they come, but even she knew that she wouldn't be able to buy her non-existent kids' love. If it was that easy, she probably would've had kids years ago.

When Elyse did picture herself as a mother, she pictured being very involved with her kids. She pictured herself excelling at it, just like she pictured herself excelling at any other endeavor that she took on. If she was going to be a mother, she would be the poster-child for it. Other women would be in awe of her mothering and ask her for advice, just like she was used to when it came to work, style, interior design, and anything else Elyse put her mind to. This is what made it so difficult for Elyse. She could picture herself being a perfect mom, and she could picture herself as a perfect partner at the firm, but she couldn't picture both of those things at the same time.

The rest of the evening flew by. Elyse and Jackie wrapped up their cocktail hour then walked the block back to the hotel for the conference welcome dinner. It didn't matter how nice of a hotel it was, dinners in banquet rooms always felt a little cheap. Like you knew your meal was going to be mediocre at best. That was why Elyse specifically requested she and Jackie have drinks at a real restaurant, where the ambiance would be more chic and upscale than banquet room #6.

Elyse was physically present for the welcome dinner but mentally felt like she was floating outside of her body, watching herself interact with all the other women like her. All the small talk was thinly veiled with competition and humble brags. Any chance to sprinkle in comments about their relative success and wealth was taken. Things like, who flew first class, who had been on the most exotic vacations, who spent more hours glued to their work phones, who did more charity work. Never one to back down from a competition, Elyse held her own in these conversations, but it was moments like these that Elyse was reminded why she was friends with Leah, Alex, Rachel and Brie. They weren't really like her, but women like her could be insufferable.

As Elyse waited for the elevator to take her back up to her hotel room, she kept going over and over what Jackie said to her and all the other small talk she made with the other women at the dinner. Elyse had always been pretty confident in her thoughts and emotions. She often didn't question them, but she just couldn't tell how she felt about her conversation with Jackie. Was Jackie right? She didn't know whether or not to feel inspired by her, or sad for her and her kids. Were her kids actually that happy and well-adjusted? It was so hard to tell when you come from money, because it's so much easier to cover up any discontentment. Was it actually all that black and white?

———

After an underwhelming day and a half at the conference, Elyse had spent her Sunday evening traveling back home. She again booked a later flight than necessary, so she would get home by the time Mark was likely in bed. She also made sure she was back in the office by seven a.m. sharp Monday morning. Not because she was eager to get back to work, but because it also meant she could avoid Mark for longer.

Elyse sat at her desk and perused her calendar, as though she hadn't already looked at it eight times the night before. This Monday, like every Monday, started with an eight a.m. meeting with her assistant Laurie to talk about her schedule for the rest of the week. It was a meeting about meetings; one of those meetings that probably wasn't necessary but made her seem important. And that's what everyone else with their own assistant did, so Elyse did it, too.

She realized her office was her comfortable place. More comfortable than her own home that she now seemed to avoid any chance she could. The home she had poured so much into. That she had meticulously decorated. The home that looked amazing but felt awful.

Her office was also more comfortable than the hotel and conference room where she spent the weekend. Elyse couldn't quite shake the discomfort she felt after speaking with Jackie. She tried to pass it off as the humid air, or the hotel food, but deep down she knew it was because Jackie's experience had shaken her, and the more she thought about it, the more it pushed her away from the idea of kids. Professionally, there was something so admirable about Jackie. But personally, there was something so harsh about her. Something unbecoming. Whatever the opposite of Rachel was, that was Jackie. Elyse couldn't quite place it, but she was pretty sure she had that quality, too.

Elyse envisioned the table she kept in her head. *Have a baby* in the left column, *Don't have a baby* in the right. Reflecting on her similarity to Jackie, she made a mental tick under the right column. Then she spent the next forty-six minutes flipping between emails and the semi-annual Nordstrom sale until Laurie walked into her office.

Laurie was old enough to be Elyse's mother and often acted as though she was, but in a warm, caring way, not an annoying, judgey way. Elyse secretly loved it. In the nearly ten years at the firm, she had seen Laurie go from nonstop talking about her kids, to nonstop talking about her grandkids. Elyse couldn't remember how many there were now. Maybe three, four, six? A more maternal person would've known.

Laurie set her pen and notepad down on Elyse's large mahogany desk as she took a seat across from her. "How was your weekend, dear?" She picked her pen and notepad back up, flipped to a fresh page and clicked her pen, ready to hang on to every word that was about to come out of Elyse's mouth, just as she did every Monday morning.

"It was nice. The conference was so good. Really inspiring," Elyse lied.

"Well, I hope you didn't work too hard! Was everything okay with your bookings? The hotel was a nightmare to communicate with," Laurie explained.

"Oh yes, everything was fine," Elyse reassured her. "What about you, Laurie, how was your weekend? Did you spend it with the grandkids?"

This was a tactic Elyse had adopted over the years. Elyse from five years ago wouldn't have reciprocated the question. She would've dove right into business. What started as a strategic move aimed at being "more likable," something the men in her office never seemed to worry about, had become genuine somewhere along the way. She wasn't sure if it was because she actually did really like Laurie and found her presence comforting, or because she had evolved as a human being.

"Oh, it was lovely!" Laurie exclaimed. "I saw all my old B school girlfriends. We probably haven't all seen each other in, gosh, ten, twelve years. Time just slips away from you, ya know? But we had dinner at one of those fancy teppanyaki restaurants, and oh goodness I think I drank too much sake. I did get to see the grandkids on Sunday, though, they are—"

"B school?" Elyse interrupted Laurie, slightly taken aback.

"Business school," Laurie responded. "That's probably not what people call it these days, though."

"Laurie, I didn't know you had a business degree," Elyse said, surprised and realizing she had no idea what Laurie's education and experience were prior to being at the firm. "I mean, you never told me, and you don't have it hanging up anywhere."

"It's actually an MBA. And I honestly don't think I could even tell you where it is," Laurie responded.

"What!?" Elyse didn't mean to sound so rude.

Her head was spinning. Her assistant was technically more educated than her, and yet here Laurie was organizing Elyse's schedule, booking her flights, and making sure she made other people's coffee just right.

"Yeah, it was me and three other women in a class of thirty men. Of course, Lillian didn't finish because she got married, and Jill accidentally got pregnant during her internship. So, yeah it was just me and Sally that made it to the end," Laurie explained with a shrug.

"Laurie, how did you end up here?" Elyse asked with genuine confusion. "Sorry, I sound like an asshole," Elyse apologized, realizing how rude her comments could be perceived.

"Of course not dear. It's fine," Laurie reassured her. "Well, I started out working in an entry-level position at a telecommunications company. Of course it was a lower position than what you'd expect with an MBA, but I figured I could work my way up. I married Harold just a few months after I graduated. It was important to me that I worked the first full year after graduating, and that I got a job before Harry and I married. Going to an interview with a wedding band was a liability back then. People would just assume that you'd be pregnant by the time you got your first paycheck, if you weren't already," Laurie said.

Elyse glanced down at her own three-carat solitaire and double diamond pavé wedding band that she proudly flaunted.

Laurie continued. "And well, Joey came along nearly a year to the date of me starting to work there. And of course, there was no paid leave back then. They were nice enough to hold my position for six weeks, but I just couldn't bear to leave Joey when he was that little. The little bugger never would take a bottle, and I was nowhere near fitting back into my office attire, so I just stayed home. We knew we wanted more kids, so it didn't make sense for me to go back to work. And less than a year later, Maria came along. And ya know, time just slips away when you're knee-deep in diapers, and then you think, hey, what's one more? And of course back then you could easily live on one income, and Harry brought in more than enough to support us. After all the kids were in school for a couple of years, I got kinda bored, so I figured it might be nice to go back to work."

"So, how did you go back?" Elyse asked, heavily invested in Laurie's story.

"Well, I started out as a part-time junior assistant for the school board," Laurie started.

"With an MBA?" Elyse quickly realized how rude that was given Laurie is still an assistant with an MBA.

Elyse realized that Laurie's story was confirming one of her deeply held concerns—taking time off work to have babies meant you were essentially creating your own glass ceiling.

"Yeah, an MBA with basically no work experience and a ten-year gap on my résumé. Recruiters weren't exactly knocking down my door," Laurie said with a scoff. "And it was nice having something part time and not too demanding, so I could pick up the kids, chaperone the odd field trip, things like that." Laurie could see Elyse's bewilderment, nearing pity.

"But don't you feel like you missed out? Or, don't you ever wonder—"

"I don't regret it, if that's what you're asking," Laurie said confidently. "I'd do it all again the same. Honestly, anyone can get a piece of paper that says they're smart and qualified if they work hard enough. But there's something about having a little person draw a terrible picture just for you. Even when they're shitty teenagers and roll your eyes at you ninety percent of the time, they still need you. More than you're needed at any job."

Elyse opened her mouth to start in.

Laurie continued before she could get a word in. "I'm not saying your work here isn't important, dear, or anyone's work anywhere isn't important, but every employee, no matter their position, is replaceable. Being a parent is the one role where you're irreplaceable." Laurie saw Elyse's expression shift from confusion to sadness. "I mean if that's what you want. If being a parent is what you want," Laurie clarified, recognizing she was talking to a married, childless thirty-five-year-old woman. "Elyse, sweetie. Are you okay?"

Elyse gave an unconvincing nod.

"It's none of my business what you do or don't do, but you seem like maybe you're having a tough time." Laurie tilted her head with concern.

When Elyse first started working at the firm, Laurie had once asked her if she had any kids. It was a question Laurie didn't think could be perceived as an insult, but she sensed that Elyse took it as one, so she never pushed the subject after that.

Elyse gave another unconvincing nod.

"Listen, I don't envy women today. Yeah, there were fewer options back in my day, but at least the choice was easier. I never had the career pressure, because Harold had a good job and his income was enough, and people didn't bat an eye at the idea of a woman being a stay-at-home mom, like they do now. I also didn't have to worry about all that gentle parenting, Montessori crap, or whatever the hell my daughter-in-law tells me is the way to do things now," Laurie said.

"Shouldn't I just know by now?" Elyse asked, as though a practical stranger could answer this agonizing, life-altering question for her. She hated that she was being this vulnerable, especially in a professional setting.

"I think women today have too many choices. And I don't mean that in an anti-feminist way. I guess I just mean, we didn't think about it that much when I was your age. It was just something you did without thinking too much about it, and before you knew it, you were pregnant. Don't be so hard on yourself, Elyse. You still have time," Laurie reassured her.

Elyse heard that a lot, and she hated it. How much time exactly? Elyse had always thrived with deadlines. Maybe someone needed to give her a deadline. Maybe she could just put it in her calendar, set an alarm or something.

After spending a solid five unnecessary minutes going through the week's priorities and schedule, Laurie left the office, leaving Elyse to sort through her many emotions while also going through the motions of meetings, emails, and spreadsheets. She realized work was the one setting where she was able to push everything else to the back of her brain and hone in on whatever task was in front of her.

On her way home, she was no longer able to compartmentalize, and she thought about the conversation with Laurie. Despite very different perspectives, she felt the exact same way after talking to Jackie—somewhat inspired, somewhat sad, and even more confused than ever.

"Hey babe, how was your day?" Mark greeted her at the door. "Did you have a good trip?"

Despite the ongoing tensions, they still had moments of normalcy, which made their situation even more challenging to navigate sometimes.

Elyse paused to set her purse and keys down, ignoring Mark's question. "Did you know that Laurie has an MBA?" It was a stupid question. If Elyse didn't know that information about her own assistant, then Mark certainly didn't know.

"Laurie, your assistant? No way? Good for her," Mark responded.

That was it? Elyse thought. She couldn't help but be annoyed with Mark's response. *Good for her.* That was all the thought he put into it. No, "hey, that must've been tough," or "why is a woman with an MBA getting your coffee?" No recognition of the pioneer that Laurie was at the time. No recognition of the sacrifices and opportunities she had lost to pop out three kids.

The longer Elyse sat in her annoyance with Mark's seemingly innocent reply, she realized she felt something deeper. To her, Mark's response wasn't just his response. It was an example of how misunderstood she felt, how unseen she felt by her husband. Like she was in this decision-making process alone.

He just didn't get it.

Twenty-Three

ALEX

"DO YOU THINK it's too late to switch to a Peppa theme?" Alex asked, indecisively.

"Yes! She's two. Her favorite thing changes every day," Andrew reminded her. "Let's just stick with the unicorns, or whatever it was that we landed on."

Alex folded her laptop down, so she could see Andrew across from her at their kitchen table. "Yeah, you're right. I just want her to have the best time. Her first birthday was nice but really that's more for the adults than the kid. She may actually remember this one."

Lola's second birthday was coming up, and Alex wanted to make sure it was as memorable as a two-year-old's birthday party could be.

"I think you might be overthinking it, babe," Andrew teased from across the table.

Was overthinking even a thing? Underthinking seemed like a much more plausible risk to Alex.

"I know, I know. I'll take it down a notch," Alex said, as she stood up from her chair and leaned over to give Andrew a quick peck.

"What time does your parents' flight get in tomorrow?" She asked, making her way into the kitchen to start the nightly task of washing Lola's many sippy cups.

"It's supposed to be three-thirty. I figured I'd grab Lola early from daycare and take her with me to get them at the airport," Andrew replied.

"Sounds good. Let me know if anything changes," Alex said.

Andrew's parents were making the nine-hour flight across the country to celebrate Lola's birthday. It was sweet that they were making the trip, but the thought of planning this party and having houseguests at the same time overwhelmed Alex. Luckily, Andrew's parents were generally laid back and having more entertainment for Lola would also make it easier for Alex to get things ready for the party.

Alex caught her phone lighting up with a message from the corner of her eye. She dried her wet soapy hands with a tea towel as she read the message. "Shit! Leah just texted, and she can't watch Lola tomorrow night." As a thank you for making the long trip, Alex and Andrew were planning on taking his parents out for dinner and had Leah lined up to babysit.

Andrew had made his way to the kitchen and took over sippy cup duty. "What about any of the other girls?"

"No. Elyse is away for a conference. I'm pretty sure Rachel is occupied with one of the kids' soccer practices or something, and Brie is honestly going through some sort of existential crisis right now and barely answers her texts," Alex said.

"Well, you know who we could ask?" Andrew said, knowing Alex wouldn't like his suggestion.

Alex shook her head. "Don't say it, Andrew."

He was right. She not only knew what he was suggesting but didn't like it.

"It's not that unreasonable to ask a grandparent to watch their grandkid for a couple of hours. Plus, Cindy's always talking about wanting to see Lola more," Andrew said, rationalizing the idea to Alex.

"Her saying that is just her way of making herself feel better. If she wanted to see her more, she would," Alex said firmly.

Andrew tilted his chin down. "Well, maybe she would if you asked her?"

He could tell he crossed a line. He generally tried to not get too involved in Alex's dealings with her mother. And as Alex liked to remind him, being the child of two emotionally healthy, loving parents meant he wasn't qualified to speak on matters related to Cindy.

Alex picked the tea towel back up to start drying the cups Andrew placed in the rack beside the sink. "Fine. I'll ask her."

Alex agreed, only because she had already picked out her outfit and what she was going to order off the menu. Surely Cindy couldn't cause long-term emotional distress for Lola in just a couple of hours. Right?

Alex hadn't seen or heard much from Cindy over the summer. Her and Dale liked to spend most of their time at an RV campground in Newport, and Alex hadn't exactly reached out, either.

Ever since she decided that she could only handle one child and was generally a substandard parent, and that Cindy was the likely root cause, she had been avoiding her mom as much as possible. It was a complicated feeling. It was a complicated relationship. It was like Alex and Cindy would take one step forward then two steps back. Alex would waver between being hopeful their relationship could be mended, to knowing that there was nothing to be mended.

Alex wasn't naïve. She knew their relationship would never look like a typical mother-daughter relationship, but she thought maybe they could reach the point where they at least had some sort of relationship. One where the thought of having to spend any time around her mother at all didn't make Alex want to drink heavily, putting her in a weird mood for a solid two weeks after seeing her.

Alex: Hey mom. Hope you've been well. Huge favor to ask and please feel free to say no if you can't do it. But our sitter bailed for tomorrow night, and we're supposed to be having dinner with Andrew's parents. Wondering if you could watch Lola for a couple of hours. Our reso isn't until 8 p.m., so I'll be there to get Lola down for bed.

Alex immediately tucked her phone away so she didn't have to deal with any response from Cindy.

Later that night, when Alex was in bed listening to her guided bedtime meditation, she heard Siri's voice interrupt her serene sleep guide to dictate a text message that just came through.

Cindy: Long time, no talk

Cindy: Guess you only text when you need something?

Cindy: But yes, of course I'd love to watch my granddaughter

Cindy: Say hi to John and Beth for me.

Andrew's parents' names were actually Jack and Betsy, but Cindy was never one to remember names. Alex hated how Cindy referred to Lola as *her* granddaughter. As though she had some sort of ownership over her. She tried not to be too annoyed with her mother, since she was doing her a favor, and it killed Alex that she was relying on Cindy for something. One, because Cindy was generally unreliable, and two, because anytime Alex did ask for something, Cindy couldn't resist acting like she was being put upon, and like Alex was taking advantage of her "generosity." But she was desperate, so rather than addressing Cindy's snide remark, she simply thanked her.

Alex: Thanks, mom. We really appreciate it!

She restarted her bedtime meditation from the beginning because just one short interaction with Cindy had undone all of her zen.

———

Alex awoke the next morning to a text from Leah.

Leah: So sorry for all the back and forth on this, but plans got changed again, so I am able to watch Lola tonight

Thank god, Alex thought to herself.

Alex: Awesome!! Thank you so much :) and let me know when I can return the favor!

Leah: Please, my mother has a chokehold on the right of first refusal to babysit Oliver

Feeling relieved she wouldn't have to rely on her mother for babysitting services, Alex texted Cindy.

Alex: Hey mom. Our sitter is now available again so no worries about tonight. Thanks again for agreeing to babysit though. We'll see you this weekend for Lola's party!

Cindy: Oh, I'm no longer needed? Thx for letting me know.

Cindy: So now that I'm free, no invite to dinner?

What a very Cindy response. Alex let out an audible sigh and pounded her phone screen harder than she needed to as she typed her reply.

Alex: Not like that at all. We just figured with Jack and Betsy having a long flight they might want to have a good meal and not something that I will likely burn.

Alex: Of course you're welcome to come. It's Fernando's at 8 p.m.

Alex typed, then deleted, then retyped the last message before pressing send. She obviously didn't want Cindy there but knew she'd look like the bad guy if she didn't extend the invitation. This is what Cindy did. She played the victim to manipulate people into doing what she wanted. It was a pattern that had created pervasive feelings of guilt, anxiety, and insecurity in Alex, at least according to her therapist.

Cindy: Fernando's...fancy! Don't worry, I won't mortify you by bringing Dale.

Another very Cindy response. Alex had expected a comment about the restaurant, which was on the pricier side. They weren't poor growing up, but they were certainly on the lower end of middle-class. Throw in Dale's weekly booze budget, combined with his sometimes lack of steady employment, and Alex was often reminded that money didn't grow on trees. And yet Cindy was often the first to judge someone else for not having something nice enough. It was a classic damned if you do, damned if you don't situation. If you go low-end or basic, Cindy judges you. If you go high-end or splurge a little, Cindy judges you.

Alex started to type a reply then stopped. It was too early to deal with this shit. She decided not to dignify Cindy's comment with a response. In just three sentences, Cindy had managed to ruin Alex's entire day. And it was only seven a.m. Alex set her phone back on her nightstand and made her way to the shower to wash away the icky feeling she often had after any interaction with her mother.

———

Alex eyed the two forks on the crisp black tablecloth, illuminated by two tealights in the center of the table. *Start from the outside in.* Alex was probably twenty-three before she ever dined at a restaurant nice enough to have more than one fork—or probably even a non-plastic fork. She could distinctly remember the sinking feeling she had when she grabbed the wrong bread plate while attending a fancy wedding with her boyfriend at the time, and how he had to tell her

"Our special for tonight is a lamb shank braised in red wine and shallots, served over garlic mash with crispy brussel sprouts. Are you ready to order or would like a few more minutes?" The waiter at Fernando's asked.

"Uh, we'll take a few more minutes if you don't mind. We're still waiting for our last guest," Andrew replied.

"Why don't we at least get a couple of orders of calamari to tide us over?" Alex said uncomfortably.

It was 8:40, and Cindy hadn't arrived yet, nor was she answering calls or texts. Jack and Betsy were likely starving, and even if they weren't—Alex was.

As the calamari arrived at their table, so did Cindy, nearly an hour late.

"Mom, you made it," Alex said, trying to hide her annoyance.

"Oh, so nice to see you again, Jack and Betsy, how was your flight?" Cindy asked, ignoring Alex's comment. *Oh, so she does remember their names*, Alex thought to herself. She could already tell that Cindy was going to be laying it on thick tonight.

"Did you order without me, sweetie?" Cindy asked, looking at the calamari on the table.

Alex bit her tongue.

The first fifteen minutes of their dinner went well. The waiter had been lurking and came to take their orders before Cindy's butt could hit her chair. There were enough basic topics to cover—the flight, Jack's recent retirement, weather differences between the coasts. But really their sets of parents were pretty much strangers, having only met a couple of times previously.

"I must say, I'm one jealous grandmother, with you getting to see Lola whenever you want," Betsy said to Cindy, referring to her close proximity. The truth was that Lola knew more of Betsy from FaceTime than she did of Cindy at all.

"Oh, it truly is a blessing. At least when Alex lets me see her. But you know how it is with your first kid," Cindy implied, speaking as though Alex wasn't seated right next to her. Alex was apparently the problem here.

"Well, you must be so proud of Alex. Andrew was telling us about all the great accomplishments she's had at the firm," Betsy continued.

"Oh yes, she really is an ambitious one. Willing to do whatever to get the job done," Cindy said.

Another thinly veiled insult from Cindy.

She didn't stop there and, in fact, leaned closer to Betsy to say, "I keep telling her, though, work isn't everything. Especially when you've got young kids."

Okay, now she was just straight up lying.

She had never said anything remotely like that to Alex. She was unaware of Alex's recent successes at work. And the fact that she was implying that Alex prioritized work over her child, from a mother who prioritized *everything* over her own kids, was infuriating.

Andrew placed his hand on Alex's leg under the table, as if to say, *I know, I know, but let it slide and let's just try to make it through this dinner in one piece.*

"Actually, I think it's great that Lola sees how hard Alex works," Andrew piped in, feeling the need to defend his wife. He also figured it would be better if he was the one to speak up rather than Alex, who he could see was getting very close to losing her composure.

"Oh yes, of course. I wasn't implying anything. But it's something to think about before baby number two comes along. That's when things actually get hard," Cindy said.

The passive-aggressiveness was palpable. The accumulation of all the little jabs felt like Alex was being sucker-punched. That was something else Alex couldn't stand about Cindy. All of her little comments, individually, seemed relatively harmless, but taken together, they added up to one giant fuck you. So, when Alex would inevitably blow up after *one little comment*, she seemed like an irrational one, not her mother. Alex, not wanting to add any fuel to the fire, decided now was not the time to let their parents in on the fact that there would be no more grandchildren from them.

"Oh, I remember those early days, when Sarah, our oldest, was a screaming toddler and Andrew was a colicky baby. They were rough for sure. But we made it through on the other end okay, I think," Betsey said, trying to participate in the conversation that was starting to get noticeably tense.

"Well, at least one of our kids made it out okay," Jack joked, elbowing Andrew softly in his side. It was sweet of Jack to try to lighten the mood, but Cindy wasn't picking up on the fact that everyone else at the table was getting uncomfortable.

"And with the way you kids parent these days, being so overly involved in everything, so caught up in the latest psycho-babble parenting trend, you really make it unnecessarily hard for yourselves," Cindy proclaimed.

Alex wouldn't have necessarily disagreed with that comment coming from someone else. Parenting today did seem extreme, but she didn't know if it was objectively so or just seemed extreme in comparison to her experience growing up. She tried not to be too much of a helicopter parent, but she also knew she didn't want to be whatever the opposite of a helicopter parent was. So Cindy.

"So, which is it, mom? Am I the helicopter parent? Or, am I missing out on raising my daughter because I care about my career?" Alex challenged her mother, trying to remain calm.

"Oh don't be so sensitive, Alex," Cindy said, completely dismissing her.

"You know, Dale and I always told the kids that they'd thank us for the tough love later, when they're independent, capable adults," Cindy continued.

Wow, really Cindy? So your parenting approach was strategic? For my benefit? Something you're proud of? Proud of not knowing a damn thing about me? Proud of the way you put Dale first every single time, even when he'd get drunk and yell and hit walls for no reason? Even when you missed prom pictures? When you didn't come to either high school or university graduations, and made me feel stupid for wanting to go myself? But of course Alex didn't say any of this out loud. They were at a nice restaurant with Andrew's nice, normal parents, and Alex had put in a lot of work over the years to ensure her in-laws thought she was a normal, well-adjusted person. So, instead, she just sat there, silent, her cheeks slightly flushed with anger and her lip curled up on one side, which if you didn't know Alex, you might just think she was smiling pleasantly, not mentally cursing you out.

Andrew took a large gulp of wine then piped in again, trying to focus the conversation on something that would give Cindy less air time. "So, Dad, now that you're retired, are you finally going to get that golf club membership?"

"Ah, we'll see if your mother lets me," Jack replied, giving Betsey a gentle, teasing nudge. "I'm going to do some volunteer work with the hospital foundation over the winter to keep me occupied and try to keep the mind working. Your mother has basically said I'm not allowed to have too much fun until she can retire next year."

"Oh, Jack, I said no such thing," Betsy said with a slight giggle.

Betsy tended to get buzzed off one glass of wine, and unlike most others, she actually turned into a sweeter version of herself when under the influence of alcohol.

Alex could see Cindy quickly losing interest in the conversation that wasn't centered around her. As the waiter came and took their plates, Cindy looked at her phone.

"Oh shoot, I didn't realize the time. I really should be going. I told Dale I'd stop at the liquor store on the way home. I'll see you Saturday," Cindy said to Andrew's parents. "Oh, and Alex, let me know how much I owe you for the check, sweetie."

Typical Cindy. Cindy and Alex both knew that the last sentence was a lie, and Cindy had no intention of paying for the dinner she invited herself to. Alex knew other adult daughters wouldn't bat an eye at paying for their mom's dinner. It wasn't paying for her dinner that bothered Alex. It was the expectation that Cindy had. As though now it was Alex's turn to take care of her, to pay her back for all those years she provided Alex with the bare minimum, legally obligated basics, like food and shelter.

"Let me walk you out mom," Alex said, getting up so quickly her chair almost tipped over.

"Sure," Cindy said skeptically.

As they stepped outside the restaurant door into the parking lot, Alex didn't hold back.

"What the actual fuck was that, Mom?"

"Excuse me, language! The fact that you would speak to your own mother like that. My god," Cindy responded.

All Alex could hear at that moment was Dale cursing the kids out practically daily. Fucking ungrateful, fucking lazy, fucking assholes, and his favorite for Alex—fucking slut. Cindy never seemed bothered by offensive language then, let alone try to stop him.

"I'm sorry, *who* the actual fuck was that? Since when did you and Dale have all this parenting advice, and since when are you proud of, or even know about any of my work accomplishments?" Alex could feel the adrenaline pumping through her veins.

Cindy's eyes narrowed. "I was being pleasant in front of your guests, dear. I thought you might appreciate that."

Alex shook her head and pursed her lips. "The fact that you can turn it on and off like that tells me you know exactly what you're doing and you just don't give a shit."

"Oh please, don't act like you don't do it, too, Alex. Putting on a little show to impress your well-to-do in-laws. We can't all be as perfect as you Alex, with your pretty face, handsome husband, and fancy job," Cindy retorted.

There was a brief silence.

"You know, Dale warned me that trying to be closer with you and my only granddaughter would end up like this. All I've done to just try to be involved and support you during the last few months, and I get no appreciation for any of it. I'm not sure how I managed to raise such an entitled brat," Cindy continued.

"A few months of half-assed effort doesn't make up for a few decades of flakiness and not giving a shit," Alex said, her tone biting.

"You don't give me any credit for what I've been through trying to raise you kids. And you were far from perfect, Alex. Running around with god knows who, doing god knows what," Cindy replied, emphasizing the last sentence.

"Please, you guys practically kicked me out of the house every opportunity you got. And that's not the point. I was the kid and you were the adult. You were the parent, but you expected us to cater to your drunk asshole of a husband. I never understood why you always chose him over us, and now that I have Lola, I know I never will," Alex said. She remained firm throughout their discussion, but now her voice was starting to get shaky.

"You know, one day, when Lola only sees you for your flaws, give me a call and tell me how that feels," Cindy said, with just an inkling of hurt coming through her voice.

"I don't think you should come Saturday," Alex said, her voice firm again.

Cindy turned around and started to make her way to her car, as Alex turned and made her way back into the restaurant.

"Alex," she heard her mother call her name from across the parking lot. She went against her better judgment and, instead of continuing back into the restaurant, turned back around to face her mother. "Just because you hate me, doesn't mean my granddaughter needs to, too," Cindy said coldly.

Alex couldn't dignify Cindy's comment with a response. Instead, she continued back to the restaurant and didn't look back.

"Okay, Lola is down for her nap. Let's get out of here," Alex said to Brie.

Lola's birthday party had just wrapped up, and after two hours of chaos, Lola was settled in for her nap. Andrew encouraged Alex to take advantage of all the extra hands to clean up after the party and get out for a bit. The party went smoothly, and Lola had a blast. Leah and Rachel came with the kids. Elyse was away for her work conference and wasn't able to make it, but surprisingly, Brie came. She liked to pretend like it wasn't her scene, but she had a reputation as fun aunt Brie that she was learning to lean into. It meant a lot to Alex that Brie came, because a two-year-old's birthday party was the last place she would've wanted to be on a Saturday afternoon if she was a childless adult.

Alex and Brie hopped into Alex's car and pulled into the nearest coffee shop.

As they carried their mugs of coffee over to the table farthest away from any other patrons, Brie asked the obvious question that she couldn't ask in front of the other party guests. "Okay, so do I want to know why Cindy wasn't there?"

"Unofficially, she was sick. Officially, she's a narcissist who I don't think I can have in my life anymore," Alex said, following it up with the details about the dinner at Fernando's.

"Damn. That is rough. But you've gotta do what's best for you," Brie reassured Alex.

"Thank you," Alex said sincerely.

When her strained relationship with her mother came up, Alex was used to most people saying things like, "but she's your *mother*," or "you only have one mother," or "but she's family." That was the best reasoning anyone could give her.

"I'm sorry, I'm an asshole. I'm bitching about my mom, and here you are dealing with your own mom shit," Alex said.

"Don't worry, I'm not going to tell you that you'll regret it one day when Cindy gets old, or gets dementia, or gets hit by a bus or whatever. The circumstances of if and how they go doesn't change what your relationship was like—is like. I got incredibly lucky to have the mom I had. She was an absolute kook, but I don't think she ever once made me feel like shit. So, that's something...I guess," Brie said.

Alex tried to feel comforted by Brie's words, but she still couldn't get her mom's comments out of her head. If Lola only saw Alex for her flaws, how would she see her? Would she see someone who's a bit of a mess and tries to cover it up with too much makeup and clothes that are too tight. Would she see someone whose contrived confidence has always been paper thin? Would she see her intense insecurities she tries to keep buried at the bottom of a wine glass. Would she see through the facade? Maybe it was best to never truly know how your kids perceive you.

Just then a wave of heat and nausea came over Alex.

"You okay?" Brie asked, noticing the visible change in Alex's appearance and demeanor. She looked pale and spaced out.

"Umm, uh yeah. I don't know what just came over me," Alex said, shaking her head.

And then it hit Alex.

"Shit, what day is it?" She asked Brie.

"Uh, Saturday. The seventh. I think," Brie replied.

"Shit."

"What?" Brie asked, realizing the answer to her own question as soon as it came out of her mouth. "Should we stop at a drugstore on the way home?"

Alex nodded.

That night after Lola was in bed and Andrew's parents had settled into the guest room for the night, Alex forced herself to get confirmation of what she already knew. After an excruciatingly long three minutes, she saw the faint but undeniable pink lines.

Shit.

How could this have happened? Well, she knew how it happened, but was the universe trying to play some sort of sick joke on her? As soon as she decided that they were done having kids, she got pregnant? Maybe she should also decide she never wants a million dollars.

At that moment Alex felt a lot of things; mostly disappointment in herself, almost like she had failed a test in school. She didn't feel happy, which made her feel guilty. But she also didn't feel sad or fearful, either.

Then, she thought of Andrew, who would definitely be excited.

Then, she thought of Lola, whose whole world would be flipped upside down.

Then, she thought of Leah who wanted nothing more than a positive pregnancy test.

Then, she threw up for the second time that day.

Twenty-Four

LEAH

"THEY WEREN'T EVEN fucking trying," was the first thing Leah said to Scott when she walked through the door as she got home from work.

"What? Who?" Scott asked, rightfully confused.

Leah haphazardly tossed her purse and keys on the entryway console and joined Scott at the kitchen table, not bothering to remove her coat or shoes.

"Alex and Andrew. She didn't even think she wanted a second," Leah explained.

Alex had texted Leah the news a couple of days after she got a positive pregnancy test. Alex still didn't know how she felt about the whole situation, but she knew it would be a sensitive topic for Leah and keeping it from her for the standard twelve weeks just felt cruel. Leah was devastated but also appreciative of the heads up. There was nothing worse than seeing someone who was showing all the early signs of pregnancy—refusing drinks, barely eating, giant boobs, a general air of mystery—coyly trying to keep an obvious secret. Leah had seen it play out many times over the last year with her cousin, a co-worker, and several Facebook friends. It wasn't rational, but it infuriated Leah. She hated picking up on the clues then anxiously awaiting to see if there'd be an obnoxiously cute pregnancy announcement a few weeks later. She almost took it personally, like these people were purposely trying to peel a Band-Aid off as slowly and painfully as possible. A true friend will just rip it off, like Alex did.

"Oh wow, Alex is pregnant?" Scott immediately regretted his slightly excited tone. He regretted it even more when he saw that Leah wasn't pissed about his response. Just pure sadness in her eyes.

That sadness made Scott feel even more guilt that he had found the last month and a half to be the happiest, most enjoyable time he could remember in a long time. year with her cousin, a co-worker, and several Facebook friends. It wasn't rational, but it infuriated Leah. She hated picking up on the clues then anxiously awaiting to see if there'd be an obnoxiously cute pregnancy announcement a few weeks later. She almost took it personally, like these people were purposely trying to peel a Band-Aid off as slowly and painfully as possible. A true friend will just rip it off, like Alex did.

After the failed embryo transfer, Leah and Scott had genetic testing done on the remaining embryo. The process took a couple of months, during which Leah insisted they still try to get pregnant the natural way. When the test results came back completely normal, it was a big relief and an even bigger amount of pressure. Everything was fine. All there was left to do was to transfer their last remaining embryo and hope for a miracle. No pressure at all.

No one was more surprised than Leah that she had actually agreed to take a couple months off from trying, mostly under the pretense that a "reset" may be good for them. Kind of like when your computer isn't working, and instead of trying to troubleshoot the issues, you just turn it off, wait a bit, then turn it back on and hope for the best. But Leah knew deep down that the real reason she agreed to the hiatus was that she was terrified to move forward with transferring their last embryo. If it didn't work again, she'd be running out of options. Options and hope.

The break from trying to get pregnant felt like a huge weight had been lifted off Scott's shoulders, but he knew that weight was growing on Leah.

He was right. And that weight was becoming unbearable for Leah. She knew she could try another round of egg retrieval. If she had some sort of guarantee, she'd do it in a heartbeat, but she just didn't know if she could handle another round of injections, hormones, waiting, moodiness, and of course, the potential heart-wrenching disappointment. And if she felt that way, she knew that Scott was absolutely feeling that way, times a million. She tried to not resent him too much for his lack of resilience; but one thing she absolutely did resent him for was his obnoxious, over-the-top, carefree happiness over the last month and a half of not trying. He was practically giddy.

"Are you okay?" Scott asked after a long silence. "I mean I know you're happy for Alex, but that was probably hard to hear."

"Yes, I'll be fine. She sent me a text because she didn't want to put me on the spot."

Scott nodded sympathetically, because what else could he really say?

"I don't feel like cooking tonight. Let's order takeout," Leah said, making her way down the hall to find Oliver playing in his room. She was a mother after all, and she had to remind herself of that several times throughout this process.

———

Two Weeks Later

Scott's complacency, combined with Alex's news had lit a new fire under Leah. After speaking with her doctors, she had concocted a new plan. Since she had a normal cycle and was now just a few days away from ovulating, she figured they'd try naturally this month, then if that didn't work, they would transfer the last embryo during her next cycle. Yes, that timing would be good based on vacation schedules and Thanksgiving plans they had made to see their families. Just in time for a Christmas baby announcement, maybe? No—Leah didn't want to be that person. The one that made all the other infertile women out there feel even shittier.

That night after putting Oliver to bed, Leah knew she had to let Scott in on their plans. Not that there was much for him to do at this point but really just out of courtesy.

"So, babe," Leah started, as she fluffed her pillow. "I was thinking that if things don't work out this month, it's probably time to transfer the last embryo." She tried to keep her tone casual, as though he wouldn't catch on if she was really nonchalant about it.

Scott, who was laying in bed watching sports highlights on his phone, turned his head so quickly Leah thought he might actually have whiplash. "What?"

Had he even been paying attention to Leah these last couple of months? It had been two months of not trying, of not having practically every conversation revolve around getting pregnant. Did he think if Leah just took a couple of months off, she would suddenly forget about the thing that had consumed them for the last almost year?

"Well, we've taken a couple months off. I'm feeling really good. We know that genetically, the embryo is fine, so I just figured it was a matter of when, not if," Leah said, trying to keep her cool.

"I didn't realize that transferring the last embryo was a done deal," Scott said.

Leah hated when he acted like this. As though his aloofness could absolve him from the responsibility of shared decision-making that was required of married adults.

"I haven't put my body and sanity through hell the last eight months to not take every opportunity. Are you really saying you don't want to do this anymore?" Leah said it as less of a question and more of a threat.

"No, that's not what I'm saying. I'm saying that this thing has consumed us for the last year, and maybe we should take a break from it for a bit. You know, enjoy the holidays."

The fucking holidays? Leah thought to herself.

"We just took a break! You act like time isn't a factor here." Leah was done trying to keep her emotions in check.

"I think we just need to clear our heads," Scott said, knowing it was a lame excuse.

There was silence. What did clear their heads even mean? *What a stupid response*, Leah thought to herself.

Scott sighed. "It's been over a year, Leah. We have an amazing kid, and quite frankly, you're missing out on that because you're so obsessed with this," Scott said what he truly thought but felt terrible saying it.

Leah was a wonderful mother, but it was true that pursuit of baby number two had taken over most of her time and energy. Mostly out of necessity. There was no such thing as casually doing IVF. The mechanics of it all took up enough time and effort as it was, but all the additional stuff—the research, the time spent on online communities, desperately trying to find answers, looking for support on down days, offering support to others on not-so-down days—took up exponentially more. It was impossible to not be consumed by it all.

Leah burst into tears. She wasn't a crier. Or a yeller. "Fuck you Scott—how can you be so dismissive. You haven't had to lift a fucking finger through this whole thing!"

"I'm hurting, too, you know. And it's not because of a baby that doesn't exist. It's because I'm watching my wife suffer, and I want her back," Scott said, with equal amounts of hurt and anger.

"Are you really asking me to choose between you and another baby? Because you don't want to hear my choice in that ultimatum," Leah said firmly. She wasn't actually prepared to leave Scott over this, not yet anyway. But she resented him enough at that moment to make him think that she would.

"No, Leah. I'm asking you to choose yourself...and the family that you actually have."

That is such bullshit, Leah thought. What did *choosing herself* even mean?

"I'm sleeping in the guestroom," Leah said, walking out of their bedroom.

Leah and Scott didn't speak for the next three days, including the day she ovulated.

Twenty-Five

BRIE

BRIE LOOKED AROUND her. The walls were bland, the lighting was harsh, and the air stale. The only semblance of character she noticed was a collage of hand-drawn pictures on a bulletin board. It would've been cute, heartwarming even if the pictures had been drawn by four-year-olds. Not eighty-four year-olds. She was being shown around the nursing home that Dora would be moving into next week. It was a sad mix of hospital meets preschool.

"And here's where we have weekly bingo. Monday night is specifically for our dementia residents. Does Dora enjoy bingo?" The chipper nurse asked.

"No." Brie was short and borderline rude in her reply.

"Oh, that's okay. We have lots to do here. We'll find something your mom enjoys," the nurse replied.

The nurse giving her a tour was doing her best to assure Brie that the facility was top-notch, "one of the best in the city." That made Brie even sadder. If this was one of the best facilities, what else was out there? Brie knew she wasn't being fair. It didn't matter how nicely decorated the place was, how warm and friendly the staff was, the air of sadness and loss lingered heavily within those four walls.

"Now, as Dora's substitute decision-maker there are some important things you'll have to think about before she moves in. All of our residents are required to have advanced care directives. So, basically what that means is what type of care Dora would want in the event of an accident or emergency. The options range from heroic interventions to DNR," the nurse explained.

"Sorry, DNR?" Brie asked.

"Do not resuscitate," the nurse said quietly. "Did Dora ever have those conversations with you or anyone in your family?"

"No, I don't think she was planning on getting dementia when she was sixty," Brie replied, regretting her biting tone.

Despite Brie's coldness, the nurse was warm and understanding. "Well, in situations like these, all you can do is put yourself in your mom's shoes and try to make the decision how she would've."

Brie knew that if she were to truly put herself in Dora's shoes, she'd be slipping her a little something so that she never had to step foot in a place like this. But that clearly wasn't an option. So that night when Brie was going through what felt like thousands of forms that all asked basically the same questions, she checked the box by DNR without hesitation.

———

The following Wednesday was one of the first truly cold mornings of the fall, where you could see your breath in the air. It was the big moving day that Brie wanted to fast-forward through.

Dora mostly cooperated with getting out the door. Brie was intentional about trying to have a calm morning with Dora. She made sure the curtains were open, letting in natural sunlight, and she played her *Dora* playlist—which was a mix of mostly Fleetwood Mac, Neil Young, and Bob Dylan—at low volume all morning. She knew better than to play any song from the 90s or later, or Dora would get agitated. Brie had become an expert in creating a calming dementia-friendly environment, and the most mundane things that most people wouldn't think twice about—patterns on rugs, wattage and placement of lamps, having the news playing on the TV in the background—had become carefully curated choices that were reflective of hours of research and time spent on dementia support group discussion boards.

Despite the conversations leading up to this day and trying to explain to Dora what was happening, she still didn't know she was moving into a nursing home. And Brie didn't have it in her to try to be honest, so that morning she just said, "Let's go for a drive, Mom."

The fact that Dora so willingly got in the car crushed Brie. The drive to the facility went by in a blur, and Brie did her best to stay mostly detached. They were greeted by a personal care worker and the nurse who had originally shown Brie around the facility. Dora was unbothered as they took the elevator up to her new home, a 10x12 room on the fourth floor. Brie unpacked her one small suitcase, which consisted mostly of clothing, a couple of funky decor items that Dora had accumulated on her travels, and two framed photos—one of Brie and Dora when Brie was a toddler, and one of them from their trip to Peru.

"There are just a couple more forms we need your signature on when you get a chance," the personal care worker said quietly, as she popped her head in the doorframe of Dora's room.

Brie was relieved. She didn't know how to actually make the transition out of the room and say goodbye to her mom, and the personal care worker had just given her an out.

"I'll see you tomorrow, Dora," Brie said, already dreading stepping foot back into this place.

Dora seemed unbothered, though, sitting on her new bed, stroking the small patchwork quilt that she brought from home. The quilt was a gift from an elderly neighbor who she'd often go have tea with and check in on regularly. Was it Mildred? Or Myrtle? Brie couldn't remember. She passed away a few years ago, and it was so striking to see Dora go from caregiver to careneeder in such a short amount of time.

Brie made her way out to the nursing station to complete the paperwork. As her pen made its last stroke of her last signature, she heard a scream come from her mom's room. She heard the call bell ring at the nursing station and saw two staff members run toward her mom's room.

Her heart froze. She wanted to just run away, but instead, she slowly walked toward her mom's room. She knew instantly that the scene in front her would be burned in her brain forever. Time slowed down as she saw the personal support worker on the floor holding her arm in pain, while one of the other, larger staff members had Dora pressed against the bed, pulling her elastic-waisted pants exposing her bare hip. Yet another staff member was holding a syringe with what Brie would remember as the largest needle she had ever seen, even though it technically wasn't. Dora didn't even notice when the giant needle pierced the skin on her hip.

The staff member who stuck the needle in her turned around to see Brie in the doorway. "Don't worry, move-in day is always tough. Every day won't be like this," she said to Brie, unfazed by what just happened.

Brie felt hot. The kind of hot that feels like you're burning from the inside out. She didn't know what to say, and even if she did know what to say, she was certain she would throw up or pass out if she opened her mouth. So instead, she just nodded.

"She's probably going to be drowsy for a while then have a good sleep. It will take a while for the Haldol to wear off, so you might as well go home. We can call you later once she's awake if you want?"

Brie nodded again, turned around, and walked as fast as she could without actually running to the elevator. She couldn't stay there a second longer.

—————

As Brie walked through the door to her house, she realized it was the first time in nearly a year that it was empty. There was no Dora. This would be her first night alone in her house in nearly a year.

She grabbed her cell phone out of her bag and quickly started running through her contact list. She knew she could call any of the girls. She had gotten texts from Rachel and Elyse throughout the day checking to see how she was doing.

Instead, to avoid the terrible mix of loneliness and guilt she was feeling, Brie texted the last number she probably should've.

Brie: Hey Brad, long time no talk ;)

Brad: Well, well, well, look who it is ;)

Brie: Let's meet up at Finnigan's. 5:30?

Brie wasn't going to beat around the bush. She needed a distraction, and she didn't have the time or energy to ease into a conversation with Brad, who she hadn't spoken to in a few months. Not because there were any hard feelings there, but because she just didn't have any reason to talk to him otherwise. And now she did.

Brad: Lol, you just expect me to drop everything to hang out with you after months of radio silence?

Brie knew he wasn't actually upset. He was just looking for a little ego boost before he inevitably said yes. Brie wasn't willing to give it to him.

Brie: I feel like going out. You in, or should I scroll down farther in my contacts?

Brie felt juvenile for how this conversation was going, and if Brad wasn't a man-child himself, she actually would've been embarrassed. But with all the other emotions of the day—sadness, anguish, relief, guilt—there just wasn't room for embarrassment, too.

Brad: You know I'm always down ;)

Brie: Consider yourself lucky, alphabetically. Getting an uber now. Text you when I'm close.

Four hours later, Brie was still at Finnigan's, five beers and two shots deep, hanging off Brad, laughing at what was probably a terrible joke. An hour later they were stumbling through Brie's front door. This certainly wasn't her finest moment, but it also probably wasn't that different from how Dora would've handled the situation—Brie took some weird comfort in knowing that.

Twenty-Six

RACHEL

"I'LL HAVE THE chicken fettuccine alfredo, please," Rachel said, handing the menu to the waiter.

She had been ordering the same dinner from the same Italian restaurant she and Sean went to every year for their anniversary dinner. Sure, their anniversary was four months ago but better late than never. Between their conflicting work schedules and the kids' activities, they were just getting around to it.

"Anything to drink with that?" the waiter followed up.

"Uh, I guess I'll get a glass of pinot grigio." Rachel ordered the wine she knew she could pronounce, not the one that she wanted the most. Based on the wine list descriptions, the Scheurebe sounded like the best option, but after trying to sound it out in her head a couple of times, she decided to stick with what she knew.

Rachel didn't even really want wine. On the rare occasions that she had a drink these days, she always opted for a beer. But she was out at probably the third fanciest Italian restaurant in Providence, and she at least knew that you order white wine with white sauces—or, at least she thought that was true.

The waiter turned to Sean. "And for you?"

Sean gave his order confidently, without hesitation. "I'll have the beef tenderloin with mashed potatoes and a glass of the cab sauv."

A few minutes later their drinks arrived.

"Here's to eight married years." Sean raised his glass, and Rachel followed suit.

It was crazy to Rachel that they had been married for eight years. What was even crazier was that they had been parents for seven of those years. They weren't one of those couples that wanted to wait, to really enjoy married life before having kids. Having kids right away was what Rachel's mom did, and her sister, and so it just seemed like that's what she was supposed to do. She hadn't really even given it much thought.

She and Sean dated for exactly two years before getting engaged and got married nine months later. And ten months after getting married, Julia came along. It was actually kind of wild to think about how little time they had spent together alone. Even in those first few years, between Sean's shift work and Rachel's reluctance to move in together before being engaged, how much time had they really spent together? Rachel didn't necessarily think this was a bad thing, or that maybe they should've waited longer to have kids, or moved in earlier. It was just a weird observation that hadn't really dawned on her until now. She hadn't realized how scarce one-on-one alone time with her husband was, until they actually had some.

"So, I think I'm going to apply for that position I was telling you about. The clinic manager one," Sean said after taking his first sip of wine.

A couple of weeks earlier, he told Rachel about the clinic manager position that was opening up. He of course asked her what she thought about him applying for it, but in the way most people asked Rachel what she thought—as less of a genuine question and more as a courtesy. Like he knew she would never actually oppose it and would instead offer unwavering support. That was exactly what Rachel did—she encouraged him to apply because of course he would be great for it. And when Sean later changed his mind and decided that maybe he didn't want the added responsibilities that came with the manager position, Rachel agreed.

"Oh, I thought you had decided you weren't going to?" Rachel asked tentatively, careful not to sound discouraging.

"Yeah, but I thought about it some more and talked to some of the guys at work about it, and they think I'd have a good chance. And let's be honest, I can't keep doing the hands-on care forever. Shift work is starting to get really old, too," Sean explained.

Rachel did her best "I'm listening intently" nod she had mastered from all her years in HR. A way to put people at ease without being too encouraging or getting anyone's hopes too high.

"I kind of thought you'd be more excited," Sean said with a hesitant grin.

"Of course I'm excited for you! You should do whatever makes you happy. And shift work is getting old for me, too," Rachel agreed.

Rachel knew that Sean would hate the manager role. The best part of his work was interacting with patients, and the least favorite part of his work was anything related to paperwork or having to deal with people issues, so basically, the two main tasks of a manager. His need to be liked, combined with his lack of directness would mean that his staff would end up eating him alive. Rachel felt guilty for thinking this, but she knew she was right. Of course she wouldn't actually say this to Sean. Doing so wouldn't qualify as the unwavering support that Rachel was there to provide.

"If I have a normal schedule for once, just think of how much easier it will be on you. I can do more of the pick-ups and drop-offs. Knowing we have the weekends means I can take the kids to their lessons and sports. It won't have to be you all the time. You could even go back to full-time hours if you really wanted to," Sean said eagerly.

Rachel felt herself clenching up. She and Sean had never actually had an intentional discussion about Rachel taking on the brunt work of the house and kids in order to accommodate Sean's schedule. They never had to have a discussion, because Rachel just did it. Sean never asked her to. There were no intense power struggles, no talks about getting extra help to relieve the burden on Rachel. She just did it. And now the thought of not being the primary parent to do all these things made Rachel feel uneasy. Sure, many people would look at her life and find it too ordinary, too selfless, but she felt an intense desire to keep things the way they were. Her current situation may not have been the most glamorous, but it was her comfort zone. And Rachel would choose comfort over glamor any day.

Sean was right. She should've been more excited at the thought of him being around more, of her getting more time to herself, of getting a break from the never-ending mental to-do list, but she wasn't. If anything, she was actually dreading it.

She swallowed and said, "Yeah, no it would be great. As long as that's what you want. I don't want you to feel like you have to apply to change your schedule. I just know how much you love the clinical work, and I don't want you to do something you don't love because you think I need a break." Rachel was trying to be honest with Sean about the realities of management without being offensive. But she was also looking for a way to keep everything as it was—the way she liked it.

"Well, I'll never know if I don't try. It's no big deal. I can always go back to just being a tech if it's not my thing," Sean said.

Rachel felt a slight sense of relief.

"Well the kids would love it! Mom can be kind of boring sometimes anyway," Rachel half-joked. "Oh, speaking of which, I should check in with my mom to see if the kids are in bed," she said, changing the subject.

"Rach, they're fine. Your mom has watched them a million times before," Sean reminded her.

That wasn't true. Yes, her mother was their go-to babysitter, but it really was only a few times a year, and Rachel tried to plan those few instances so that the kids were in bed by the time they left.

"Come on. Let's just focus on us tonight," Sean said as he reached across the table to hold Rachel's hand. It was one of those touches that almost felt foreign. She could feel his eyes searching for hers. *Oh my god, was he flirting?* Did he really expect her to just flip the switch from unsexy household logistics to whatever it was that made her remember how much she was actually still attracted to her husband?

Rachel looked up to meet his gaze, gave an embarrassed sigh, and put her phone back in her bag.

"Plus, the extra money wouldn't hurt, either. Maybe next year's anniversary dinner can be in Italy instead of an Italian restaurant?" Sean suggested hopefully.

There was that clenching feeling again. In the last seven years, she and Sean had only had one overnight away from the kids when they were both at a friend's wedding. Between the odd girls' trips or guys' weekends, they both had individual nights away. But there was always peace of mind knowing that one parent was home with the kids. At least for Sean. Rachel tended to keep her overnights as short as possible. The reason for this wasn't money. They were both practical with money, some may even say frugal, but a few months of intentional saving and cutting back on expenses and they'd be able to do a European holiday, no problem. If it wasn't money, then what was it?

Rachel was overwhelmed. All this talk about fancy vacations, Sean doing more, and her being able to do less, made her feel a deep sense of panic. She knew most other women in her situation would be welcoming, even excited about these possibilities, but she liked her life just fine the way it was. Change just wasn't her thing, even if it was a good change.

"But seriously, Rach. You've been holding this family together and deserve some time to yourself," Sean said sincerely.

"Yeah, no, that would be a dream," she lied.

"When's the application due? I can help you with your cover letter if you want," Rachel offered. Not because she was a good wife, but because she was a good HR professional who had been through enough terrible résumés and interviews that she owed it to her profession to not let Sean be one of them.

Shit, she thought to herself. He probably will get it then.

The rest of their dinner was thankfully less focused on Rachel's new found freedom and more about Sean and his plans to try to get more biking in during summer, maybe train for a triathlon. And lots of conversations about the kids. How the fall fair went. Julia's newly acquired second grade attitude. How Henry was adjusting to school.

In the absence of anything Rachel felt was notable about her own life, she updated Sean on Elyse and Mark, Leah and Scott, Brie and her mom, and Alex's pregnancy. If she didn't have the kids and her friends' lives to talk about, she wondered if she'd have anything to talk about at all.

Twenty-Seven

A FOOD COURT CHRISTMAS

IT WAS ONLY midway through November, but between holiday office parties, kids' Christmas concerts, and extended family obligations, everyone's calendars were full. So, instead of getting dressed up and going to dinner, or planning a fun girls' night in, they decided that spending an afternoon Christmas shopping would be the most practical solution. And even then, time was limited, and they all had different lists. So, they decided to divide and conquer and then meet up in the food court for a late lunch.

Rachel and Leah mostly stuck to toy stores and were focused on getting stuff for the kids. Elyse and Alex were more focused on early holiday sales for themselves and stuck to clothing and makeup. And Brie bopped around between the two groups because she hated malls in general. They didn't fit her anti-mass consumerism aesthetic. She preferred eco-friendly, vintage, local, artisan-type vibes that generally weren't found inside of a Target. Plus, her disdain for malls would also hide the fact that she had come to realize that it would be her first Christmas without her mom. Yes, Dora was still around physically, but Brie wasn't prepared to spend Christmas in a nursing home, pretending like Dora had any idea of who she was, or that it was even Christmas.

Brie made her way into the toy store, spotting Leah and Rachel. She started browsing and filling a cart of toys for her friends' kids. Brie was willing to relax her anti-consumerism philosophy for her honorary nieces and nephews. Plus, the anarchist in her wanted to make sure they got the fun, impractical stuff that their parents wouldn't buy. Toy guns, glitter art, and Pop Rock candy, it was.

"Brie, that is way too much stuff, really. The kids get so much already. You don't need to get them anything. Let alone three or four things," Rachel reassured her when she saw the amount of items Brie had in her cart.

"And oh god, please, nothing with small parts," Leah begged. "Seriously, I don't know where I'm going to put all this shit.

"Well, that's for you to worry about. Not fun Aunt Brie," she teased. "And don't forget about the goat."

"What?" Rachel asked, confused.

"I'm getting all the kids a donation in their names, for a goat to feed families in Nigeria," Brie explained.

"That's kind of messed up, Brie. I mean Oliver is pretty into barnyard animals, but I don't think he's quite ready to hear about the fate of them," Leah joked.

"Well, too late! It's already done," Brie informed her.

Meanwhile, in Sephora, Elyse and Alex were perusing all the latest anti-aging skincare products.

"I heard this one is really good. Jennifer Aniston has apparently used it for years," Elyse said, picking up the tiniest, most expensive bottle of face serum on the shelf. "I'm trying to ward off

Botox for as long as possible, but I'm not sure how much longer I can go," Elyse explained.

"Ugh, I would kill for some Botox right about now," Alex said.

"So, why don't you just do it?" Elyse asked.

Alex fell silent, because she realized she hadn't let the cat out of the bag to Rachel and Elyse. Brie and Leah were the only ones who knew. Brie knew because she was there when Alex found out, and Alex felt compelled to tell Leah in the gentlest way possible, as soon as possible. She knew how much Leah struggled with pregnancy announcements and wanted to give her the time and space to let it settle in. Every time someone announced they were pregnant, it just reminded Leah that she wasn't.

Alex had zero expectations for Leah to be excited for her, especially when Alex wasn't even sure if she was excited for herself. Leah, being the true friend she was, congratulated Alex but was also completely honest, too. *I'm a little sad. But my happiness for you is bigger than my sadness for myself*, Leah had said. Alex was almost relieved that Leah's response was not over-the-top enthusiasm. She much preferred a genuine, vulnerable response to a fake one. It was a response that reassured Alex of just how deep her friendship with Leah was.

Alex wasn't necessarily trying to keep it a secret. She just wanted to wait as close as possible to twelve weeks to let people know. And if she was being really honest with herself, it was easier to try not to think about it since she still wasn't one-hundred percent sure if it was what she wanted. She didn't think she would actually make *that* decision at this point in her life, but it was a comfort knowing she still technically had options.

"Oh my god, you're not pregnant, are you?" Elyse asked, finally catching on.

For most other women, reluctance to Botox wouldn't have been much of a pregnancy clue, but for Alex, who has been using anti-aging products since she was in early twenties—it was.

Alex gave a slight, single nod.

"Wow. I thought you guys decided you were done?" Elyse followed up.

"We did. We just probably decided a little too late. I'm still only nine weeks, so it's early. But yeah...oops!" Alex said with a light shrug.

"Well, how are you feeling about it?" Elyse asked.

"Honestly, I try not to think about it. I had such a tough time after Lola was born, and the thought of doing it all again..." Alex trailed off.

Elyse put a moisturizer bottle back on the shelf and turned to face Alex. "Yeah, but you came out on the other end. You're doing great now, right?"

"Well, yeah, I feel a lot better. More like myself. I just...I don't know. I don't know what I'm doing. And all this stuff with my mom just makes me question if I'm even capable of being a good mom myself," Alex admitted. "And the thought of two. Like if I have to split my attention, will I be a worse mom? Will I become Cindy?"

"Oh my god, don't be so ridiculous, Alex. You are not Cindy. How can you even question that?" Elyse said, practically scolding Alex for being so ridiculous. "You're a wonderful mother to Lola, and you'll be a wonderful mother to this new little one, too."

She wasn't the warm and fuzzy type, but she knew when and how to give her friends the confidence boost they needed at the appropriate times.

"Thank you, Elyse," Alex smiled at her. "Any updates with you and Mark? You wanna be pregnancy buddies?" She joked.

"Ha! Hardly. Mark wishes. It's like we've been in a year-long argument. And honestly the more he pushes the more it makes me not want to. Which is probably terrible to say," Elyse admitted.

"Is that about not wanting a baby, or not wanting to lose an argument?" Alex asked astutely.

"Touché!" Elyse agreed. "I don't know. I still feel like I have lots of time. I figure the more years of success I have at work, I can use those good years as leverage, and everyone at the firm will have to ignore the hot mess I'd be after having a baby."

"Oh, come on, Elyse. If I can do it, so can you. Not that I'm a partner or anything," Alex said, trying to be encouraging but knowing Elyse's career aspirations were likely much higher than hers.

"Well, I figure I'll either be an amazing executive and a shitty mom, or a good mom and a shitty executive," Elyse said jokingly but honestly.

"Hey, it could be worse. You could be shitty at both," Alex said, referring to her stuffy debacle, even though it was months ago.

"Oh, it's a quarter after. Let's meet up with the rest of the girls," Elyse said, catching the time on her phone.

———

After ordering their respective meals at different restaurants, the girls piled their trays at a table in the middle of the food court.

"Shoot, look at the time. I've only got another half-hour before I have to pick up Julia," Rachel wrinkled her nose in disappointment.

"Already?" Alex asked.

"I know. I feel like I barely got anything done that I needed to," Rachel replied, looking slightly defeated.

Elyse let out a single breathy laugh. "God, what happened to us? We used to be fun. I didn't just imagine that, right? Now we can barely find a couple of hours to all get together. And don't get me wrong, I love a Panera salad as much as the next, but when did we get so, so—

"Boring?" Alex found Elyse's words for her.

Leah chuckled. "Seriously. Let's start looking at beach dates. It's like seven months away. Surely we can find a time that works for everyone."

"And if not, Costco has a cafeteria, right?" Brie joked.

They all laughed, probably harder than was warranted.

Leah caught her breath and waved her hand. "Okay, okay, before we have to leave, let's do some rapid-fire life updates then. I'll go first. I've spent the last almost year sinking drugs, money, and my sanity into baby number two with no luck, but Scott wants to stop because it's too hard...*for him*. What about you Rach?"

"Well, all I do is think about my kids' snacks and activities, while I do the job of a director and get paid like an assistant," Rachel said.

Brie chimed in, "My only family member doesn't even know who I am, and my snotty grad students are giving me shit for not supporting them enough."

"Oh, me next," Elyse said. "My marriage is falling apart because my baby fever-infected husband would rather me barefoot and pregnant than bringing in six figures or actually having an intellectual thought."

"Speaking of pregnant, guess who is accidentally knocked up after she definitely decided she's not fit to parent one, let alone two, kids? Oh yeah, I have also cut Cindy out of my life for good," Alex said.

There was a brief moment of reserved excitement for Alex's news, as if to ask her permission if it was okay to be excited since it wasn't exactly what she had planned on.

"It's okay. You can be excited. It's slowly starting to sink in for me," Alex said, sensing the others' trepidation.

"Well, look at us, all just thriving," Leah said, as she held up her fountain soda cup.

The rest of the girls raised their paper cups, giggling with ear-to-ear smiles—because amidst all their misfortunes, they were grateful they had each other to lean on, even if it was mostly through texts, memes, and rushed mall food court lunches—and they all cheers'd. It wasn't champagne and it wasn't a fancy restaurant, and there wasn't much to celebrate, aside from Alex's unplanned pregnancy, but it was one of their more memorable toasts in their nearly twenty years of friendship.

December 2023

230

Twenty-Eight

Rachel

"MAKE SURE THEY have their water bottles and don't forget their car snacks. Do you guys have to pee before you go?" Rachel instructed Sean and asked her kids all in one breath.

Sean was getting the kids packed up to have a fun Saturday afternoon with their dad: mini-golf, fast food for lunch, and if there was no fighting, maybe a stop at the toy store. It had been a couple of months since Sean applied for the clinical manager role at the hospital, and with Rachel basically writing his cover letter, updating his résumé that hadn't been touched in a decade, and coaching him through some likely interview questions, it came as no surprise to her that he got the job.

Previous Saturdays he was usually either working, recovering from a night shift, or gearing up for a night shift. So, Rachel always took the reins and scheduled the kids' activities around not disturbing his erratic sleep schedule and including him in family activities when it worked. All Sean had to do was show up, like an invited guest. But not this Saturday. It was his first weekend of working a Monday-to-Friday, nine-to-five schedule, and his first order of business in his new role was to dedicate the weekend to the kids and give Rachel a break. A break that not only she didn't ask for but one that she'd rather not have. She was already a little sad to be missing the fun and worried that Sean wouldn't know about all the little tricks and tips she had managed to develop over the years to have smooth outings with the kids. But why would he know any of it? It's not like she had ever shared her parental wisdom with him, but surely that wasn't on purpose. Right?

"Rach, don't worry. I've got it. They'll be fine." He gave her a reassuring, bordering-on-overconfident grin.

"Okay guys, give Mommy hugs and kisses goodbye." Both kids ran over and fell into her. Rachel gave them extra hard squeezes and lingered in the hugs a little too long. She knew it was a bit dramatic for them only being gone for a few hours.

"Enjoy your time, babe. And if you go out, don't rush back!" Sean insisted. "Did you decide on what you're going to do? Spa? Shopping? Lunch?"

"Haven't decided yet. I guess I'll just see where the afternoon takes me!" Rachel said, knowing it wasn't likely she was going to do any of those things.

Once she heard the car leave the driveway, she followed the dog upstairs where he quickly curled up on his bed and fell asleep instantly. Clearly, he was embracing this quiet alone time more than Rachel was.

The house felt eerie and unfamiliar being so empty on a Saturday. There was no one screaming for Mommy, no messes or spills to clean up. At least no obvious ones anyway. No quarrels to break up. She couldn't quite place this feeling, but she knew she didn't like it. It was something between uneasiness and panic.

Instead of going to a spa or going shopping, or even just meeting one of the girls for lunch, like she had told Sean she would probably do with her new found freedom, she walked around her creepily quiet house and just saw remnants of Julia and Henry.

She walked into Julia's room, instinctively putting the dirty clothes on the floor beside the hamper into the hamper and looked around. Julia's toy bins were filled with a mix of Barbies and animals. Julia wanted to be a vet but not just any vet, a world famous one that has her own TV show. Julia loved telling everyone that and beamed with pride when she did. When did people lose that unabashed confidence in themselves, she wondered. When does reality set in? Who knows though, maybe she really would be a world famous vet with her own TV show one day. Does anyone actually end up doing what they want to do when they're seven?

Rachel tried to recall what she wanted to be when she was seven. She couldn't remember, but she definitely knew it wasn't to sit in an office cubicle doing mostly unnecessary paperwork and attending even more unnecessary meetings.

Would she even want Julia to want to be like her? That seemed like a loaded question for any parent to ask themselves. It wasn't that Rachel didn't like herself. She thought she turned out just fine. But she also wasn't exactly a world famous veterinarian.

She walked across the hall into Henry's room. It was much more chaotic than Julia's room, just like Henry was. She stepped on a Lego that hadn't made it into the Lego bin. Luckily, her feet had practically developed calluses to adapt to all the stray Legos and she barely felt it. What would Henry think of her as a grown man? Oh god. What would a future daughter-in-law think of her? Rachel made herself snap out of it and threw the few remaining pieces of

Legos in a bin. She quickly tried to hush her inner voice and texted Leah.

Rachel: Cleaning out Henry's room. Does Oliver want some wooden puzzles?

She quickly snapped a picture with her phone and sent it to Leah. Anytime she found herself dreading her own kids growing up, she reached out to someone with younger kids, and usually offered them a hand-me-down, or asked how they were doing with the latest parenting trials and tribulations. Things like, "How's the nap regression going, stick in there, mama! Don't worry about potty training, they'll do it when they're ready! They all have tantrums. I'd be more worried if they didn't." It was as if she had a ridiculous insatiable need to care for babies and toddlers, the neediest of the human species.

Just as she sent the text to Leah, she got a text from Sean. It was a selfie with all three of them with French fries placed in the corners of their mouths pretending to be walruses with silly grins. It was adorable. Rachel started to tear up.

Seriously, what was wrong with her? Why wasn't she happier right now? Most women would kill for an afternoon to themselves while their doting husband and engaged father entertained the kids. Somehow having the afternoon to herself was less appealing to her than doling out snacks, coloring, and playing Legos. Instead of relaxing, she was alone with her thoughts, which she realized almost never happened, and it made her uncomfortable. And if there's one thing Rachel hated, it was discomfort.

———

Two hours later, she was still mindlessly straightening out Henry's room. She switched the Lego bin with the dinky car bin, and switched the pants drawer with the pajamas drawer in his dresser. Really pointless stuff that didn't change the look or functionality of his room but kept Rachel's hands and mind occupied.

As she closed the last dresser drawer, she heard the garage open and the high-pitched voices quickly filled the empty house. "Mooooooommy, we brought you a milkshake!" Henry screamed.

Her whole body unclenched at the sounds of chaos downstairs. Coats and shoes being strewn about, the damn dog's yelpy bark.

She made her way downstairs to greet her family. She tried to look for obvious signs of distress. Did Sean look overwhelmed by the chaos? Was one of the kids disappointed? Any physical signs that there had been tears earlier? But all she saw was her two happy, healthy kids excited from a fun afternoon with their loving father. What more could she ask for, really?

"Did you guys have fun?" She asked, making sure to sound excited.

"Yaaaaaa! And Daddy says we can go again next weekend!" Julia informed her mother.

"Oh, great! That will be fun," Rachel lied through a tight-lipped smile.

"I want a snack," Henry whined.

His high-pitched demand instantly released the tension in Rachel's body. In some twisted way, the same things about having kids that used to grate on her were now so familiar that they had actually become not only tolerable but comforting. All was right in the world again.

"What do you say?" Rachel prompted, even though she was already cutting up an apple.

"Please!"

Twenty-Nine

ALEX

ALEX HAD FINALLY started to come out of her first trimester misery. It was barely tolerable the first time around, but add in taking care of a toddler, and this time around she was exponentially more exhausted—physically, mentally, and emotionally.

She was doing her best to find the joy in this second pregnancy, mostly for Andrew, but it felt performative. However, she felt she needed to make up for the fact that she said she didn't want any more kids, and now here she was with a tiny baby bump that was already trying to make its existence known. Not like her pregnancy with Lola when she was desperately trying to look pregnant up until twenty-four weeks when she finally popped.

It was an easy pregnant body to embrace because it was basically her normal body with the addition of a perfectly round baby bump and a few extra cup sizes that Alex had proudly flaunted. This second time around though, it felt like she put on ten pounds the second she got a positive pregnancy test. And those pounds were unfortunately more evenly dispersed than just in her boobs and belly.

When Alex told Andrew that she was pregnant, he couldn't help but express his pure joy and excitement. *Must be nice*, Alex had thought to herself.

"Guess it was meant to be," he had said.

Once he saw the grim expression on her face, he realized that Alex did not have the same thought.

"What are you thinking, babe?" He asked, wanting to be supportive of Alex, yet knowing she struggled postpartum with Lola and had been going through a lot with her mother. But now that he knew she was pregnant, he realized that he wasn't so apathetic about a second baby after all. It turned out that he was really, really excited.

"I mean, this isn't what we planned. It's actually the exact opposite of what we planned..." Alex trailed off.

She was saying more with her silence than she did with her words. She didn't want to actually say the word *abortion* out loud, but she also wanted to make it clear that it wasn't completely out of the question for her.

"Are you...is that something..." Andrew was fumbling his words.

"I mean, I've thought about it," Alex answered honestly.

"And which way are you leaning?" Andrew asked, also not actually wanting to use the word abortion.

"My knee-jerk feeling is I just want to make it go away, but when I actually think about it, like deep, deep down, I don't think I'd actually do...that," she said with a downward gaze and a queasiness in her stomach that she knew wasn't from morning sickness.

Andrew tried to not look too visibly relieved, but Alex could see that he was.

"I mean do happily married thirty-five-year-olds even get abortions?" Alex said, half-joking.

Andrew sighed. "Well, if I'm being completely honest, I do really want us to have this baby. I felt indifferent when there wasn't a second baby to be had, but now, knowing that it exists..."

"I know," Alex said, nodding in agreement.

"What made you so sure that you don't want a second?" Andrew asked, gently, trying to make sure he wasn't coming off as pushy.

"I just...I worry I won't be good at it. That i'm already not good at it and having two will make me doubly not good at it," Alex said, choking back tears.

The look of surprise on Andrew's face reminded Alex of how much she had kept from him. That he didn't even know that she had been dealing with these feelings for months. She felt simultaneous guilt and relief for finally being honest.

"Alex, are you crazy? You don't see how Lola looks at you. I would kill for her to look at me that way. I know she loves me, but you...you're her whole world," Andrew said, genuinely.

Alex let a few tears fall. That was one of the nicest things someone had ever said to her. She didn't say it out loud, but that was the moment she decided this baby probably was meant to be.

This pregnancy started to feel more real, and she felt her first twinge of excitement when they found out they were having another little girl. Alex liked to think she would have been just as happy if it was a boy, but at least she didn't need to find out the hard way.

She and Andrew decided to make the trip to the West Coast to spend the holidays with Andrew's parents and his sister's family. Alex wasn't initially sold on the idea but thought if they were going to do it, now would be the time before Lola can really remember celebrating at home.

With a growing family, she wanted to start to establish those holiday traditions—the consistent things that her kids could look forward to and rely on happening. The things that other, well-adjusted people seemed to speak about so fondly. She knew they would have a great time with Andrew's family, and honestly, she was in the mood to be hosted and not have to worry about cleaning her house and pretending like she gave a shit about cooking a nice meal.

But when she started to picture the future, a future with two kids, she saw Christmas morning in their own home, gathered around a Christmas tree decorated with lots of tacky homemade ornaments the kids made, staying in their pajamas all day, and cozying up at night to watch a Christmas movie together. It was an image, that at one time, seemed so unrealistic to Alex, and now it was within reach. It was an image that mostly conjured up happiness and pride, and a little bit of trepidation. Because when you come from dysfunction, the thought of contentment feels undeserved and ill-fitting, kind of like you're wearing someone else's shoes. Shoes that, even though they might technically be the right size for you, just feel uncomfortable and aren't quite your style.

Choosing to make the trip across the country also gave her a reason to not think twice about her mom. An upcoming holiday always heightened Alex's anxiety. Holidays were for family, and everyone else talked so nonchalantly about their plans with cousins, parents, in-laws. It was always a stark reminder of what she didn't have, and she always found herself in the position of feeling like maybe she should reach out. Invite her mom. Make some sort of gesture. Maybe if they just started to act like a normal family they would actually become one.

Alex and her mom still hadn't spoken since the dinner at Fernando's. Which also meant that her mom still didn't know she was pregnant. At this point, basically everyone knew, but she just couldn't bring herself to tell her mother. She didn't want her to know. She knew that seemed extreme, but maybe it was just her protective maternal instincts kicking in.

———

It was late in the morning on Christmas day, and Alex was sipping her second cup of coffee, pretending like it wasn't decaf. Their Christmas morning with Andrew's family had been both relaxing—and chaotic—with three excited kids under one roof. It was sweet to see Lola with her two older cousins who she had only met one other time. It was one of those moments when Alex felt guilty for originally not wanting to expand their family, like she was depriving Lola of a guaranteed lifelong best friend.

She glanced down at her phone and did the time zone math, realizing it was well into the afternoon back home. She had a slew of messages from the girls wishing everyone a Merry Christmas, with lots of pictures of excited kids and tired moms, and one of Brie on a beach looking tanned and relaxed.

She also saw the message from her mother.

Cindy: Merry Christmas to you, Andrew, and Lola. I know things have been weird, but I hope you guys have a wonderful day.

Cindy: And I left a gift for Lola on your doorstep. Hope she likes it.

Her mom didn't even know they were on the other side of the country. She didn't know because Alex didn't tell her. Alex didn't tell her because she had cut her out of her life. She had cut her out because Cindy was a bad mother, or maybe, Alex was a bad daughter, or maybe it was both.

Cindy didn't even know she was going to be a grandmother again.

Alex felt her mind spiraling. It was eleven in the morning and she was pregnant so reaching for a glass of wine wasn't going to be an option. Alex went through her mental checklist she usually did when she found her anxious mind taking hold of her. Okay Alex, focus on what you can control. It's Christmas. Lola is what matters most. Take care of the gift, then get off your phone and deal with this mom shit later.

She texted her neighbor across the street.

Alex: Merry Christmas! Sorry to bother you but wondering if you would mind popping the gift on our doorstep into the garage when you get a chance...unless the porch pirates have already gotten to it :)

Neighbor Nancy: Just checked. It's still there. I'll run over now and grab it :)

Alex: Thanks so much! Merry Christmas 🎄

As Alex settled into her middle seat, with Lola gazing out the plane window on her left, and Andrew heavily invested in a game of solitaire on her right, she felt an ache in her jaw and noticed that she had been clenching it for who knows how long. They were waiting for the plane to take off and sitting on the tarmac was one of the worst parts of traveling. She decided the best distraction was to scroll through her phone, looking at all the cute pictures she had captured of Lola over the last five days.

It had been a nice visit, and the change of scenery made it easier for Alex to forget about her mom's Christmas text, which she now had to revisit. She had done a good job of stuffing it to the back of her mind but sitting on a tarmac with nothing to do meant she couldn't avoid it as easily.

She read the text, over and over, as if there was some hidden message in it she could try to uncover. She wondered what her mom was actually feeling at the moment she sent it. Was it genuinely hurt? Alex hoped not. Because if it was, that meant that she was to blame. Was it resentment? Was it a way to point out the fact that Alex hadn't reached out to wish her a Merry Christmas? Was it because she was pissed that she hadn't gotten a thank you for the gift that Alex didn't know about?

She was so annoyed with herself. The back and forth of whether or not to continue a relationship with her mother was exhausting. When she made the decision to cut her mom out completely, it felt freeing. Less so because she wouldn't be seeing or talking to Cindy, and more so because a decision had been made. A decision that allowed clarity. Like she almost had a blueprint for the rest of her life based on that decision. It was the uncertainty, more than the outcome, that drove Alex crazy. When it came to her mother, she found it simpler to analyze the situation in black and white terms; Cindy is either in, or she's out. But she knew it was never that straightforward, and that most people came in shades of gray.

She tried to channel her therapist while sitting on the tarmac. Her feelings could still be valid, and her mom could still feel hurt at the same time. Those things were not mutually exclusive. She looked down at her phone and started typing.

Alex: Hey mom, hope you had a good Christmas.

She was intentional in typing *you* and not *you and Dale*. Her feelings toward her mother were always fluid and messy and confusing, but her feelings toward her stepdad were crystal clear. Fuck that guy.

She started to type "sorry" but then deleted it. What was she sorry for? Sorry that she missed her dropping off the gift? Sorry she hadn't contacted her or tried to see her over the holidays? Sorry she had cut her out of her life? Sorry that she hated her, and yet deeply needed to feel loved by her? Sorry for all of it? Sorry for none of it? Sorry was much too loaded of a word to start out with.

Alex: We're actually just flying home from Andrew's parents' house, so Lola hasn't opened her gift yet. But thank you for dropping it off.

This is where Alex would normally feel compelled to follow up with an invite of some sort, but instead, she left it at that. She sent a quick photo of Lola on Christmas Day then quickly turned her phone to airplane mode as the flight attendants were instructing.

She started pressing the screen in front of her to find a movie to watch during the flight. She was looking for something light, maybe a rom-com or a non-murder-focused documentary. Something that would be distracting but not mentally or emotionally taxing. After a few minutes of indecisiveness, she found a documentary about dolphins. She pressed play and tried not to think about what messages may await her on the other end of the flight.

———

Alex clenched as the little airplane in the corner of her phone disappeared from the screen. Her phone immediately vibrated with three text messages she had missed while in the air; two in the girls' group chat and one from her co-worker Pam wishing her a Merry Christmas. And zero from Cindy. Alex unclenched, feeling relieved that there was no cryptic or passive aggressive message from her mother for her to try to overanalyze. Cindy lived rent-free in her brain. Alex shouldn't have been surprised by this. Paying rent was never Cindy's strong suit.

Alex practically tripped over the large box wrapped in green paper with red and pink candy canes and a giant silver bow on top, as she walked through the front door. Her neighbor must have thought she was doing Alex a favor by bringing it in the house and not the garage. She wasn't.

Before she could bend over to pick it up, she saw Lola's eyes light up. Alex was really hoping to not have to deal with whatever it was that Cindy got for Lola—mostly for selfish reasons. She didn't want to deal with an overly excited, jet-lagged toddler who was now even more likely to fight bedtime. And even more so, she didn't want to get worked up over what the gift was. If there was anyone who could make a toddler's Christmas gift actually be a thinly veiled insult to her, it was Cindy.

Alex, fully expecting the box to contain something like a potty to insinuate that Lola should be potty trained by now, was surprised to see a very plain, very appropriate gift for a two-year-old. A baby doll, a coloring book with some crayons, and a tiara and magic wand. Under another layer of tissue, there was a piece of pink satin fabric sticking out. Alex pulled the tissue back and saw the small pink satin dress with puffy sleeves and mesh train attached to the shoulders. It was clearly an older dress that had been worn before, but it would work perfectly with her new tiara and wand to play dress-up. As she lifted the dress out of the box, a piece of paper that must have been in the bottom of the box fell out.

Alex picked it and read it silently to herself.

Thought you might like to have this for Lola. This was yours when you were about Lola's age. Dressing up in this and pretending to be a princess was your favorite thing to do. You once wore this for a week straight, you even insisted on sleeping in it and wearing it to the grocery store. I held onto it hoping to have a granddaughter one day. Hope she enjoys it as much as you did.

Cindy had kept the dress this whole time, waiting to be able to pass it on. It was so *not* a Cindy thing to do.

Shit, Alex thought to herself. Am I the asshole?

Thirty

LEAH

THE DAY AFTER Christmas, Leah, Scott and Oliver piled into a shuttle to catch their flight to Mexico. It was Leah's surprise Christmas gift to the family. She knew it had been a hard year for everybody, and they were all beach people who questioned why they lived in a temperate climate where it snowed five months of the year. So, for the next seven days, they would relax, swim, play in the sand, and ring in a new year that they hoped would be kinder to them.

Since their fight and subsequent silent treatments, Leah and Scott had come to an unspoken agreement that they'd pause the fight, focus on the holidays, and resume in the new year. This was obviously good news for Scott, and even Leah had to admit that ignoring the situation was becoming a more desirable option than addressing it. She wasn't sure if she was starting to actually feel differently about it all, or if she was just so freaking tired from thinking about it, planning around it, and fighting with Scott about it.

When she planned the Mexico trip, Leah made a promise to herself that she would be present during it. Like, actually present for it. Not just waiting for the opportune time to start planning to try to get pregnant again. Not constantly doing mental math to figure out cycles, costs, or age gaps between two kids—the mental math that had consumed her entire last year. Not analyzing everything that Scott said or didn't say as some sort of hidden message about babies and fertility. Instead, she had promised herself that she'd put no pressure on herself to make a decision about next steps. 2024 Leah could think about that. 2023 Leah, at least what was left of her after being ravaged by infertility, would be fully enjoying the moments and family in front of her.

Sure, she had promised herself that so many times over the last year—*be in the moment, forget about the hurt of the past months, don't dwell on the future.* She had done it all: meditation, intention-setting, mantras, you name it. None of it ever actually worked, so Leah was skeptical that she'd be able to follow through on that promise during this vacation. But there was something about stepping off the plane and breathing in the tropical air that made her feel different. In fact, she was so in the moment that she didn't even stop to reflect on whether or not she was in the moment until a day-and-a-half into the vacation.

Scott had asked her where she wanted to have dinner. It caught her by surprise when she realized she hadn't even thought about it. Normally she would've given a decision like that all the thought. And, normally, decisions seemingly unrelated to fertility, like where to have dinner, would always lead there. It was like the neural paths in Leah's brain were a poorly designed city with a mess of one-way streets that only led to one destination: infertility. At least they had been for the last year. Until now. At first, she thought it may have been a fluke, or maybe it was the poolside margaritas, but the longer they were on vacation, the more Leah was starting to believe maybe there were other destinations, or at least other paths, with nicer scenery. Paths she could get used to. Paths she'd like to stay on.

"Mooooooommmy, look at me!" Oliver said excitedly, interrupting her thoughts as he went down the waterslide, screaming with joy as Scott caught him at the bottom.

They were having a pool day. It was their third day at the resort, and they had gotten into the routine of mornings and afternoons spent at either the pool or the beach, a late afternoon nap for everyone depending on how they felt, then either more pool time, or going to see a show, or the zoo, or other amenities they had on the resort. It was Oliver's turn tonight, so Leah was expecting to eat at the pizza place.

That was another thing she had been enjoying. Just eating to eat. To nourish and enjoy. Not thinking about how every little chemical or micronutrient might be impacting her fertility.

After a yummy pizza supper and putting Oliver to bed, which was so much easier when he had been playing outside all day, she and Scott, confined to their room, sat on their balcony enjoying room service cocktails, talking about everything and nothing—their jobs, updates with their respective friend groups and families, their takes on the latest political scandals—just genuinely enjoying each other's company.

That one-on-one time with Scott on the balcony made Leah realize how little they had connected over the last year. How few actual conversations they had, but she also knew with a young kid it was fairly normal for most conversations to be transactional in nature. *Can you pick Oliver up? We need more milk. When is this bill due?* Between the necessary transactional conversations, and the many, many conversations about fertility, embryos, and cycles, she realized they had no other space for conversations where they were actually connecting. Learning about what was going on in each other's lives, outside of Oliver and fertility things.

They agreed that a vacation like this at least once a year was absolutely necessary. They even talked about the possibility of doing a weekend getaway, just the two of them. She also realized that the part of her that is a wife had done a shit job over the last year. Not that Scott had done his best work as a husband during that time period, either. She wasn't sure if it was from coming off all the hormones, the tropical climate, or her third cocktail of the night, but she felt content. Not just content but truly happy.

———

It was their last full day at the resort. Oliver had chosen the beach over the pool. It was his goal to spend the entire day there. So, Leah loaded up with some to-go sandwiches and endless snacks, and got a start on her third book of the vacation. Luckily, Scott was a big kid and simply lying on the beach wasn't really his thing. That meant while he spent the bulk of the time with Oliver, splashing in the water, building sand castles, and having endless races along the shore, Leah got to lay back, read her book, and pop in and out of the water at her leisure.

She had to admit, now that Oliver was three and was a bit more independent, how much easier life had gotten, and how nice it was to have a kid you could have somewhat of a conversation with. One that had developed his own unique interests, mostly space and dinosaurs at the moment, and wanted to share those interests. One that wanted to help Mommy and Daddy whenever he could. Leah wasn't naïve; she knew these things wouldn't necessarily last, and there were of course the tough moments of irrational tantrums and power struggles, but she was really enjoying this stage. More than she had ever enjoyed the baby stage. Obviously, she would embrace it fully if they were lucky enough to have that experience again, but the deep-rooted need to experience it one more time was slowly fading for her. And she felt so much lighter.

As she laid on the beach reading her book glancing up to catch glimpses of Scott and Oliver splashing in the water, she saw a wholeness to her life—a simplicity that she couldn't appreciate until now. She had spent so much time wrapped up in the minutiae of infertility—the timing, the drugs, the hormones, the appointments, the monthly disappointment—that she couldn't see what an incredibly beautiful, amazing life she had right in front of her. She was finally able to block out all the trees and enjoy her forest.

———

That night after Oliver went to bed, Leah and Scott opened a bottle of wine and sat on the balcony.

"What?" Scott asked, noticing Leah's longing stare at him.

Leah set her wine glass on the table beside her, grabbed Scott's hand, and let out a happy sigh. "I think...I think I'm ready to accept that we're a family of three. A really great one."

It felt like the weight of a hundred negative pregnancy tests was lifted off her shoulders.

Scott's visible relief was palpable. "You sure, babe? We don't need to make any final decisions right now."

"I know. I just wanted you to know that you and Oliver are enough. More than enough. You're everything."

"Is this the pinot talking?" Scott joked, tipping his wine glass toward her.

He was right to be skeptical. Every time Leah said she was going to take a break, or not think so much, or try so hard to get pregnant, she usually just became more obsessed with getting pregnant than she was before.

"Maybe," she replied honestly. "I need you to do me a favor, though."

"Of course," Scott said, concerned about what she was about to ask of him.

"I'm sure I'll always be a little sad about not having a second baby, no matter how happy you and Oliver make me. I need you to let me be a little sad sometimes," Leah explained.

"I mean, I never want to see you sad, but if that's what you need," Scott replied, staring into her eyes.

Leah nodded. "It is."

She realized that the more she fought her emotions and tried to control everything, the more miserable she was. She made a promise to herself that she would start to give in to her emotions, to really *feel* them. She was finally ready to work her way through infertility and not around it.

"Here's to our next chapter," she said, raising her wine glass.

"I'll cheers to that," Scott said, clinking his wine glass against hers and leaned in to kiss Leah's sun-kissed cheek.

Thirty-One

BRIE

"FLIGHT 273 TO San Juan, Puerto Rico is now boarding," the airline agent announced over her handheld speaker.

Brie watched people frantically form an ever-growing line. What a weird social concept, she thought. People think if they get in line quicker, they'll somehow make it to their destination sooner. The first person and the last person to board all land at the same time. What perplexed her even more were the people who didn't originally get in line. The followers. The ones who become frantic by contagion and follow suit.

Brie proudly boarded the plane last and was happy to find an empty seat between her and the other passenger in her row. One perk of flying on Christmas Eve.

Despite having invites from all the girls to spend Christmas with them, and despite the judgmental look the nurses gave her when she declined the Christmas Day luncheon at the nursing home, Brie was spending her Christmas alone, taking her third solo vacation in the last two months. She also didn't want to tell her friends that the last thing she wanted to do was wake up to the sound of happy, overexcited children. She could've gone to Elyse's, but the tension between her and Mark, combined with the stuffiness of both their families sounded even worse than a chaotic kid-filled Christmas.

Since Dora moved into the nursing home, Brie had taken a leave of absence from work. She quickly found that having nothing to occupy her mind was the worst thing she could've done. So, instead of using the time to visit her mom, which she kept to no more than an hour, no more than once a week, she did what she loved most: travel. Brie was always a good solo traveler, something Dora encouraged her to do. If she wasn't traveling with Dora, she was traveling alone. She loved meeting locals and other solo travelers on vacation—typically men. One fling per vacation had become standard for Brie. She never truly set out to do that. It just kept happening until it became a pattern.

———

The combination of welcome champagne and jet lag meant that Brie slept through most of Christmas. She woke up late in the afternoon to a photo-clogged group chat of excited kids and mounds of wrapping paper. It was only ever the kids in the photos, maybe a dad here and there, but she knew her friends were probably looking frazzled and disheveled, and so Christmas memories of them would remain undocumented. The exception of course being Elyse, who was childless and perfectly put together in front of her professionally decorated Christmas tree with her and Mark having the largest, fakest smiles on their faces.

She knew her friends thought she was having a sad Christmas, but the holiday didn't mean much to Brie. She and Dora never really did a traditional Christmas, and it usually looked very different year to year. Dora was either scooping her off to some exotic location, or if they stuck around, ended up volunteering at a homeless shelter serving meals. Brie always found that to be so contradictory about Dora. She frowned upon people who flaunted their wealth and didn't use it to help others. While she certainly wasn't materialistic, she also didn't hesitate to spend her money and used it to her advantage to curate the lifestyle she wanted, which was apparently a lot of travel and not a lot of retirement savings, which Brie didn't learn until the in-depth financial review that comes with nursing home admission.

Dora didn't hesitate on a lot of things. Some would say she was impulsive. From the outside, Brie could seem that way, too, but the truth of the matter was that she was much more calculated than Dora, and as soon as she started making any real money after grad school, the first thing she did was start a 401k and some modest investments.

One of the hardest parts of grieving Dora was taking her off the pedestal that Brie had put her on. As fearful as it was to acknowledge Dora's flaws, making her more human and less perfect had started to comfort Brie. Maybe Dora didn't have all the answers. Maybe her way of life wasn't the only one. Brie admittedly felt a bit lost without the Dora blueprint to follow. Maybe it wasn't so bad to be a bit conventional, a bit less impulsive, a bit more boring.

That night Brie found herself drinking a beer alone on the beach and watching the sunset.

As she started walking back up to her room, she could feel the eyes of the hot bartender on her, as they had been every time she had passed by him earlier in the day.

"Another round?" he asked, not trying to hide the fact that he was flirting with how close he leaned in. "It's on the house."

Brie hesitated. She knew where this would lead, and for one of the first times in her adult life she took the path of more resistance. She decided she wasn't in the mood for mediocre, meaningless sex with a stranger. *Sorry Dora*, she thought to herself.

"No thanks. I'm good for the night," she replied.

The rest of the week, Brie woke up earlier than usual, drank less than usual, and did some hikes. She read books, chatted with strangers, and for the first time, started to feel the fogginess of the last year clear away. It was a bit of a departure from how Dora would've done a trip like this, but maybe this is how Brie does trips now.

Brie always thought being strong meant emulating her mother, but the more distance she had from Dora, as hard as it was, the more she realized being strong in her own way was actually a little different. She had learned so much from Dora, so much she would take with her, that is ingrained in her, but she realized she didn't have to take everything from Dora.

Thirty-Two

ELYSE

IT HAD BEEN just under a year since Elyse had made partner. She wanted to feel amazing, but the truth was, the novelty was starting to wear off. She spent way too much time with assholes, she had realized. Asshole clients—assholes she worked with, whose egos were larger than their annual bonuses. She had started to avoid any unnecessary social activities, often making excuses for why she couldn't join her all-male colleagues for a booze-filled lunch of steak and one-upmanship. The only person she found herself wanting to have a conversation with was Laurie, who reminded her of Rachel—thirty years later.

For the first time since she could remember, Elyse was slipping out of the office early on a Friday afternoon. It would likely go unnoticed as most of the partners would be doing the same to go to one of the aforementioned lunches. She wouldn't be joining them, though.

Elyse was driving alone for the next two hours to a luxury lakeside resort in Connecticut where she was meeting Mark. The weekend getaway was an early Christmas gift from Mark's parents. One that neither one of them would've booked, but it would've been too awkward to turn it down. So, here they were, just the two of them in the most luxurious romantic suite, both dreading the next two-and-a-half days.

———

The first couple of hours were pleasant enough, but the elephant in the room followed them everywhere they went and took up all the available space.

In true form, Mark was the one to break the silence. Elyse never did.

His forehead crinkled creating deep wrinkles that Elyse had never noticed before. "What are we going to do, babe?"

It was the saddest she had ever heard Mark's voice. It wasn't anger or resentment. It was exasperation and defeat. Elyse knew this because she felt the same way.

"I don't know." Elyse surprised herself by starting to cry. "I love you so much, I really do. I'm just scared we want different things. I don't want to make you hate me, but I feel like I already have, and I don't—" Elyse sighed. "I don't know how to be the person you want me to be."

"I could never hate you, Elyse," Mark said. "God, if I hated you this situation would honestly be so much easier. I don't want you to be any different. I just want us to be a family. And I know, I know it's not fair that you're the one who has to do the heavy lifting upfront, but I mean that's mostly biology. I can't really do anything about that. Trust me, if I could I would."

"The truth is..." She paused to try to swallow the giant lump in her throat. "The truth is I'm scared I won't be good at it, and that if you see me not be good at it, then you'll feel differently about me." Elyse felt the simultaneous relief of finally admitting this out loud, and the growing weight of understanding what this admission would likely mean for her future with Mark.

"Of course you'll be good at it. How could you doubt that?" Mark asked, shaking his head slightly.

"I'm not actually worried about not being a good mom. I'm worried about not caring enough to be a good mom. I'm not like your mom, or your sister, or like Rachel. I'd rather spend my energy on things that I'm good at, like work. And having a baby right now is basically in direct conflict with that," Elyse explained.

"I know this is crazy, but I swear I will never stop trying to make it up to you if we can have a baby. Please Elyse," Mark begged, sounding desperate and pitiful.

"Mark, you can't bribe me into being a mom," Elyse said, again needing to be the realistic one of the two.

"No, I'm serious. I will take paternity leave. I will change every single diaper. We can hire a nanny. We can hire a surrogate. Adopt. We can do this any way possible that works for you."

Taking the time away during the baby phase, no matter how short, wasn't Elyse's concern. It was all the phases that would follow that worried her. Toddlers were annoying and more work than babies. She dreaded the thought of weekends spent at soccer games and PTA meetings instead of nice restaurants, and puberty seemed like a nightmare. Maybe an early-to-mid-twenties adult child wouldn't be so bad, she thought to herself.

Elyse realized that she wasn't being as honest with herself, and by extension, Mark.

But for now, they would open their $300 bottle of wine and enjoy it in their $1000 a night suite. Tomorrow they'd get their couples' massage and read their respective books by the fire, overlooking a beautiful lake and have the obligatory vacation sex. Then they would drive back to their beautiful home and face their ugly reality.

———

Elyse arrived home from the resort before Mark. It didn't surprise her since she was generally a faster driver than him. Since they had taken separate vehicles, they were able to avoid an uncomfortable drive home, but Elyse knew they couldn't continue to avoid the uncomfortable dinners, the uncomfortable breakfasts, the uncomfortable sharing of a sink when they brushed their teeth before bed, the uncomfortable lives they were living together but incredibly separate.

Rather than dwell on the obvious, Elyse began unpacking her overnight bag. She always unpacked immediately whenever she returned from a trip. Not unpacking just seemed uncivilized to her. She tried to think about what Mark usually does, and she realized she didn't know because she just automatically unpacked for him. She wondered what he would do if she actually gave him the chance. *You know what, I'm not going to unpack for him this time,* she thought to herself—another one of her little tests.

Once she was done unpacking, she busied herself with laundry and tidying up their already-tidy home. Her friends with kids always complained about how impossible it was to ever have a clean home—toys everywhere, never-ending laundry, mystery stickiness on every surface—and here she was desperate to find a hidden mess, or a disorganized cupboard, anything to keep her hands and mind busy. With no luck, she settled on steaming her unwrinkled outfits she had already selected for the week.

By the time she finished steaming her casual Friday outfit, she realized that it had been almost two hours since she got home, and Mark still wasn't there.

Elyse: Where are you???

Maybe he stopped to get some groceries for the week? Even then, he should definitely be home by now. Elyse tried calling his number. It went straight to voicemail. Mark's phone was always on the brink of dying. *If he listened to me and just charged his damn phone every night, this wouldn't happen*, Elyse thought to herself

Elyse started to go through her contacts. Who would know where Mark is? Where would Mark go? The more she thought about it the more she realized how out of character this is for him. He always lets her know where he's going, even the quick little errands. And now it was two hours later, she had no response from him and all she could think was how this was his fault for not just charging his phone. She could feel panic starting to set in. What if something happened? The roads were clear and traffic wasn't bad. She looked at Twitter for any signs of potential car accidents—nothing. She called his sister.

"Hi, Elyse," Sarah greeted her. "He's here. I was just about to text you," she said, before Elyse could even ask.

Elyse felt immediate relief. Then annoyance, bordering on anger. "Oh, oh that's what I figured," she said nonchalantly. "Let me guess, his phone is dead?"

"Bingo," Sarah replied.

Elyse could hear Mark in the background playing with his niece and nephew.

"Don't worry, he's leaving soon. I have to kick him out before he gets the kids too riled up before bedtime," Sarah said.

"Oh, okay tell him to drive safe," Elyse replied.

As she ended the call with Sarah, she replayed the sound of Mark's voice in the background playing with the kids in her head. There was a jubilance in his voice Elyse hadn't heard in a long time. She was making him miserable and she knew it. And she knew she couldn't keep making the person she loved most in the world so unhappy. She knew Mark would never be the one to call it quits. She knew what she had to do, and she knew it would crush them both.

After the longest twenty minutes of her life, Mark walked through the front door. Before he could even get his shoes off, Elyse started in.

"I can't keep doing this to you, Mark. You're unhappy, and I'm the reason, and—"

"No, Elyse," Mark interrupted her. In just those two words, his tone shifted from angry to pure sorrow. "Don't make this about me being unhappy, like it's my fault or something."

"Listen Mark, I'm not trying to fight right now. God knows we've done enough of that. We're on two different pages—we're not even in the same book. I love you too much to keep doing this to you. I'm sorry I can't give you what you want..."

Mark tossed his hands in the air. "So, it's a no, then? No babies? You finally made up your mind?" His eyebrows lifted, less out of anger and more to try to stop the tears from pouring out of them.

Holy shit, I'm in the middle of ending our marriage, and his first thought is about babies, Elyse thought to herself. It solidified her decision even more.

"No," she replied, shaking her head to stave off the tears she could feel welling. "It's not a no. It's an I don't know, but I'm okay not knowing, at least for now. And you're not, and I can't keep you...trapped in this marriage. You deserve to be a dad, and I—" Elyse started to cry. "I deserve to keep not knowing."

Mark nodded solemnly. "I know how much you love this house. I'll go to a hotel for now, and then we can figure the rest out."

"It's already late. Just stay here. Please?" Elyse asked.

Mark nodded again.

Elyse wasn't sure what she expected Mark's reaction to be. It felt like it should have been more—bigger, louder, more intense—but with such a long, slow, painful build-up, it was bound to be anti-climactic. Like instead of ripping the Band-Aid off a year ago when maybe they probably should've, they'd just been picking at it, peeling it away slowly to cause the most amount of pain for the longest amount of time. Either way, the wound was finally exposed, and could finally breathe, and maybe even, in time, heal on its own— on their own.

Without speaking, they put on their pajamas, brushed their teeth side-by-side at their double vanity, and crawled into their king-sized bed. Mark held Elyse in his arms, and she let him. She tried to make sure she took in everything about him—his smell, his scratchy stubble, his strong forearms, the tiny scar he had on his left elbow from getting stitches as a kid.

The next day, Mark moved out.

Part Three
Middle Ages

October 2028

Thirty-Three

BACK TO THE BEACH

THE GIRLS GROUP CHAT:

Elyse: Can't wait to see you ladies this weekend! Our check-in is 3 p.m. on Friday. I'm still not sure what time I'll be able to get away, but I'll text you when I'm on my way. When are you guys planning on getting there?

Alex: I was planning on getting there right at 3!

Elyse: @Alex must be nice to be your own boss :P

Rachel: I likely won't be there until 6:30-7ish. Henry has a basketball tournament. If they make it to the finals, he'll be playing at 4. If not, I should be able to get there around 4:30ish.

Brie: Really hope he loses Rach. I'm down Alex, wanna drive together?

Alex: Sure!

Brie: Alex and I can get a head start on making the weekend's signature drink...spicy Metamucil margaritas

Elyse: Alex and Brie, since you'll be there earlier can you grab the cake? I ordered from that bakery on Washington that Leah loves

Brie: Of course. Anything for Leah's 40th!

Elyse: I'll bring Leah!

They had taken nearly a decade off, but the girls finally all found the time and headspace to get back to their annual girls' beach weekend. This time, actually at the beach and for a full weekend.

Alex and Brie arrived at the rental house which sat directly on Misquamicut Beach just after 3:30 p.m. and promptly poured themselves a glass of rosé. Sure, they'd drink water for the next three hours to pace themselves but such a momentous occasion needed to start with a drink.

"Cheers to my first weekend sleeping in six years," Alex joked.

"How depressing," Brie said, as she clinked glasses with Alex. "Is this your first overnight away from Maren?" She asked.

Maren, Alex's youngest daughter, was eight months old. After having her second daughter, Lainey, Alex found her groove in motherhood. So much so, that her and Andrew decided on more babies and honestly weren't quite sure yet if they were done. For

Alex, everything was somehow less scary and overwhelming with three than it was with one.

"Hell no! Andrew and I got a hotel downtown for our anniversary a couple of months ago," Alex said.

"And you still didn't sleep in?" Brie, whose wake-up time was still never before 8:30 a.m., and only if it was absolutely necessary, asked.

"No, I meant to, but we ended up having way too much wine, and I ended up waking up early to throw up and be a miserable hungover mess," Alex said.

After all these years, Alex was still a bit of a messy drunk and never quite figured out how to hold her liquor.

"Well, there's still hope for this weekend," Brie said. "Cheers to Andrew for holding down the fort. Who would've thought that out of all of us, you'd end up with the most kids?" Brie had maintained her commitment to a child-free life.

"Definitely not me!" Alex said genuinely.

In between Lainey and Maren, Alex also decided her professional skills were better used elsewhere. She started her own boutique PR consulting firm where she could pick and choose the projects and clients she took on. She had also grown to love the small daytime events and despise the nightlife-focused events. She happily donated all of her mini dresses, which she proudly still fit into but just didn't feel comfortable in, to some of her younger Vibe coworkers before branching out on her own.

Alex loved being a girl mom and parading her girls around in adorable matching outfits and taking them out for special girls' days consisting of shopping and getting pedicures. Her own family brought her so much joy that she spent as little time as possible thinking about her mom. It was one of those issues that the more she tried to "fix" it, the worse it made her feel, so she did everything she could to accept the relationship with her mom the way it was and protect her own space. At least that's what her therapist had told her.

Over the last five years, she had a handful of times when she had cut her mom out of her life "for good." After the last time, she decided that the finality of it all, the feeling like she was making a huge decision over and over again, was overwhelming and unhealthy, another insight from her therapist. So, instead of treating everything as a big decision, Alex would periodically take some space from her mom, without the pressure of feeling like she had to make some sort of final decision. It also made it less stressful when she inevitably would allow her mother back into her life.

Her therapist also taught her to set some boundaries, even if they were implied. One of those boundaries was that she was never alone with her mother. Having her around when the kids were around was the perfect buffer and took some of the pressure off of the two of them. So, even though it wasn't exactly a happy ending for her and her mother, it was a good enough ending, and sometimes that's the best you can ask for.

Alex and Brie spent the next few hours getting things ready for the rest of the girls to arrive. They stopped at a corner store and grabbed some snacks, and among the very limited wine selection, they lucked out and found a bottle of Opus One, Leah's favorite wine. A very random corner store find, but they figured it was meant to be and paid the jacked up price to celebrate their friend.

Back at the beach house, as they were putting together a charcuterie board to help offset some of the wine, Rachel arrived.

Brie glanced at the clock, noting it was nearly 6:30 p.m. "So, Henry made it to the finals then? Did they win?" She asked.

"No, they didn't make it to the finals. I had to deal with another issue. Julia got her period. I had to spend more time calming Sean down than her," Rachel said. "How is she old enough to get her period? How am *I* old enough to have a daughter who is old enough to get her period."

"God, I don't want to think about it. I'll be a mess when the time comes for my girls." Alex loved saying that, *my girls*.

Rachel, being the most experienced parent, had subtly become the group leader when it came to all things parenting. It was simultaneously a role she loved and a role she didn't want. She loved being able to give her friends perspective, calm their parenting anxieties, and take their kids off their hands for a few hours every now and then. As it turned out, all that ambition and perfectionism that most of the other girls had, and that Rachel lacked, served her well in parenting. She was able to be much more laid back and often mellowed her friends out a bit about the latest parenting trend they felt they were failing at.

But she had to admit, these pre-teen years were not her favorite. She didn't feel like she was in her natural element like she did when they were toddlers and school-aged. Being needed less by her kids, or at least in very different ways, was a hard transition for Rachel. Whenever she felt bored, or even worse, unwanted by her kids, she found herself pouring into others with small children. Like she was trying to get that feeling of being needed and important, second-hand. Of course, others just thought it was her being the incredibly supportive and selfless friend she had always been.

At one point, she even contemplated trying for a third. But she knew Sean would probably be less enthusiastic about it, and she also knew it wasn't a sustainable solution. Because that kid would also grow up, and roll their eyes at her, and tell her she was, like, so not cool.

The director position at Rachel's work had come up a couple of times over the last five years—once when Lina got promoted to a VP role and again when Lina's replacement left after only a year. Rachel still hadn't applied, but next time she would, she had told herself.

"When I got my first period, Dora made me drink this weird honey, herb, and raw egg concoction, then I had to dance with her outside with a flower crown on. After that, she gave me a glass of red wine," Brie shared.

"Dora would," Alex said. "Also, it kinda sounds like Dora may have invented Coachella."

Brie smiled at Alex's comment. Somewhere over the last five years, thoughts of Dora in her earlier days had become a source of smiles and happy memories and were no longer painful reminders of what Brie had lost.

It had been almost five years since Dora moved into a long-term care facility, and three-and-a-half years since she passed away at sixty-three. Her official cause of death was pneumonia. Which was just another way of saying that her dementia progressed so far, so quickly, that the rest of her body started to wither away, just like her brain. But you can't write that on a death certificate, so the pneumonia that she caught, after having back-to-back respiratory infections that took a toll on her increasingly frail body, was the straw that broke the camel's back.

Brie was thankful that she didn't live long in the facility. Although the staff was welcoming and caring, Dora would've hated everything about it. The institutional feel, the rules, the infantilization of adults. Luckily, by the time Dora moved in, she was so far removed from her true self that she didn't seem to mind, and even seemed to grow fond of the childish sing-alongs and activities. This made Brie feel even guiltier than if she had gone into the facility and hated every second of it.

After her mother passed, Brie took a sabbatical for a research position in Wales for six months. Being in a completely different environment was exactly what she needed. She had even thought about staying there permanently. But the friends she had made there were just surface-level friends. Nothing could replace her decades'-old friendships waiting for her at home.

The girls were not at all surprised when the first thing Brie did when she got home from Wales was move herself back to College Hill, into a funky apartment. They *were* surprised to see that Brie had not come home empty-handed. The second thing Brie did when she got home was start the paperwork for Rhys to come to the U.S. on a work visa.

Brie and Rhys met in a dingy pub in Cardiff. He was seventeen years older than Brie and had a teenage daughter. The process of getting visas was a bit trickier since he was coming with his daughter, and the fact that, for many reasons, Brie didn't want to live with Rhys right away. The most important of which was that teenage girls terrified her. Luckily, Bronwyn was now twenty and had gone off to college at New York University. Brie no longer feared her and felt more like a big sister or friend than a stepmother-type, which she was much more comfortable with.

The rest of the girls were skeptical when Brie brought Rhys and Bronwyn over so quickly. Between Brie's impulsivity, general disdain for commitment and grieving her mother's death, no one had put much weight into their relationship lasting. But four years later, it seemed like Rhys might be the one to stick. The girls also found great humor in the fact that to this day Brie had never had an age-appropriate boyfriend in her adult life.

Of course, Brie and Rhys did things their own way. They were legally married for visa purposes, but Brie refused to make a big deal out of it. She didn't even tell anyone they got married at the courthouse until a couple of months after the fact. And she vehemently declined Elyse's offer to throw an intimate, low-key celebration dinner. They still wore wedding bands but also never referred to each other as husband and wife. They preferred common-law partners, even though they were technically husband and wife.

Brie had built her own little family with Rhys and Bronwyn, but more importantly, had realized that her family was who she decided it was, and she had too many wonderful people in her life to fret about not having any blood relatives that she knew. How Dora seemed so content raising Brie on her own, yet surrounded by many close friends and honorary family members she had accumulated made a lot more sense to Brie now.

Elyse finally arrived, just as everyone was sitting down for supper. "Sorry, Sam wouldn't let me leave the house and who am I to say no? He's like the love of my life."

"Elyse, I swear Sam has been the best thing ever for you. You're such a softie now," Alex said.

After Mark moved out, he and Elyse lived separately for three months; he in an Airbnb just outside the city, and Elyse in their townhouse. Elyse would never openly admit that they were separated or broken up. And it wouldn't be difficult since the girls and one of Mark's coworkers were the only ones who knew about it. They even managed to fake a family Easter dinner they co-hosted at the townhouse. They stayed in communication every day, which simultaneously made dealing with the split easier and harder. They texted and called, and for a change, talked about nothing important. *How was your day? What did you have for lunch? How's work going?* When the important stuff, like babies, were off the table, things were so much easier.

After a few months of living separately, talking every day but not actually seeing each other, Elyse couldn't stand it anymore. Why was Mark not coming back? Was he really going to make her be the one to budge? Oh god, what if he met someone else? Was that technically allowed? The solitude was driving her mad, and she truly did miss him.

When she pictured her future, she still couldn't tell if there was a baby in it, but that picture always had Mark in it. She physically just couldn't get him out of the picture, as much as she tried. Elyse finally reached out to Mark to invite him over for a glass of wine. She had no idea what she was going to say, or what to expect but was relieved when he started crying five seconds after she opened the door and gave her one of the tightest hugs she had ever experienced.

Their first month back together was rocky. They knew they needed each other but didn't know how to move forward. Mark was still desperate to be a father, and Elyse still didn't feel ready. So, they took the approach only two wealthy individuals with a decent understanding of the law could do. They decided to freeze embryos and put an agreement in place. If after five years they weren't used, Mark would have legal custody over them and could find a surrogate if he wanted. After a year of going through the medical and legal process to freeze embryos, Elyse felt even less ready, but slowly, after another couple of years Elyse finally decided to bite the bullet.

Elyse never found herself yearning for a baby the way Mark did, but she did get to the point where the thought of having a baby was tolerable. She still didn't know how it would all work in terms of trying to be her best at work and her best as a mother, but Elyse had succeeded at most things in her life, so she decided to trust herself that she could figure this out too, even if she didn't have a meticulously laid out plan to follow. Mark was patient and didn't pressure Elyse, either. Knowing that someday, someway, he would be a father, made it easier to wait. Rather than putting all of his energy into pressuring Elyse, he put it into simply hoping that his future as a father would include her, too.

She was surprised how agreeable she was to pregnancy and motherhood, without it becoming her whole identity. Elyse's perfectionism also began to ease. Luckily for Elyse, her confidence had always outweighed her perfectionism, so letting go a bit wasn't as difficult as it would have been for most Type A perfectionists. Somewhere along the lines, faking it until she made it had become genuine. Just like in her professional career, she was more self-assured as a mother based on her own experience. It was funny the effect motherhood had. For some, it's the loosening up they need, for others it's the beginning of stress and worry they never would have imagined.

After giving birth, Elyse returned to work earlier than planned. She was itching to get back and hated feeling like her sole purpose was lactation. It was also clear that Mark was more than happy to stay at home with Sam for the first year. They had found the dynamic that worked best for them. Babies were okay, but Elyse was really enjoying this new toddler phase. She figured her professional experience dealing with self-centered, irrational people made parenting a toddler fairly easy and much more rewarding.

Someone else might have questioned what all the fuss was about. Was it worth putting off for so long? Was it worth almost losing Mark over? But Elyse knew that if it would have happened any other way, it wouldn't have actually been her decision, and that would've strained their relationship beyond repair. Although she had no regrets, she still couldn't help but feel the odd pang of guilt when she saw Mark with Sam. She had denied Mark that father role, the indescribable love for so long. He was happier than she had ever seen him. Much happier than she alone could've made him.

The girls finished up dinner just as the sun was beginning to set.

"I guess now's probably the time. Should I go get Leah?" Elyse asked.

The girls nodded.

Elyse went into her room and carefully removed the marble box that contained Leah's ashes from her overnight bag.

Thirty-Four

LEAH

IT HAD BEEN five years since Leah and Scott decided to forego baby number two and that their family was perfectly complete as it was. It brought a new sense of levity to their family, and as much as Leah hated to admit it, she was happy to be able to make up for the year-and-a-half she spent only giving Oliver a fraction of the attention he deserved.

It had been four years since Leah was diagnosed with ovarian cancer. Of all the tests and scans, injections, and blood work that Leah went through in trying to get pregnant a second time, she had grown numb to it all and had forgotten that any of it could mean anything. After accepting defeat, she mentioned at her annual check-up the following year some menstrual irregularities, which she attributed to her body adjusting after being bombarded with drugs and hormone cocktails. Her doctor ordered more bloodwork and a scan just in case. It was probably nothing, or could even possibly be the signs of early menopause.

The news shocked everybody and shook Scott to his core. Weren't they still young? How was this happening? Leah was young and healthy and didn't feel sick, surely this couldn't be right, or couldn't be serious. Surely she would come out on the other end with this one.

It had been three years since the most devastating news was delivered. Words like Stage 4, spread, untreatable, comfort measures, were the only words Scott could remember from those conversations. The next six months were spent wavering between denial and also trying to make the best of the time Leah had left while she was feeling well. They took Oliver to Disney, did a family trip to Hawaii, and rented a beach house for the entire summer. Every time Leah caught a glimpse of Oliver's childhood excitement during those special moments at amusement parks, on the beach, or eating an ice cream cone, she tried so hard to burn those images into her mind. They were the only things that she wanted to take with her when it was her time to go.

It had been two years since Leah decided that a medically assisted death was the best option for her and her family. After six months of not being able to experience life how she wanted and growing weaker and more tired, and worse, to not see as many smiles and glow on Oliver's face, Leah had the conversation with Scott, with her doctors, with her friends. She was grateful that medically assisted death was legalized in Rhode Island, just a year before she ended up doing it. She didn't want to lose anymore of her strength and ability to exist in the moment and be present. She wanted all the time in the world with her son, but she just couldn't stand him having memories of her being a shell of herself; she only wanted him to have the Disney, beach, and ice cream memories of her.

It had been just over a year-and-a-half since the girls had surrounded Leah at her bedside, each with a glass of wine in their hands, spending the afternoon reminiscing on their favorite times.

Leah had strict instructions that only happy tears were allowed, and the girls mostly followed suit. In true Leah form, she made sure there were more laughs than anything else. The goodbyes were the longest, hardest, most awkward ones. None of them wanted to leave, but they knew Leah needed rest.

The next day would be her last, and she had promised Oliver a day of ice cream, Legos, and movies. She went through the day in a blur, like she was floating outside of her body. As if time was standing still and rushing by all at once. Every time she found her thoughts drifting to what tomorrow would be like for Oliver and Scott, for her family and friends, for the rest of the world, she forced herself back into the present moment. She tried to consume her husband and son with all her senses—how they looked, the smell of Oliver's bubble gum-flavored ice cream, the feeling of Scott's scratchy stubble against her skin, the sound of Legos clicking together.

She was simultaneously the happiest and saddest she had ever been tucking Oliver into bed one last time, obviously indescribably sad that she wouldn't be able to be part of his world anymore but happy that she got to be for the cruelly short amount of time she had. And proud. So proud that she and Scott had created such a perfect son. Scott didn't want Leah to do any of the manual labor that comes along with the bedtime routine, but she insisted. And by some miracle—and a lot of drugs—Leah made sure she was the one to pull the sheets over Oliver and fluff his pillow, just like he liked it.

Oliver was almost seven at the time—too old to be shielded from the harsh reality, and too young to really know how to process it. Leah's biggest concern was how this time would shape Oliver. Would he be able to grow from it—have it give him a deeper appreciation for family and life in general? Or, would it crush him? Would it make him lose faith in humanity? Would he make bad choices? Would it be the beginning of many difficult times in his life? Leah couldn't bear to think of the latter and had made Scott and her friends promise they would do everything within their power and tap into every possible resource to make sure that didn't happen.

That night, she laid in Oliver's bed with him, reading all his favorite stories. He actually did most of the reading which was perfect because Leah wasn't sure she'd have the energy to read them. Neither one of them wanted the moment to end, because they knew there weren't going to be anymore. Leah had gone over in her head a million times what her last words to her son would be. How could she say goodbye without actually saying goodbye? How could she ever convey to him how much she loved him? She had decided that her last words to him would not be about her but about him.

"Being your mom is the best thing I've ever done," Leah said. The words she repeated over and over in her head had finally been said out loud.

"Mommy, I know you have to go away and can't come back. But do you think, if you get a chance, you could maybe try?" Oliver asked. It was such a seven-year-old question.

Leah nodded and squeezed his hand. "Mommy, can you lay with me until I fall asleep?" It had been a while since Oliver had asked her to do that.

"Of course. Anything for you," she said, squeezing his hand even harder, and he curled into her.

Oliver tried to stay awake, but after twenty minutes, he was in a deep sleep. Leah was glad. Leaving Oliver's room when he was asleep felt like less of a goodbye than if he was awake.

After a couple of hours of lying with Scott in their bed, mostly in silence, just lying and holding onto each other, she called the doctor to come complete the process.

As the doctor carefully filled a syringe, Leah looked up at Scott and said, "We didn't quite grow old together, but I tried really hard."

Scott choked back tears. He had cried so many of them over the last four years, and he didn't want to have these last few moments with his wife be engulfed by his own sadness.

"You and Oliver are going to be okay, because you have to be, alright?" Leah said, as though it was a demand.

Scott nodded in agreement.

"Of all the stupid things I did in college, you were the best one," Leah said, with a tearful grin.

Scott surprised himself by letting out a little laugh. Leah felt a great sense of pride that the last thing she would hear was her husband's laughter that she had caused.

Once Leah peacefully faded out of consciousness, the doctor quietly announced the official time of death to Scott. He nodded silently, got up and walked across the bedroom he had shared with Leah for so many years, and into their en suite bathroom. He shut the door, turned on the shower, and let out the biggest, most tortured sounding wail.

Thirty-Five

LIFE'S A BEACH

THE GIRLS STOOD on the beach looking out on the ocean, each with their own little jar of Leah.

Leah had left each of them a letter with personalized instructions. Her wish was not so much to have her ashes spread at the beach but to make sure that they all took the time to get back to the beach, to foster the friendships that meant so much to her. The ones that were strong enough that they could get put on the backburner for a few months or years while they were going through the motions of life.

Her notes to the girls were short and sweet, and perfectly tailored to each of them. In just a few sentences, they were meaningful, profound, and made each one of them laugh more than they cried.

Her words to Elyse, who was very pregnant at the time of her passing, was to know that her unapologetic ambition was her strength, not her weakness, and if there was anyone who could "do it all" and look amazing while doing it, it was her; that she was sad she wouldn't be able to see her become a mom, but she knew how amazing she'd be. How she knew all those surface-level characteristics were how Elyse showed her love for her friends, that Leah never once doubted.

Her message to Rachel was that her selflessness and loyalty had never gone unnoticed, and the world needed more Rachels. Even though it felt like she may not take up much space in this world, the impact she had on her friends' lives was immeasurable. That she could only hope that Rachel experienced half the joy, comfort, support, and friendship she had provided to Leah and the rest of the girls.

Her parting words to Alex were to know how proud she was for how far Alex had come. For being such an amazing mother, that she could mother herself and her two beautiful girls. She had built a beautiful life, one Leah was honored to have been a part of. She fully expected, no, demanded that fun, party girl Alex make an appearance at the beach weekend.

Her message to Brie was that she is one of the most beautiful souls Leah had ever met, and she loved how wonderfully weird she is. She was so happy that Brie and Rhys found each other. Even though she knew that Brie is 1000% enough for herself, having someone else to make it 1001% isn't so bad. She would always be fun Aunt Brie, and though motherhood wasn't something Brie was looking to experience, she could be a step-grandmother in just a few years. And everyone knew Brie would kill it as a grandmother.

Watching their friend die was the realest, most grown up thing they had done. All the weddings, houses, jobs, even being parents, still never really felt that grown up. Like everyone was just faking it. But this...this was a reality check that none of them wanted.

In the immediate months that followed, each of the women responded to their grief in ways that, although they seemed different, were actually quite similar.

Alex opened her own PR firm and decided if baby number three was going to happen that it should be now; Brie started spending the occasional night at Rhys' place instead of always making him come to hers; Rachel instituted more family time and took more pictures of the kids; and Elyse cut out red meat and finally started meditating, which she swears she can do while watching reality TV. All little things to make them feel like they actually had even just an ounce of control over their lives.

The void of Leah was huge. Not just because she was their friend, a wife, a mother, an effortless professional with a brilliant mind, so smart she didn't have to try to seem smart and important. Not just because she had the best dry wit that none of the other women could pull off. But because she was the equilibrium of their group. She balanced out Elyse and Rachel's prudishness with what some would call Alex and Brie's abrasiveness.

One by one, they each approached the shore to release their own little piece of Leah into the ocean and took a moment to talk to their friend.

Alex told Leah about Maren. How her middle name was Leah, and even though she's still just a baby, she could tell that Maren was going to have the same quick wit that Leah had.

Elyse gave her an update on Sam, who arrived just weeks after Leah passed. How she was surprised how much she loved being a boy mom, and how there were so many little things that Sam did, that she wondered if Oliver did them, too. How, even months later, she still finds herself reaching for her phone multiple times a day to ask Leah.

Brie told her about the latest political scandal and what was going on in the news. She also let her know that Scott seemed like he was doing better, and not to worry, he does give Oliver vegetables sometimes. Her and Rhys were planning on taking Scott and Oliver to a Brown Bears hockey game next weekend. Brie pulled a few strings and arranged for Oliver to ride the Zamboni at intermission.

Rachel told Leah that Oliver was doing good. He was at her house last weekend to play with Henry, and he is getting so tall, loves soccer, and wants to try-out for the school team next year. He is always so polite, too. She knew that Leah would want to know that.

After each of them spread the last physical remnants of Leah and had a moment, they walked along the beach toward the house in silence.

Brie stopped and turned around to face the water, finally breaking the silence. "So, this is forty, huh?"

Rachel slowed her pace and turned her gaze toward the water, smirking. "I guess."

"So, how was everyone's thirties?" Alex asked, putting her arm around Rachel's shoulder.

It seemed like the type of question Leah would've asked the group at that moment. Somewhat seriously, somewhat sarcastically, given the sullen mood of the evening.

"A lot more therapy than I would've thought," Elyse said.

"Didn't you only go like twice?" Alex asked.

"I meant what I said," Elyse replied with a raised eyebrow.

"Hey, the only people who escape their thirties without therapy are the ones who need it the most," Brie said.

"I actually think my thirties were kinda the best," Rachel said, thinking back to Julia and Henry as babies, toddlers, and all of the "firsts."

All four of them were now facing the gentle waves of the Atlantic Ocean, where they had just left their friend.

"What about you, Alex? How was your thirties?" Brie asked.

"Nothing like I expected," said Alex.

Reader Discussion Guide

1. Which main character did you relate to the most and why?

2. Which character do you think showed the most growth over the span of the twelve years covered in the book?

3. Part three updates the reader on how the rest of the women's thirties panned out. Did any of the women's decisions (or lack thereof) in part three surprise you? If so, why?

4. Unlike the rest of her friends, Rachel is lower maintenance, less of a perfectionist, and some may even view her as less ambitious. However, she is also generally the most content—trying to keep her life the same, rather than change it. Do you think this comes from a deep-seated comfort with herself, not feeling like she has to prove herself to others, or insecurities and reservations about putting herself out there more? Or, can it be a mix of both?

5. Throughout the book, Elyse struggles with whether or not she wants to have a baby, and more specifically, how a baby would

interfere with her career. Her conversations with Jackie Andrews and her assistant Laurie both nudge Elyse toward not wanting children, despite them having vastly different approaches to career and motherhood—Jackie willingly sacrificed her relationship with her kids for her career, and Laurie sacrificed her career for her kids. Do you think Jackie and Laurie's experiences are still relevant today for millennial women? What do you think Elyse's experience as a working mother will be?

6. Brie has always admired her mother and her free-spirited lifestyle. It isn't until Dora's decline that Brie really starts to reflect on her mother, not just as her mom but as a person. Realizing that Dora had insecurities, and maybe her lifestyle was more out of necessity than choice, makes Brie question if she should be following the "Dora blueprint" so closely. How has your perception of your parents changed as you get older? Does seeing them as people first and parents second make you rethink any of their life choices? Any of your life choices?

7. Alex's dysfunctional relationship with her mother skews her perception of her own abilities as a mother, and Alex realizes that a lot of her anxious tendencies are rooted in her upbringing. Do you think it would be easier for Alex to just cut her mother out of her life completely? Why do you think she can't?

8. Dealing with fertility issues puts a strain on Leah and Scott's relationship. She ultimately decides in Mexico that she no longer wants to continue to pursue baby number two.

Unfortunately for Leah, she only has about a year between making this decision and learning of her cancer diagnosis. Had Leah not gotten sick and ultimately passed away, how do you think she and Scott would've moved on from Mexico? Do you think Leah was truly done with trying to have another baby, or do you think the issue would continue to impact her and Scott's relationship?

9. This story is told predominantly from the perspectives of the women, but many of the issues they face are just as impactful to their husbands' lives. What do you think their perspectives are? Which of the husband's inner monologue would you most like to hear?

10. What do you think their forties have in store for these women? Who are you rooting for the most?

Acknowledgements

FIRST AND FOREMOST, I must thank Krys and imPRESS Millennial Books for holding my hand throughout this entire process. When I first started writing this story, I had no idea how to publish a book, and quite frankly, I probably still don't. This story would have never been told without you patiently guiding me through every step of the publishing journey, while editing it, too!

THANK YOU TO MY BETA READERS. Not only did you pull so much more out of this story but you also gave me a crash course in how to be a writer at the same time.

TO THE IMB CREW, thank you so much for being such a supportive, encouraging community. I've learned so much from you all, and I can only hope that one day I can pay it forward and show the same level of support and encouragement to other first-time authors who have no idea what they're doing.

THANK YOU TO ERIN, LINDA AND SHELLY, for lending your personal experience to make sure parts of this story were genuine and relatable.

TO MY CLOSEST FAMILY AND FRIENDS, acquaintances, friends of friends, and anyone else who showed enthusiasm and interest in this book, simply based on who wrote it, thank you. Your support means everything to me, and even if you only came for the author, I hope you stayed for the story.

TO RYAN, VERA & CHARLIE, you are my favorite part of my thirties, and my love for you is endless.

TO ELYSE, RACHEL, BRIE, ALEX, AND LEAH, thank you for practically writing yourselves. Thank you for personifying the parts of me (which parts, I'll never tell), the parts of so many other women in their thirties, and the parts of society that make this phase of life so intense, yet so boring, yet so messy, yet so important, yet so fun, yet so hard, yet so fulfilling.

www.ingramcontent.com/pod-product-compliance
Lightning Source LLC
Chambersburg PA
CBHW031251120726
47906CB00003B/697